The Mystery of
31 New Inn

The Mystery of
31 New Inn

R. Austin Freeman

ÆGYPAN PRESS

The Mystery of 31 New Inn
A publication of
ÆGYPAN PRESS

www.aegypan.com

To My Friend
Bernard E. Bishop

Preface

Commenting upon one of my earlier novels, in respect of which I had claimed to have been careful to adhere to common probabilities and to have made use only of really practicable methods of investigation, a critic remarked that this was of no consequence whatever, so long as the story was amusing.

Few people, I imagine, will agree with him. To most readers, and certainly to the kind of reader for whom an author is willing to take trouble, complete realism in respect of incidents and methods is an essential factor in maintaining the interest of a detective story. Hence it may be worth while to mention that Thorndyke's method of producing the track chart, described in Chapters II and III, has been actually used in practice. It is a modification of one devised by me many years ago when I was crossing Ashanti to the city of Bontuku, the whereabouts of which in the far interior was then only vaguely known. My instructions were to fix the positions of all towns, villages, rivers and mountains as accurately as possible; but finding ordinary methods of surveying impracticable in the dense forest which covers the whole region, I adopted this simple and apparently rude method, checking the distances whenever possible by astronomical observation.

The resulting route-map was surprisingly accurate, as shown by the agreement of the outward and homeward tracks, It was published by the Royal Geographical Society, and incorporated in the map of this region compiled by the Intelligence Branch of the War Office, and it formed the basis of the map which accompanied my volume of *Travels in Ashanti and Jaman*. So that Thorndyke's plan must be taken as quite a practicable one.

New Inn, the background of this story, and one of the last surviving inns of Chancery, has recently passed away after upwards of four centuries of newness. Even now, however, a few of the old, dismantled houses (including perhaps, the mysterious 31) may be seen from the Strand peeping over the iron roof of the skating rink which has displaced the picturesque hall, the pension-room and the garden. The postern gate, too, in Houghton Street still remains, though the arch is bricked up inside. Passing it lately, I made the rough sketch which appears on next page, and which shows all that is left of this pleasant old London backwater.

R.A.F.
GRAVESEND

Chapter I

The Mysterious Patient

*A*s I look back through the years of my association with John Thorndyke, I am able to recall a wealth of adventures and strange experiences such as falls to the lot of very few men who pass their lives within hearing of Big Ben. Many of these experiences I have already placed on record; but it now occurs to me that I have hitherto left unrecorded one that is, perhaps, the most astonishing and incredible of the whole series; an adventure, too, that has for me the added interest that it inaugurated my permanent association with my learned and talented friend, and marked the close of a rather unhappy and unprosperous period of my life.

Memory, retracing the journey through the passing years to the starting-point of those strange events, lands me in a shabby little ground-floor room in a house near the Walworth end of Lower Kennington Lane. A couple of framed diplomas on the wall, a card of Snellen's test-types and a stethoscope lying on the writing-table, proclaim it a doctor's consulting-room; and my own position in the round-backed chair at the said table, proclaims me the practitioner in charge.

It was nearly nine o'clock. The noisy little clock on the mantelpiece announced the fact, and, by its frantic ticking, seemed as anxious as I to get the consultation hours over. I glanced wistfully at my mud-splashed boots and wondered if I might yet venture to assume the slippers that peeped coyly from under the shabby sofa. I even allowed my thoughts to wander to the pipe that reposed in my coat pocket. Another minute and I could turn down the surgery gas and shut the outer door. The fussy little clock gave a sort of preliminary cough or hiccup, as if it should say: "Ahem! ladies and gentlemen, I am about to strike." And at that moment, the bottle-boy opened the door and, thrusting in his head, uttered the one word: "Gentleman."

Extreme economy of words is apt to result in ambiguity. But I understood. In Kennington Lane, the race of mere men and women appeared to be extinct. They were all gentlemen — unless they were ladies or children — even as the Liberian army was said to consist entirely of generals. Sweeps, laborers, milkmen, costermongers — all were impartially invested by the democratic bottle-boy with the rank and title of *armigeri*. The present nobleman appeared to favor the aristocratic recreation of driving a cab or job-master's carriage, and, as he entered the room, he touched his hat, closed the door somewhat carefully, and then, without remark, handed me a note which bore the superscription "Dr. Stillbury."

"You understand," I said, as I prepared to open the envelope, "that I am not Dr. Stillbury. He is away at present and I am looking after his patients."

"It doesn't signify," the man replied. "You'll do as well."

On this, I opened the envelope and read the note, which was quite brief, and, at first sight, in no way remarkable.

"Dear Sir," it ran,
"Would you kindly come and see a friend of mine who is staying with me? The bearer of this will give you further particulars and convey you to the house.
"Yours truly, H. Weiss."

There was no address on the paper and no date, and the writer was unknown to me.

"This note," I said, "refers to some further particulars. What are they?"

The messenger passed his hand over his hair with a gesture of embarrassment. "It's a ridicklus affair," he said, with a contemptuous laugh. "If I had been Mr. Weiss, I wouldn't have had nothing to do with it. The sick gentleman, Mr. Graves, is one of them people what can't abear doctors. He's been ailing now for a week or two, but nothing would induce him to see a doctor. Mr. Weiss did everything he could to persuade him, but it was no go. He wouldn't. However, it seems Mr. Weiss threatened to send for a medical man on his own account, because, you see, he was getting a bit nervous; and then Mr. Graves gave way. But only on one condition. He said the doctor was to come from a distance and was not to be told who he was or where he lived or anything about him; and he made Mr. Weiss promise to keep to that condition before he'd let him send. So Mr. Weiss promised, and, of course, he's got to keep his word."

"But," I said, with a smile, "you've just told me his name — if his name really is Graves."

"You can form your own opinion on that," said the coachman.

"And," I added, "as to not being told where he lives, I can see that for myself. I'm not blind, you know."

"We'll take the risk of what you see," the man replied. "The question is, will you take the job on?"

Yes; that was the question, and I considered it for some time before replying. We medical men are pretty familiar with the kind of person who "can't abear doctors," and we like to have as little to do with him as possible. He is a thankless and unsatisfactory patient. Intercourse with him is unpleasant, he gives a great deal of trouble and responds badly to treatment. If this had been my own practice, I should have declined the case off-hand. But it was not my practice. I was only a deputy. I could not lightly refuse work which would yield a profit to my principal, unpleasant though it might be.

As I turned the matter over in my mind, I half unconsciously scrutinized my visitor — somewhat to his embarrassment — and I liked his appearance as little as I liked his mission. He kept his station near the door, where the light was dim — for the illumination was concentrated on the table and the patient's chair — but I could see that he had a somewhat sly, unprepossessing face and a greasy, red moustache that seemed out of character with his rather perfunctory livery; though this was mere prejudice. He wore a wig, too — not that there was anything discreditable in that — and the thumb-nail of the hand that held his hat bore disfiguring traces of some injury — which, again, though unsightly, in no wise reflected on his moral character. Lastly, he watched me keenly with a mixture of anxiety and sly complacency that I found distinctly unpleasant. In a general way, he impressed me disagreeably. I did not like the look of him at all; but nevertheless I decided to undertake the case.

"I suppose," I answered, at length, "it is no affair of mine who the patient is or where he lives. But how do you propose to manage the business? Am I to be led to the house blindfolded, like the visitor to the bandit's cave?"

The man grinned slightly and looked very decidedly relieved.

"No, sir," he answered; "we ain't going to blindfold you. I've got a carriage outside. I don't think you'll see much out of that."

"Very well," I rejoined, opening the door to let him out, "I'll be with you in a minute. I suppose you can't give me any idea as to what is the matter with the patient?"

"No, sir, I can't," he replied; and he went out to see to the carriage.

I slipped into a bag an assortment of emergency drugs and a few diagnostic instruments, turned down the gas and passed out through the surgery. The carriage was standing at the curb, guarded by the coachman and watched with deep interest by the bottle-boy. I viewed it with mingled curiosity and disfavor. It was a kind of large brougham, such as is used by some commercial travelers, the usual glass windows being replaced by wooden shutters intended to conceal the piles of sample-boxes, and the doors capable of being locked from outside with a railway key.

As I emerged from the house, the coachman unlocked the door and held it open.

"How long will the journey take?" I asked, pausing with my foot on the step.

The coachman considered a moment or two and replied:

"It took me, I should say, nigh upon half an hour to get here."

This was pleasant hearing. A half an hour each way and a half an hour at the patient's house. At that rate it would be half-past ten before I was home again, and then it was quite probable that I should find some other untimely messenger waiting on the doorstep. With a muttered anathema on the unknown Mr. Graves and the unrestful life of a *locum tenens*, I stepped into the uninviting vehicle. Instantly the coachman slammed the door and turned the key, leaving me in total darkness.

One comfort was left to me; my pipe was in my pocket. I made shift to load it in the dark, and, having lit it with a wax match, took the opportunity to inspect the interior of my prison. It was a shabby affair. The moth-eaten state of the blue cloth cushions seemed to suggest that it had been long out of regular use; the oilcloth floor-covering was worn into holes; ordinary internal fittings there were none. But the appearances suggested that the crazy vehicle had been prepared with considerable forethought for its present use. The inside handles of the doors had apparently been removed; the wooden shutters were permanently fixed in their places; and a paper label, stuck on the transom below each window, had a suspicious appearance of having been put there to cover the painted name and address of the job-master or livery-stable keeper who had originally owned the carriage.

These observations gave me abundant food for reflection. This Mr. Weiss must be an excessively conscientious man if he had considered that his promise to Mr. Graves committed him to such extraordinary precautions. Evidently no mere following of the letter of the law was enough to satisfy his sensitive conscience. Unless he had reasons for sharing Mr. Graves's unreasonable desire for secrecy — for one could not suppose that these measures of concealment had been taken by the patient himself.

The further suggestions that evolved themselves from this consideration were a little disquieting. Whither was I being carried and for what purpose? The idea that I was bound for some den of thieves where I might be robbed and possibly murdered, I dismissed with a smile. Thieves do not make elaborately concerted plans to rob poor devils like me. Poverty has its compensations in that respect. But there were other possibilities. Imagination backed by experience had no difficulty in conjuring up a number of situations in which a medical man might be called upon, with or without coercion, either to witness or actively to participate in the commission of some unlawful act.

Reflections of this kind occupied me pretty actively if not very agreeably during this strange journey. And the monotony was relieved, too, by other distractions. I was, for example, greatly interested to notice how, when one sense is in abeyance, the other senses rouse into a compensating intensity of perception. I sat smoking my pipe in darkness which was absolute save for the dim glow from the smoldering tobacco in the bowl, and seemed to be cut off from all knowledge of the world without. But yet I was not. The vibrations of the carriage, with its hard springs and iron-tired wheels, registered accurately and plainly the character of the roadway. The harsh rattle of granite setts, the soft bumpiness of macadam, the smooth rumble of wood-pavement, the jarring and swerving of crossed tram-lines; all were easily recognizable and together sketched the general features of the neighborhood through which I was passing. And the sense of hearing filled in the details. Now the hoot of a tug's whistle told of proximity to the river. A sudden and brief hollow reverberation announced the passage under a railway arch (which, by the way, happened several times during the journey); and, when I heard the familiar whistle of a railway-guard followed by the quick snorts of a skidding locomotive, I had as clear a picture of a heavy passenger-train moving out of a station as if I had seen it in broad daylight.

I had just finished my pipe and knocked out the ashes on the heel of my boot, when the carriage slowed down and entered a covered way — as I could tell by the hollow echoes. Then I distinguished the clang of heavy wooden gates closed behind me, and a moment or two later the carriage door was unlocked and opened. I stepped out blinking into a covered passage paved with cobbles and apparently leading down to a mews; but it was all in darkness, and I had no time to make any detailed observations, as the carriage had drawn up opposite a side door which was open and in which stood a woman holding a lighted candle.

"Is that the doctor?" she asked, speaking with a rather pronounced German accent and shading the candle with her hand as she peered at me.

I answered in the affirmative, and she then exclaimed:

"I am glad you have come. Mr. Weiss will be so relieved. Come in, please."

I followed her across a dark passage into a dark room, where she set the candle down on a chest of drawers and turned to depart. At the door, however, she paused and looked back.

"It is not a very nice room to ask you into," she said. "We are very untidy just now, but you must excuse us. We have had so much anxiety about poor Mr. Graves."

"He has been ill some time, then?"

"Yes. Some little time. At intervals, you know. Sometimes better, sometimes not so well."

As she spoke, she gradually backed out into the passage but did not go away at once. I accordingly pursued my inquiries.

"He has not been seen by any doctor, has he?"

"No," she answered, "he has always refused to see a doctor. That has been a great trouble to us. Mr. Weiss has been very anxious about him. He will be so glad to hear that you have come. I had better go and tell him. Perhaps you will kindly sit down until he is able to come to you," and with this she departed on her mission.

It struck me as a little odd that, considering his anxiety and the apparent urgency of the case, Mr. Weiss should not have been waiting to receive me. And when several minutes elapsed without his appearing, the oddness of the circumstance impressed me still more. Having no desire, after the journey in the carriage, to sit down, I whiled away the time by an inspection of the room. And a very curious room it was; bare, dirty, neglected and, apparently, unused. A faded carpet had been flung untidily on the floor. A small, shabby table stood in the middle of the room; and beyond this, three horsehair-covered chairs and a chest of drawers formed the entire set of furniture. No pictures hung on the moldy walls, no curtains covered the shuttered windows, and the dark drapery of cobwebs that hung from the ceiling to commemorate a long and illustrious dynasty of spiders hinted at months of neglect and disuse.

The chest of drawers — an incongruous article of furniture for what seemed to be a dining room — as being the nearest and best lighted object received most of my attention. It was a fine old chest of nearly black mahogany, very battered and in the last stage of decay, but originally a piece of some pretensions. Regretful of its fallen estate, I looked it over with some interest and had just observed on its lower corner a little label bearing the printed inscription "Lot 201" when I heard footsteps descending the stairs. A moment later the door opened and a shadowy figure appeared standing close by the threshold.

"Good evening, doctor," said the stranger, in a deep, quiet voice and with a distinct, though not strong, German accent. "I must apologize for keeping you waiting."

I acknowledged the apology somewhat stiffly and asked: "You are Mr. Weiss, I presume?"

"Yes, I am Mr. Weiss. It is very good of you to come so far and so late at night and to make no objection to the absurd conditions that my poor friend has imposed."

"Not at all," I replied. "It is my business to go when and where I am wanted, and it is not my business to inquire into the private affairs of my patients."

"That is very true, sir," he agreed cordially, "and I am much obliged to you for taking that very proper view of the case. I pointed that out to my friend, but he is not a very reasonable man. He is very secretive and rather suspicious by nature."

"So I inferred. And as to his condition; is he seriously ill?"

"Ah," said Mr. Weiss, "that is what I want you to tell me. I am very much puzzled about him."

"But what is the nature of his illness? What does he complain of?"

"He makes very few complaints of any kind although he is obviously ill. But the fact is that he is hardly ever more than half awake. He lies in a kind of dreamy stupor from morning to night."

This struck me as excessively strange and by no means in agreement with the patient's energetic refusal to see a doctor.

"But," I asked, "does he never rouse completely?"

"Oh, yes," Mr. Weiss answered quickly; "he rouses from time to time and is then quite rational, and, as you may have gathered, rather obstinate. That is the peculiar and puzzling feature in the case; this alternation between a state of stupor and an almost normal and healthy condition. But perhaps you had better see him and judge for yourself. He had a rather severe attack just now. Follow me, please. The stairs are rather dark."

The stairs were very dark, and I noticed that they were without any covering of carpet, or even oilcloth, so that our footsteps resounded dismally as if we were in an empty house. I stumbled up after my guide, feeling my way by the hand-rail, and on the first floor followed him into a room similar in size to the one below and very barely furnished, though less squalid than the other. A single candle at the farther end threw its feeble light on a figure in the bed, leaving the rest of the room in a dim twilight.

As Mr. Weiss tiptoed into the chamber, a woman — the one who had spoken to me below — rose from a chair by the bedside and quietly left the room by a second door. My conductor halted, and looking fixedly at the figure in the bed, called out:

"Philip! Philip! Here is the doctor come to see you."

He paused for a moment or two, and, receiving no answer, said: "He seems to be dozing as usual. Will you go and see what you can make of him?"

I stepped forward to the bedside, leaving Mr. Weiss at the end of the room near the door by which we had entered, where he remained, slowly and noiselessly pacing backwards and forwards in the semi-obscurity. By the light of the candle I saw an elderly man with good features and a refined, intelligent and even attractive face, but dreadfully emaciated, bloodless and sallow. He lay quite motionless except for the scarcely perceptible rise and fall of his chest; his eyes were nearly closed, his features relaxed, and, though he was not actually asleep, he seemed to be in a dreamy, somnolent, lethargic state, as if under the influence of some narcotic.

I watched him for a minute or so, timing his slow breathing by my watch, and then suddenly and sharply addressed him by name; but the only response was a slight lifting of the eyelids, which, after a brief, drowsy glance at me, slowly subsided to their former position.

I now proceeded to make a physical examination. First, I felt his pulse, grasping his wrist with intentional brusqueness in the hope of rousing him from his stupor. The beats were slow, feeble and slightly irregular, giving clear evidence, if any were needed, of his generally lowered vitality. I listened carefully to his heart, the sounds of which were very distinct through the thin walls of his emaciated chest, but found nothing abnormal beyond the feebleness and uncertainty of its action. Then I turned my attention to his eyes, which I examined closely with the aid of the candle and my ophthalmoscope lens, raising the lids somewhat roughly so as to expose the whole of the irides. He submitted without resistance to my rather ungentle handling of these sensitive structures, and showed no signs of discomfort even when I brought the candle-flame to within a couple of inches of his eyes.

But this extraordinary tolerance of light was easily explained by closer examination; for the pupils were contracted to such an extreme degree that only the very minutest point of black was visible at the center of the grey iris. Nor was this the only abnormal peculiarity of the sick man's eyes. As he lay on his back, the right iris sagged down slightly towards its center, showing a distinctly concave surface; and, when I contrived to produce a slight but quick movement of the eyeball, a perceptible undulatory movement could be detected. The patient had, in fact, what is known as a tremulous iris, a condition that is seen in cases where the crystalline lens has been extracted for the cure of cataract, or where it has become accidentally displaced, leaving the iris unsupported. In the present case, the complete condition of the iris made it clear that the ordinary extraction operation had not been performed, nor was I able, on the closest inspection with the aid of my lens, to find any trace of the less common "needle operation." The inference was that the patient had suffered from the accident known as "dislocation of the lens"; and this led to the further inference that he was almost or completely blind in the right eye.

This conclusion was, indeed, to some extent negatived by a deep indentation on the bridge of the nose, evidently produced by spectacles, and by marks which I looked for and found behind the ears, corresponding to the hooks or "curl sides" of the glasses. For those spectacles which are fitted with curl sides to hook over the ears are usually intended to be worn habitually, and this agreed with the indentation on the nose; which was deeper than would have been accounted for by the merely occasional use of spectacles for reading. But if only one eye was useful, a single eye-glass would have answered the purpose; not that there was any weight in this objection, for a single eye-glass worn constantly would be much less convenient than a pair of hook-sided spectacles.

As to the nature of the patient's illness, only one opinion seemed possible. It was a clear and typical case of opium or morphine poisoning. To this conclusion all his symptoms seemed to point with absolute certainty. The coated tongue, which he protruded slowly and tremulously in response to a command bawled in his ear; his yellow skin and ghastly expression; his contracted pupils and the stupor from which he could hardly be roused by the roughest handling and which yet did not amount to actual insensibility; all these formed a distinct and coherent group of symptoms, not only pointing plainly to the nature of the drug, but also suggesting a very formidable dose.

But this conclusion in its turn raised a very awkward and difficult question. If a large — a poisonous — dose of the drug had been taken, how, and by whom had that dose been administered? The closest scrutiny of the patient's arms and legs failed to reveal a single mark such as would be made by a hypodermic needle. This man was clearly no common morphinomaniac; and in the absence of the usual sprinkling of needle marks, there was nothing to show or suggest whether the drug had been taken voluntarily by the patient himself or administered by someone else.

And then there remained the possibility that I might, after all, be mistaken in my diagnosis. I felt pretty confident. But the wise man always holds a doubt in reserve. And, in the present case, having regard to the obviously serious condition of the patient, such a doubt was eminently disturbing. Indeed, as I pocketed my stethoscope and took a last look at the motionless, silent figure, I realized that my position was one of extraordinary difficulty and perplexity. On the one hand my suspicions — aroused, naturally enough, by the very unusual circumstances that surrounded my visit — inclined me to extreme reticence; while, on the other, it was evidently my duty to give any information that might prove serviceable to the patient.

As I turned away from the bed Mr. Weiss stopped his slow pacing to and fro and faced me. The feeble light of the candle now fell on him, and I saw him distinctly for the first time. He did not impress me favorably. He was a thickset, round-shouldered man, a typical fair German with tow-colored hair, greased and brushed down smoothly, a large, ragged, sandy beard and coarse, sketchy features. His nose was large and thick with a bulbous end, and inclined to a reddish purple, a tint which extended to the adjacent parts of his face as if the color had run. His eyebrows were large and beetling, overhanging deep-set eyes, and he wore a pair of spectacles which gave him a somewhat owlish expression. His exterior was unprepossessing, and I was in a state of mind that rendered me easily receptive of an unfavorable impression.

"Well," he said, "what do you make of him?" I hesitated, still perplexed by the conflicting necessities of caution and frankness, but at length replied:

"I think rather badly of him, Mr. Weiss. He is in a very low state."

"Yes, I can see that. But have you come to any decision as to the nature of his illness?"

There was a tone of anxiety and suppressed eagerness in the question which, while it was natural enough in the circumstances, by no means allayed my suspicions, but rather influenced me on the side of caution.

"I cannot give a very definite opinion at present," I replied guardedly. "The symptoms are rather obscure and might very well indicate several different conditions. They might be due to congestion of the brain, and, if no other explanation were possible, I should incline to that view. The alternative is some narcotic poison, such as opium or morphia."

"But that is quite impossible. There is no such drug in the house, and as he never leaves his room now, he could not get any from outside."

"What about the servants?" I asked.

"There are no servants excepting my housekeeper, and she is absolutely trustworthy."

"He might have some store of the drug that you are not aware of. Is he left alone much?"

"Very seldom indeed. I spend as much time with him as I can, and when I am not able to be in the room, Mrs. Schallibaum, my housekeeper, sits with him."

"Is he often as drowsy as he is now?"

"Oh, very often; in fact, I should say that is his usual condition. He rouses up now and again, and then he is quite lucid and natural for, perhaps, an hour or so; but presently he becomes drowsy again and dozes off, and remains asleep, or half asleep, for hours on end. Do you know of any disease that takes people in that way?"

"No," I answered. "The symptoms are not exactly like those of any disease that is known to me. But they are much very like those of opium poisoning."

"But, my dear sir," Mr. Weiss retorted impatiently, "since it is clearly impossible that it can be opium poisoning, it must be something else. Now, what else can it be? You were speaking of congestion of the brain."

"Yes. But the objection to that is the very complete recovery that seems to take place in the intervals."

"I would not say very complete," said Mr. Weiss. "The recovery is rather comparative. He is lucid and fairly natural in his manner, but he is still dull and lethargic. He does not, for instance, show any desire to go out, or even to leave his room."

I pondered uncomfortably on these rather contradictory statements. Clearly Mr. Weiss did not mean to entertain the theory of opium poisoning; which was natural enough if he had no knowledge of the drug having been used. But still —

"I suppose," said Mr. Weiss, "you have experience of sleeping sickness?"

The suggestion startled me. I had not. Very few people had. At that time practically nothing was known about the disease. It was a mere pathological curiosity, almost unheard of excepting by a few practitioners in remote parts of Africa, and hardly referred to in the text-books. Its connection with the trypanosome-bearing insects was as yet unsuspected, and, to me, its symptoms were absolutely unknown.

"No, I have not," I replied. "The disease is nothing more than a name to me. But why do you ask? Has Mr. Graves been abroad?"

"Yes. He has been traveling for the last three or four years, and I know that he spent some time recently in West Africa, where this disease occurs. In fact, it was from him that I first heard about it."

This was a new fact. It shook my confidence in my diagnosis very considerably, and inclined me to reconsider my suspicions. If Mr. Weiss was lying to me, he now had me at a decided disadvantage.

"What do you think?" he asked. "Is it possible that this can be sleeping sickness?"

"I should not like to say that it is impossible," I replied. "The disease is practically unknown to me. I have never practiced out of England and have had no occasion to study it. Until I have looked the subject up, I should not be in a position to give an opinion. Of course, if I could see Mr. Graves in one of what we may call his 'lucid intervals' I should be able to form a better idea. Do you think that could be managed?"

"It might. I see the importance of it and will certainly do my best; but he is a difficult man; a very difficult man. I sincerely hope it is not sleeping sickness."

"Why?"

"Because — as I understood from him — that disease is invariably fatal, sooner or later. There seem to be no cure. Do you think you will be able to decide when you see him again?"

"I hope so," I replied. "I shall look up the authorities and see exactly what the symptoms are — that is, so far as they are known; but my impression is that there is very little information available."

"And in the meantime?"

"We will give him some medicine and attend to his general condition, and you had better let me see him again as soon as possible." I was about to say that the effect of the medicine itself might throw some light on the patient's condition, but, as I proposed to treat him for morphine poisoning, I thought it wiser to keep this item of information to myself. Accordingly, I confined myself to a few general directions as to the care of the patient, to which Mr. Weiss listened attentively. "And," I concluded, "we must not lose sight of the opium question. You had better search the room carefully and keep a close watch on the patient, especially during his intervals of wakefulness."

"Very well, doctor," Mr. Weiss replied, "I will do all that you tell me and I will send for you again as soon as possible, if you do not object to poor Graves's ridiculous conditions. And now, if you will allow me to pay your fee, I will go and order the carriage while you are writing the prescription."

"There is no need for a prescription," I said. "I will make up some medicine and give it to the coachman."

Mr. Weiss seemed inclined to demur to this arrangement, but I had my own reasons for insisting on it. Modern prescriptions are not difficult to read, and I did not wish Mr. Weiss to know what treatment the patient was having.

As soon as I was left alone, I returned to the bedside and once more looked down at the impassive figure. And as I looked, my suspicions revived. It was very like morphine poisoning; and, if it was morphine, it was no common, medicinal dose that had been given. I opened my bag and took out my hypodermic case from which I extracted a little tube of atropine tabloids. Shaking out into my hand a couple of the tiny discs, I drew down the patient's under-lip and slipped the little tablets under his tongue. Then I quickly replaced the tube and dropped the case into my bag; and I had hardly done so when the door opened softly and the housekeeper entered the room.

"How do you find Mr. Graves?" she asked in what I thought a very unnecessarily low tone, considering the patient's lethargic state.

"He seems to be very ill," I answered.

"So!" she rejoined, and added: "I am sorry to hear that. We have been anxious about him."

She seated herself on the chair by the bedside, and, shading the candle from the patient's face — and her own, too — produced from a bag that hung from her waist a half-finished stocking and began to knit silently and with the skill characteristic of the German housewife. I looked at her attentively (though she was so much in the shadow that I could see her but indistinctly) and somehow her appearance prepossessed me as little as did that of the other members of the household. Yet she was not an ill-looking woman. She had an excellent figure, and the air of a person of good social position; her features were good enough and her coloring, although a little unusual, was not unpleasant. Like Mr. Weiss, she had very fair hair, greased, parted in the middle and brushed down as smoothly as the painted hair of a Dutch doll. She appeared to have no eyebrows at all — owing, no doubt, to the light color of the hair — and the doll-like character was emphasized by her eyes, which were either brown or dark grey, I could not see which. A further peculiarity consisted in a "habit spasm," such as one often sees in nervous children; a periodical quick jerk of the head, as if a cap-string or dangling lock were being shaken off the cheek. Her age I judged to be about thirty-five.

The carriage, which one might have expected to be waiting, seemed to take some time in getting ready. I sat, with growing impatience, listening to the sick man's soft breathing and the click of the house-keeper's knitting-needles. I wanted to get home, not only for my own sake; the patient's condition made it highly desirable that the remedies should be given as quickly as possible. But the minutes dragged on, and I was on the point of expostulating when a bell rang on the landing.

"The carriage is ready," said Mrs. Schallibaum. "Let me light you down the stairs."

She rose, and, taking the candle, preceded me to the head of the stairs, where she stood holding the light over the baluster-rail as I descended and crossed the passage to the open side door. The carriage was drawn up in the covered way as I could see by the faint glimmer of the distant candle; which also enabled me dimly to discern the coachman standing close by in the shadow. I looked round, rather expecting to see Mr. Weiss, but, as he made no appearance, I entered the carriage. The door was immediately banged to and locked, and I then heard the heavy bolts of the gates withdrawn and the loud creaking of hinges. The carriage moved out slowly and stopped; the gates slammed to behind me; I felt the lurch as the coachman climbed to his seat and we started forward.

My reflections during the return journey were the reverse of agreeable. I could not rid myself of the conviction that I was being involved in some very suspicious proceedings. It was possible, of course, that this feeling was due to the strange secrecy that surrounded my connection with this case; that, had I made my visit under ordinary conditions, I might have found in the patient's symptoms nothing to excite suspicion or alarm. It might be so, but that consideration did not comfort me.

Then, my diagnosis might be wrong. It might be that this was, in reality, a case of some brain affection accompanied by compression, such as slow hemorrhage, abscess, tumor or simple congestion. These cases were very difficult at times. But the appearances in this one did not consistently agree with the symptoms accompanying any of these conditions. As to sleeping sickness, it was, perhaps a more hopeful suggestion, but I could not decide for or against it until I had more knowledge; and against this view was the weighty fact that the symptoms did exactly agree with the theory of morphine poisoning.

But even so, there was no conclusive evidence of any criminal act. The patient might be a confirmed opium-eater, and the symptoms heightened by deliberate deception. The cunning of these unfortunates is proverbial and is only equaled by their secretiveness and mendacity. It would be quite possible for this man to feign profound stupor so long as he was watched, and then, when left alone for a few minutes, to nip out of bed and help himself from some secret store of the drug. This would be quite in character with his objection to seeing a doctor and his desire for secrecy. But still, I did not believe it to be the true explanation. In spite of all the various alternative possibilities, my suspicions came back to Mr. Weiss and the strange, taciturn woman, and refused to budge.

For all the circumstances of the case were suspicious. The elaborate preparations implied by the state of the carriage in which I was traveling; the make-shift appearance of the house; the absence of ordinary domestic servants, although a coachman was kept; the evident desire of Mr. Weiss and the woman to avoid thorough inspection of their persons; and, above all, the fact that the former had told me a deliberate lie. For he had lied, beyond all doubt. His statement as to the almost continuous stupor was absolutely irreconcilable with his other statement as to the patient's willfulness and obstinacy and even more irreconcilable with the deep and comparatively fresh marks of the spectacles on the patient's nose. That man had certainly worn spectacles within twenty-four hours, which he would hardly have done if he had been in a state bordering on coma.

My reflections were interrupted by the stopping of the carriage. The door was unlocked and thrown open, and I emerged from my dark and stuffy prison opposite my own house.

"I will let you have the medicine in a minute or two," I said to the coachman; and, as I let myself in with my latchkey, my mind came back swiftly from the general circumstances of the case to the very critical condition of the patient. Already I was regretting that I had not taken more energetic measures to rouse him and restore his flagging vitality; for it would be a terrible thing if he should take a turn for the worse and die before the coachman returned with the remedies. Spurred on by this alarming thought, I made up the medicines quickly and carried the hastily wrapped bottles out to the man, whom I found standing by the horse's head.

"Get back as quickly as you can," I said, "and tell Mr. Weiss to lose no time in giving the patient the draft in the small bottle. The directions are on the labels."

The coachman took the packages from me without reply, climbed to his seat, touched the horse with his whip and drove off at a rapid pace towards Newington Butts.

The little clock in the consulting-room showed that it was close on eleven; time for a tired G.P. to be thinking of bed. But I was not sleepy. Over my frugal supper I found myself taking up anew the thread of my meditations, and afterwards, as I smoked my last pipe by the expiring surgery fire, the strange and sinister features of the case continued to obtrude themselves on my notice. I looked up Stillbury's little reference library for information on the subject of sleeping sickness, but learned no more than that it was "a rare and obscure disease of which very little was known at present." I read up morphine poisoning and was only further confirmed in the belief that my diagnosis was correct; which would have been more satisfactory if the circumstances had been different.

For the interest of the case was not merely academic. I was in a position of great difficulty and responsibility and had to decide on a course of action. What ought I to do? Should I maintain the professional secrecy to which I was tacitly committed, or ought I to convey a hint to the police?

Suddenly, and with a singular feeling of relief, I bethought myself of my old friend and fellow-student, John Thorndyke, now an eminent authority on Medical Jurisprudence. I had been associated with him temporarily in one case as his assistant, and had then been deeply impressed by his versatile learning, his acuteness and his marvelous resourcefulness. Thorndyke was a barrister in extensive practice, and so would be able to tell me at once what was my duty from a legal point of view; and, as he was also a doctor of medicine, he would understand the exigencies of medical practice. If I could find time to call at the Temple and lay the case before him, all my doubts and difficulties would be resolved.

Anxiously, I opened my visiting-list to see what kind of day's work was in store for me on the morrow. It was not a heavy day, even allowing for one or two extra calls in the morning, but yet I was doubtful whether it would allow of my going so far from my district, until my eye caught, near the foot of the page, the name of Burton. Now Mr. Burton lived in one of the old houses on the east side of Bouverie Street, less than five minutes' walk from Thorndyke's chambers in King's Bench Walk; and he was, moreover, a "chronic" who could safely be left for the last. When I had done with Mr. Burton I could look in on my friend with a very good chance of catching him on his return from the hospital. I could allow myself time for quite a long chat with him, and, by taking a hansom, still get back in good time for the evening's work.

This was a great comfort. At the prospect of sharing my responsibilities with a friend on whose judgment I could so entirely rely, my embarrassments seemed to drop from me in a moment. Having entered the engagement in my visiting-list, I rose, in greatly improved spirits, and knocked out my pipe just as the little clock banged out impatiently the hour of midnight.

Chapter II

Thorndyke Devises a Scheme

*A*s I entered the Temple by the Tudor Street gate the aspect of the place smote my senses with an air of agreeable familiarity. Here had I spent many a delightful hour when working with Thorndyke at the remarkable Hornby case, which the newspapers had called "The Case of the Red Thumb Mark"; and here had I met the romance of my life, the story whereof is told elsewhere. The place was thus endeared to me by pleasant recollections of a happy past, and its associations suggested hopes of happiness yet to come and in the not too far distant future.

My brisk tattoo on the little brass knocker brought to the door no less a person than Thorndyke himself; and the warmth of his greeting made me at once proud and ashamed. For I had not only been an absentee; I had been a very poor correspondent.

"The prodigal has returned, Polton," he exclaimed, looking into the room. "Here is Dr. Jervis."

I followed him into the room and found Polton — his confidential servant, laboratory assistant, artificer and general "familiar" — setting out the tea-tray on a small table. The little man shook hands cordially with me, and his face crinkled up into the sort of smile that one might expect to see on a benevolent walnut.

"We've often talked about you, sir," said he. "The doctor was wondering only yesterday when you were coming back to us."

As I was not "coming back to them" quite in the sense intended I felt a little guilty, but reserved my confidences for Thorndyke's ear and replied in polite generalities. Then Polton fetched the teapot from the laboratory, made up the fire and departed, and Thorndyke and I subsided, as of old, into our respective armchairs.

"And whence do you spring from in this unexpected fashion?" my colleague asked. "You look as if you had been making professional visits."

"I have. The base of operations is in Lower Kennington Lane."

"Ah! Then you are 'back once more on the old trail'?"

"Yes," I answered, with a laugh, "'the old trail, the long trail, the trail that is always new.'"

"And leads nowhere," Thorndyke added grimly.

I laughed again; not very heartily, for there was an uncomfortable element of truth in my friend's remark, to which my own experience bore only too complete testimony. The medical practitioner whose lack of means forces him to subsist by taking temporary charge of other men's practices is apt to find that the passing years bring him little but grey hairs and a wealth of disagreeable experience.

"You will have to drop it, Jervis; you will, indeed," Thorndyke resumed after a pause. "This casual employment is preposterous for a man of your class and professional attainments. Besides, are you not engaged to be married and to a most charming girl?"

"Yes, I know. I have been a fool. But I will really amend my ways. If necessary, I will pocket my pride and let Juliet advance the money to buy a practice."

"That," said Thorndyke, "is a very proper resolution. Pride and reserve between people who are going to be husband and wife, is an absurdity. But why buy a practice? Have you forgotten my proposal?"

"I should be an ungrateful brute if I had."

"Very well. I repeat it now. Come to me as my junior, read for the Bar and work with me, and, with your abilities, you will have a chance of something like a career. I want you, Jervis," he added, earnestly. "I must have a junior, with my increasing practice, and you are the junior I want. We are old and tried friends; we have worked together; we like and trust one another, and you are the best man for the job that I know. Come; I am not going to take a refusal. This is an ultimatum."

"And what is the alternative?" I asked with a smile at his eagerness.

"There isn't any. You are going to say yes."

"I believe I am," I answered, not without emotion; "and I am more rejoiced at your offer and more grateful than I can tell you. But we must leave the final arrangements for our next meeting — in a week or so, I hope — for I have to be back in an hour, and I want to consult you on a matter of some importance."

"Very well," said Thorndyke; "we will leave the formal agreement for consideration at our next meeting. What is it that you want my opinion on?"

"The fact is," I said, "I am in a rather awkward dilemma, and I want you to tell me what you think I ought to do."

Thorndyke paused in the act of refilling my cup and glanced at me with unmistakable anxiety.

"Nothing of an unpleasant nature, I hope," said he.

"No, no; nothing of that kind," I answered with a smile as I interpreted the euphemism; for "something unpleasant," in the case of a young and reasonably presentable medical man is ordinarily the equivalent of trouble with the female of his species. "It is nothing that concerns me personally at all," I continued; "it is a question of professional responsibility. But I had better give you an account of the affair in a complete narrative, as I know that you like to have your data in a regular and consecutive order."

Thereupon I proceeded to relate the history of my visit to the mysterious Mr. Graves, not omitting any single circumstance or detail that I could recollect.

Thorndyke listened from the very beginning of my story with the closest attention. His face was the most impassive that I have ever seen; ordinarily as inscrutable as a bronze mask; but to me, who knew him intimately, there was a certain something — a change of color, perhaps, or an additional sparkle of the eye — that told me when his curious passion for investigation was fully aroused. And now, as I told him of that weird journey and the strange, secret house to which it had brought me, I could see that it offered a problem after his very heart. During the whole of my narration he sat as motionless as a statue, evidently committing the whole story to memory, detail by detail; and even when I had finished he remained for an appreciable time without moving or speaking.

At length he looked up at me. "This is a very extraordinary affair, Jervis," he said.

"Very," I agreed; "and the question that is agitating me is, what is to be done?"

"Yes," he said, meditatively, "that is the question; and an uncommonly difficult question it is. It really involves the settlement of the antecedent question: What is it that is happening at that house?"

"What do you think is happening at that house?" I asked.

"We must go slow, Jervis," he replied. "We must carefully separate the legal tissues from the medical, and avoid confusing what we know with what we suspect. Now, with reference to the medical aspects of the case. The first question that confronts us is that of sleeping sickness, or Negro-lethargy as it is sometimes called; and here we are in a difficulty. We have not enough knowledge. Neither of us, I take it, has ever seen a case, and the extant descriptions are inadequate. From what I know of the disease, its symptoms agree with those in your case in respect of the alleged moroseness and in the gradually increasing periods of lethargy alternating with periods of apparent recovery. On the other hand, the disease is said to be confined to Negroes; but that probably means only that Negroes alone have hitherto been exposed to the conditions that produce it. A more important fact is that, as far as I know, extreme contraction of the pupils is not a symptom of sleeping sickness. To sum up, the probabilities are against sleeping sickness, but with our insufficient knowledge, we cannot definitely exclude it."

"You think that it may really be sleeping sickness?"

"No; personally I do not entertain that theory for a moment. But I am considering the evidence apart from our opinions on the subject. We have to accept it as a conceivable hypothesis that it may be sleeping sickness because we cannot positively prove that it is not. That is all. But when we come to the hypothesis of morphine poisoning, the case is different. The symptoms agree with those of morphine poisoning in every respect. There is no exception or disagreement whatever. The common sense of the matter is therefore that we adopt morphine poisoning as our working diagnosis; which is what you seem to have done."

"Yes. For purposes of treatment."

"Exactly. For medical purposes you adopted the more probable view and dismissed the less probable. That was the reasonable thing to do. But for legal purposes you must entertain both possibilities; for the hypothesis of poisoning involves serious legal issues, whereas the hypothesis of disease involves no legal issues at all."

"That doesn't sound very helpful," I remarked.

"It indicates the necessity for caution," he retorted.

"Yes, I see that. But what is your own opinion of the case?"

"Well," he said, "let us consider the facts in order. Here is a man who, we assume, is under the influence of a poisonous dose of morphine. The question is, did he take that dose himself or was it administered to him by some other person? If he took it himself, with what object did he take it? The history that was given to you seems completely to exclude the idea of suicide. But the patient's condition seems equally to exclude the idea of morphinomania. Your opium-eater does not reduce himself to a state of coma. He usually keeps well within the limits of the tolerance that has been established. The conclusion that emerges is, I think, that the drug was administered by some other person; and the most likely person seems to be Mr. Weiss."

"Isn't morphine a very unusual poison?"

"Very; and most inconvenient except in a single, fatal dose, by reason of the rapidity with which tolerance of the drug is established. But we must not forget that slow morphine poisoning might be eminently suitable in certain cases. The manner in which it enfeebles the will, confuses the judgment and debilitates the body might make it very useful to a poisoner whose aim was to get some instrument or document executed, such as a will, deed or assignment. And death could be produced afterwards by other means. You see the important bearing of this?"

"You mean in respect of a death certificate?"

"Yes. Suppose Mr. Weiss to have given a large dose of morphine. He then sends for you and throws out a suggestion of sleeping sickness. If you accept the suggestion he is pretty safe. He can repeat the process until he kills his victim and then get a certificate from you which will cover the murder. It was quite an ingenious scheme — which, by the way, is characteristic of intricate crimes; your subtle criminal often plans his crime like a genius, but he generally executes it like a fool — as this man seems to have done, if we are not doing him an injustice."

"How has he acted like a fool?"

"In several respects. In the first place, he should have chosen his doctor. A good, brisk, confident man who 'knows his own mind' is the sort of person who would have suited him; a man who would have jumped at a diagnosis and stuck to it; or else an ignorant weakling of alcoholic tendencies. It was shockingly bad luck to run against a cautious scientific practitioner like my learned friend. Then, of course, all this secrecy was sheer tomfoolery, exactly calculated to put a careful man on his guard; as it has actually done. If Mr. Weiss is really a criminal, he has mismanaged his affairs badly."

"And you apparently think that he is a criminal?"

"I suspect him deeply. But I should like to ask you one or two questions about him. You say he spoke with a German accent. What command of English had he? Was his vocabulary good? Did he use any German idioms?"

"No. I should say that his English was perfect, and I noticed that his phrases were quite well chosen even for an Englishman."

"Did he seem to you 'made up' in any way; disguised, I mean?"

"I couldn't say. The light was so very feeble."

"You couldn't see the color of his eyes, for instance?"

"No. I think they were grey, but I couldn't be sure."

"And as to the coachman. He wore a wig, you said. Could you see the color of his eyes? Or any peculiarity by which you could recognize him?"

"He had a malformed thumb-nail on his right hand. That is all I can say about him."

"He didn't strike you as resembling Weiss in any way; in voice or features?"

"Not at all; and he spoke, as I told you, with a distinct Scotch accent."

"The reason I ask is that if Weiss is attempting to poison this man, the coachman is almost certain to be a confederate and might be a relative. You had better examine him closely if you get another chance."

"I will. And that brings me back to the question, What am I to do? Ought I to report the case to the police?"

"I am inclined to think not. You have hardly enough facts. Of course, if Mr. Weiss has administered poison 'unlawfully and maliciously' he has committed a felony, and is liable under the Consolidation Acts of 1861 to ten years' penal servitude. But I do not see how you could swear an information. You don't know that he administered the poison — if poison has really been administered — and you cannot give any reliable name or any address whatever. Then there is the question of sleeping sickness. You reject it for medical purposes, but you could not swear, in a court of law, that this is not a case of sleeping sickness."

"No," I admitted, "I could not."

"Then I think the police would decline to move in the matter, and you might find that you had raised a scandal in Dr. Stillbury's practice to no purpose."

"So you think I had better do nothing in the matter?"

"For the present. It is, of course, a medical man's duty to assist justice in any way that is possible. But a doctor is not a detective; he should not go out of his way to assume police functions. He should keep his eyes and ears open, and, though, in general, he should keep his own counsel, it is his duty to note very carefully anything that seems to him likely to bear on any important legal issues. It is not his business officiously to initiate criminal inquiries, but it is emphatically his business to be ready, if called upon, to assist justice with information that his special knowledge and opportunities have rendered accessible to him. You see the bearing of this?"

"You mean that I should note down what I have seen and heard and say nothing about it until I am asked."

"Yes; if nothing further happens. But if you should be sent for again, I think it is your duty to make further observations with a view, if necessary, to informing the police. It may be, for instance, of vital importance to identify the house, and it is your duty to secure the means of doing so."

"But, my dear Thorndyke," I expostulated, "I have told you how I was conveyed to the house. Now, will you kindly explain to me how a man, boxed up in a pitch-dark carriage, is going to identify anyplace to which he may be carried?"

"The problem doesn't appear to me to present any serious difficulties," he replied.

"Doesn't it?" said I. "To me it looks like a pretty solid impossibility. But what do you suggest? Should I break out of the house and run away up the street? Or should I bore a hole through the shutter of the carriage and peep out?"

Thorndyke smiled indulgently. "The methods proposed by my learned friend display a certain crudity inappropriate to the character of a man of science; to say nothing of the disadvantage of letting the enemy into our counsels. No, no, Jervis; we can do something better than that. Just excuse me for a minute while I run up to the laboratory."

He hurried away to Polton's sanctum on the upper floor, leaving me to speculate on the method by which he proposed that a man should be enabled, as Sam Weller would express it, "to see through a flight of stairs and a deal door"; or, what was equally opaque, the wooden shutters of a closed carriage.

"Now," he said, when he returned a couple of minutes later with a small, paper-covered notebook in his hand, "I have set Polton to work on a little appliance that will, I think, solve our difficulty, and I will show you how I propose that you should make your observations. First of all, we have to rule the pages of this book into columns."

He sat down at the table and began methodically to rule the pages each into three columns, two quite narrow and one broad. The process occupied some time, during which I sat and watched with impatient curiosity the unhurried, precise movements of Thorndyke's pencil, all agog to hear the promised explanation. He was just finishing the last page when there came a gentle tap at the door, and Polton entered with a satisfied smile on his dry, shrewd-looking face and a small board in his hand.

"Will this do, sir?" he asked.

As he spoke he handed the little board to Thorndyke, who looked at it and passed it to me.

"The very thing, Polton," my friend replied. "Where did you find it? It's of no use for you to pretend that you've made it in about two minutes and a half."

Polton smiled one of his queer crinkly smiles, and remarking that "it didn't take much making," departed much gratified by the compliment.

"What a wonderful old fellow that is, Jervis," Thorndyke observed as his factotum retired. "He took in the idea instantly and seems to have produced the finished article by magic, as the conjurers bring forth rabbits and bowls of goldfish at a moment's notice. I suppose you see what your *modus operandi* is to be?"

I had gathered a clue from the little appliance — a plate of white fret-wood about seven inches by five, to one corner of which a pocket-compass had been fixed with shellac — but was not quite clear as to the details of the method.

"You can read a compass pretty quickly, I think?" Thorndyke said.

"Of course I can. Used we not to sail a yacht together when we were students?"

"To be sure we did; and we will again before we die. And now as to your method of locating this house. Here is a pocket reading-lamp which you can hook on the carriage lining. This notebook can be fixed to the board with an India-rubber band — thus. You observe that the thoughtful Polton has stuck a piece of thread on the glass of the compass to serve as a lubber's line. This is how you will proceed. As soon as you are locked in the carriage, light your lamp — better have a book with you in case the light is noticed — take out your watch and put the board on your knee, keeping its long side exactly in a line with the axis of the carriage. Then enter in one narrow column of your notebook the time, in the other the direction shown by the compass, and in the broad column any particulars, including the number of steps the horse makes in a minute. Like this."

He took a loose sheet of paper and made one or two sample entries on it in pencil, thus —

"9:40. S.E. Start from home.
9:41 S.W. Granite setts.
9:43. S.W. Wood pavement. Hoofs 104.
9:47. W. by S Granite crossing. Macadam —

and so on. Note every change of direction, with the time; and whenever you hear or feel anything from outside, note it, with the time and direction; and don't forget to note any variations in the horse's pace. You follow the process?"

"Perfectly. But do you think the method is accurate enough to fix the position of a house? Remember, this is only a pocket-compass with no dial, and it will jump frightfully. And the mode of estimating distance is very rough."

"That is all perfectly true," Thorndyke answered. "But you are over-looking certain important facts The track-chart that you will produce can be checked by other data. The house, for instance, has a covered way by which you could identify it if you knew approximately where to look for it. Then you must remember that your carriage is not traveling over a featureless plain. It is passing through streets which have a determined position and direction and which are accurately represented on the ordnance map. I think, Jervis, that, in spite of the apparent roughness of the method, if you make your observations carefully, we shall have no trouble in narrowing down the inquiry to a quite small area. If we get the chance, that is to say."

"Yes, if we do. I am doubtful whether Mr. Weiss will require my services again, but I sincerely hope he will. It would be rare sport to locate his secret burrow, all unsuspected. But now I must really be off."

"Good-bye, then," said Thorndyke, slipping a well-sharpened pencil through the rubber band that fixed the notebook to the board. "Let me know how the adventure progresses — if it progresses at all — and remember, I hold your promise to come and see me again quite soon in any case."

He handed me the board and the lamp, and, when I had slipped them into my pocket, we shook hands and I hurried away, a little uneasy at having left my charge so long.

Chapter III

"A Chiel's Amang Ye Takin' Notes"

The attitude of the suspicious man tends to generate in others the kind of conduct that seems to justify his suspicions. In most of us there lurks a certain strain of mischief which trustfulness disarms but distrust encourages. The inexperienced kitten which approaches us confidingly with arched back and upright tail, soliciting caresses, generally receives the gentle treatment that it expects; whereas the worldly-wise tom-cat, who, in response to friendly advances, scampers away and grins at us suspiciously from the fancied security of an adjacent wall, impels us to accelerate his retreat with a well-directed clod.

Now the proceedings of Mr. H. Weiss resembled those of the tom-cat aforesaid and invited an analogous reply. To a responsible professional man his extraordinary precautions were at once an affront and a challenge. Apart from graver considerations, I found myself dwelling with unholy pleasure on the prospect of locating the secret hiding place from which he seemed to grin at me with such complacent defiance; and I lost no time and spared no trouble in preparing myself for the adventure. The very hansom which bore me from the Temple to Kennington Lane was utilized for a preliminary test of Thorndyke's little apparatus. During the whole of that brief journey I watched the compass closely, noted the feel and sound of the road-material and timed the trotting of the horse. And the result was quite encouraging. It is true that the compass-needle oscillated wildly to the vibration of the cab, but still its oscillations took place around a definite point which was the average direction, and it was evident to me that the data it furnished were very fairly reliable. I felt very little doubt, after the preliminary trial, as to my being able to produce a moderately intelligible track-chart if only I should get an opportunity to exercise my skill.

But it looked as if I should not. Mr. Weiss's promise to send for me again soon was not fulfilled. Three days passed and still he made no sign. I began to fear that I had been too outspoken; that the shuttered carriage had gone forth to seek some more confiding and easy-going practitioner, and that our elaborate preparations had been made in vain. When the fourth day drew towards a close and still no summons had come, I was disposed reluctantly to write the case off as a lost opportunity.

And at that moment, in the midst of my regrets, the bottle-boy thrust an uncomely head in at the door. His voice was coarse, his accent was hideous, and his grammatical construction beneath contempt; but I forgave him all when I gathered the import of his message.

"Mr. Weiss's carriage is waiting, and he says will you come as quickly as you can because he's took very bad tonight."

I sprang from my chair and hastily collected the necessaries for the journey. The little board and the lamp I put in my overcoat pocket; I overhauled the emergency bag and added to its usual contents a bottle of permanganate of potassium which I thought I might require. Then I tucked the evening paper under my arm and went out.

The coachman, who was standing at the horse's head as I emerged, touched his hat and came forward to open the door.

"I have fortified myself for the long drive, you see," I remarked, exhibiting the newspaper as I stepped into the carriage.

"But you can't read in the dark," said he.

"No, but I have provided myself with a lamp," I replied, producing it and striking a match.

He watched me as I lit the lamp and hooked it on the back cushion, and observed:

"I suppose you found it rather a dull ride last time. It's a longish way. They might have fitted the carriage with an inside lamp. But we shall have to make it a quicker passage tonight. Governor says Mr. Graves is uncommon bad."

With this he slammed the door and locked it. I drew the board from my pocket, laid it on my knee, glanced at my watch, and, as the coachman climbed to his seat, I made the first entry in the little book.

"8:58. W. by S. Start from home. Horse 13 hands."

The first move of the carriage on starting was to turn round as if heading for Newington Butts, and the second entry accordingly read:

"8:58.30. E. by N."

But this direction was not maintained long. Very soon we turned south and then west and then south again. I sat with my eyes riveted on the compass, following with some difficulty its rapid changes. The needle swung to and fro incessantly but always within a definite arc, the center of which was the true direction. But this direction varied from minute to minute in the most astonishing manner. West, south, east, north, the carriage turned, "boxing" the compass until I lost all count of direction. It was an amazing performance. Considering that the man was driving against time on a mission of life and death urgency, his carelessness as to direction was astounding. The tortuousness of the route must have made the journey twice as long as it need have been with a little more careful selection. At least so it appeared to me, though, naturally, I was not in a position to offer an authoritative criticism.

As far as I could judge, we followed the same route as before. Once I heard a tug's whistle and knew that we were near the river, and we passed the railway station, apparently at the same time as on the previous occasion, for I heard a passenger train start and assumed that it was the same train. We crossed quite a number of thoroughfares with tram-lines — I had no idea there were so many — and it was a revelation to me to find how numerous the railway arches were in this part of London and how continually the nature of the road-metal varied.

It was by no means a dull journey this time. The incessant changes of direction and variations in the character of the road kept me most uncommonly busy; for I had hardly time to scribble down one entry before the compass-needle would swing round sharply, showing that we had once more turned a corner; and I was quite taken by surprise when the carriage slowed down and turned into the covered way. Very hastily I scribbled down the final entry ("9:24. S.E. In covered way"), and having closed the book and slipped it and the board into my pocket, had just opened out the newspaper when the carriage door was unlocked and opened, whereupon I unhooked and blew out the lamp and pocketed that too, reflecting that it might be useful later.

As on the last occasion, Mrs. Schallibaum stood in the open doorway with a lighted candle. But she was a good deal less self-possessed this time. In fact she looked rather wild and terrified. Even by the candlelight I could see that she was very pale and she seemed unable to keep still. As she gave me the few necessary words of explanation, she fidgeted incessantly and her hands and feet were in constant movement.

"You had better come up with me at once," she said. "Mr. Graves is much worse tonight. We will wait not for Mr. Weiss."

Without waiting for a reply she quickly ascended the stairs and I followed. The room was in much the same condition as before. But the patient was not. As soon as I entered the room, a soft, rhythmical gurgle from the bed gave me a very clear warning of danger. I stepped forward quickly and looked down at the prostrate figure, and the warning gathered emphasis. The sick man's ghastly face was yet more ghastly; his eyes were more sunken, his skin more livid; "his nose was as sharp as a pen," and if he did not "babble of green fields" it was because he seemed to be beyond even that. If it had been a case of disease, I should have said at once that he was dying. He had all the appearance of a man *in articulo mortis.* Even as it was, feeling convinced that the case was one of morphine poisoning, I was far from confident that I should be able to draw him back from the extreme edge of vitality on which he trembled so insecurely.

"He is very ill? He is dying?"

It was Mrs. Schallibaum's voice; very low, but eager and intense. I turned, with my finger on the patient's wrist, and looked into the face of the most thoroughly scared woman I have ever seen. She made no attempt now to avoid the light, but looked me squarely in the face, and I noticed, half-unconsciously, that her eyes were brown and had a curious strained expression.

"Yes," I answered, "he is very ill. He is in great danger."

She still stared at me fixedly for some seconds. And then a very odd thing occurred. Suddenly she squinted — squinted horribly; not with the familiar convergent squint which burlesque artists imitate, but with external or divergent squint of extreme near sight or unequal vision. The effect was quite startling. One moment both her eyes were looking straight into mine; the next, one of them rolled round until it looked out of the uttermost corner, leaving the other gazing steadily forward.

She was evidently conscious of the change, for she turned her head away quickly and reddened somewhat. But it was no time for thoughts of personal appearance.

"You can save him, doctor! You will not let him die! He must not be allowed to die!"

She spoke with as much passion as if he had been the dearest friend that she had in the world, which I suspected was far from being the case. But her manifest terror had its uses.

"If anything is to be done to save him," I said, "it must be done quickly. I will give him some medicine at once, and meanwhile you must make some strong coffee."

"Coffee!" she exclaimed. "But we have none in the house. Will not tea do, if I make it very strong?"

"No, it will not. I must have coffee; and I must have it quickly."

"Then I suppose I must go and get some. But it is late. The shops will be shut. And I don't like leaving Mr. Graves."

"Can't you send the coachman?" I asked.

She shook her head impatiently. "No, that is no use. I must wait until Mr. Weiss comes."

"That won't do," I said, sharply. "He will slip through our fingers while you are waiting. You must go and get that coffee at once and bring it to me as soon as it is ready. And I want a tumbler and some water."

She brought me a water-bottle and glass from the wash-stand and then, with a groan of despair, hurried from the room.

I lost no time in applying the remedies that I had to hand. Shaking out into the tumbler a few crystals of potassium permanganate, I filled it up with water and approached the patient. His stupor was profound. I shook him as roughly as was safe in his depressed condition, but elicited no resistance or responsive movement. As it seemed very doubtful whether he was capable of swallowing, I dared not take the risk of pouring the liquid into his mouth for fear of suffocating him. A stomach-tube would have solved the difficulty, but, of course, I had not one with me. I had, however, a mouth-speculum which also acted as a gag, and, having propped the patient's mouth open with this, I hastily slipped off one of the rubber tubes from my stethoscope and inserted into one end of it a vulcanite ear-speculum to serve as a funnel. Then, introducing the other end of the tube into the gullet as far as its length would permit, I cautiously poured a small quantity of the permanganate solution into the extemporized funnel. To my great relief a movement of the throat showed that the swallowing reflex still existed, and, thus encouraged, I poured down the tube as much of the fluid as I thought it wise to administer at one time.

The dose of permanganate that I had given was enough to neutralize any reasonable quantity of the poison that might yet remain in the stomach. I had next to deal with that portion of the drug which had already been absorbed and was exercising its poisonous effects. Taking my hypodermic case from my bag, I prepared in the syringe a full dose of atropine sulfate, which I injected forthwith into the unconscious man's arm. And that was all that I could do, so far as remedies were concerned, until the coffee arrived.

I cleaned and put away the syringe, washed the tube, and then, returning to the bedside, endeavored to rouse the patient from his profound lethargy. But great care was necessary. A little injudicious roughness of handling, and that thready, flickering pulse might stop forever; and yet it was almost certain that if he were not speedily aroused, his stupor would gradually deepen until it shaded off imperceptibly into death. I went to work very cautiously, moving his limbs about, flicking his face and chest with the corner of a wet towel, tickling the soles of his feet, and otherwise applying stimuli that were strong without being violent.

So occupied was I with my efforts to resuscitate my mysterious patient that I did not notice the opening of the door, and it was with something of a start that, happening to glance round, I perceived at the farther end of the room the shadowy figure of a man relieved by two spots of light reflected from his spectacles. How long he had been watching me I cannot say, but, when he saw that I had observed him, he came forward — though not very far — and I saw that he was Mr. Weiss.

"I am afraid," he said, "that you do not find my friend so well tonight?"

"So well!" I exclaimed. "I don't find him well at all. I am exceedingly anxious about him."

"You don't — er — anticipate anything of a — er — anything serious, I hope?"

"There is no need to anticipate," said I. "It is already about as serious as it can be. I think he might die at any moment."

"Good God!" he gasped. "You horrify me!"

He was not exaggerating. In his agitation, he stepped forward into the lighter part of the room, and I could see that his face was pale to ghastliness — except his nose and the adjacent red patches on his cheeks, which stood out in grotesquely hideous contrast. Presently, however, he recovered a little and said:

"I really think — at least I hope — that you take an unnecessarily serious view of his condition. He has been like this before, you know."

I felt pretty certain that he had not, but there was no use in discussing the question. I therefore replied, as I continued my efforts to rouse the patient:

"That may or may not be. But in any case there comes a last time; and it may have come now."

"I hope not," he said; "although I understand that these cases always end fatally sooner or later."

"What cases?" I asked.

"I was referring to sleeping sickness; but perhaps you have formed some other opinion as to the nature of this dreadful complaint."

I hesitated for a moment, and he continued: "As to your suggestion that his symptoms might be due to drugs, I think we may consider that as disposed of. He has been watched, practically without cessation since you came last, and, moreover, I have myself turned out the room and examined the bed and have not found a trace of any drug. Have you gone into the question of sleeping sickness?"

I looked at the man narrowly before answering, and distrusted him more than ever. But this was no time for reticence. My concern was with the patient and his present needs. After all, I was, as Thorndyke had said, a doctor, not a detective, and the circumstances called for straight-forward speech and action on my part.

"I have considered that question," I said, "and have come to a perfectly definite conclusion. His symptoms are not those of sleeping sickness. They are in my opinion undoubtedly due to morphine poisoning."

"But my dear sir!" he exclaimed, "the thing is impossible! Haven't I just told you that he has been watched continuously?"

"I can only judge by the appearances that I find," I answered; and, seeing that he was about to offer fresh objections, I continued: "Don't let us waste precious time in discussion, or Mr. Graves may be dead before we have reached a conclusion. If you will hurry them up about the coffee that I asked for some time ago, I will take the other necessary measures, and perhaps we may manage to pull him round."

The rather brutal decision of my manner evidently daunted him. It must have been plain to him that I was not prepared to accept any explanation of the unconscious man's condition other than that of morphine poisoning; whence the inference was pretty plain that the alternatives were recovery or an inquest. Replying stiffly that I "must do as I thought best," he hurried from the room, leaving me to continue my efforts without further interruption.

For some time these efforts seemed to make no impression. The man lay as still and impassive as a corpse excepting for the slow, shallow and rather irregular breathing with its ominous accompanying rattle. But presently, by imperceptible degrees, signs of returning life began to make their appearance. A sharp slap on the cheek with the wet towel produced a sensible flicker of the eyelids; a similar slap on the chest was followed by a slight gasp. A pencil, drawn over the sole of the foot, occasioned a visible shrinking movement, and, on looking once more at the eyes, I detected a slight change that told me that the atropine was beginning to take effect.

This was very encouraging, and, so far, quite satisfactory, though it would have been premature to rejoice. I kept the patient carefully covered and maintained the process of gentle irritation, moving his limbs and shoulders, brushing his hair and generally bombarding his deadened senses with small but repeated stimuli. And under this treatment, the improvement continued so far that on my bawling a question into his ear he actually opened his eyes for an instant, though in another moment, the lids had sunk back into their former position.

Soon after this, Mr. Weiss reentered the room, followed by Mrs. Schallibaum, who carried a small tray, on which were a jug of coffee, a jug of milk, a cup and saucer and a sugar basin.

"How do you find him now?" Mr. Weiss asked anxiously.

"I am glad to say that there is a distinct improvement," I replied. "But we must persevere. He is by no means out of the wood yet."

I examined the coffee, which looked black and strong and had a very reassuring smell, and, pouring out half a cupful, approached the bed.

"Now, Mr. Graves," I shouted, "we want you to drink some of this."

The flaccid eyelids lifted for an instant but there was no other response. I gently opened the unresisting mouth and ladled in a couple of spoonfuls of coffee, which were immediately swallowed; whereupon I repeated the proceeding and continued at short intervals until the cup was empty. The effect of the new remedy soon became apparent. He began to mumble and mutter obscurely in response to the questions that I bellowed at him, and once or twice he opened his eyes and looked dreamily into my face. Then I sat him up and made him drink some coffee from the cup, and, all the time, kept up a running fire of questions, which made up in volume of sound for what they lacked of relevancy.

Of these proceedings Mr. Weiss and his housekeeper were highly interested spectators, and the former, contrary to his usual practice, came quite close up to the bed, to get a better view.

"It is really a most remarkable thing," he said, "but it almost looks as if you were right, after all. He is certainly much better. But tell me, would this treatment produce a similar improvement if the symptoms were due to disease?"

"No," I answered, "it certainly would not."

"Then that seems to settle it. But it is a most mysterious affair. Can you suggest any way in which he can have concealed a store of the drug?"

I stood up and looked him straight in the face; it was the first chance I had had of inspecting him by any but the feeblest light, and I looked at him very attentively. Now, it is a curious fact — though one that most persons must have observed — that there sometimes occurs a considerable interval between the reception of a visual impression and its complete transfer to the consciousness. A thing may be seen, as it were, unconsciously, and the impression consigned, apparently, to instant oblivion; and yet the picture may be subsequently revived by memory with such completeness that its details can be studied as though the object were still actually visible.

Something of this kind must have happened to me now. Preoccupied as I was, by the condition of the patient, the professional habit of rapid and close observation caused me to direct a searching glance at the man before me. It was only a brief glance — for Mr. Weiss, perhaps embarrassed by my keen regard of him, almost immediately withdrew into the shadow — and my attention seemed principally to be occupied by the odd contrast between the pallor of his face and the redness of his nose and by the peculiar stiff, bristly character of his eyebrows. But there was another fact, and a very curious one, that was observed by me subconsciously and instantly forgotten, to be revived later when I reflected on the events of the night. It was this:

As Mr. Weiss stood, with his head slightly turned, I was able to look through one glass of his spectacles at the wall beyond. On the wall was a framed print; and the edge of the frame, seen through the spectacle-glass, appeared quite unaltered and free from distortion, magnification or reduction, as if seen through plain window-glass; and yet the reflections of the candle-flame in the spectacles showed the flame upside down, proving conclusively that the glasses were concave on one surface at least. The strange phenomenon was visible only for a moment or two, and as it passed out of my sight it passed also out of my mind.

"No," I said, replying to the last question; "I can think of no way in which he could have effectually hidden a store of morphine. Judging by the symptoms, he has taken a large dose, and, if he has been in the habit of consuming large quantities, his stock would be pretty bulky. I can offer no suggestion whatever."

"I suppose you consider him quite out of danger now?"

"Oh, not at all. I think we can pull him round if we persevere, but he must not be allowed to sink back into a state of coma. We must keep him on the move until the effects of the drug have really passed off. If you will put him into his dressing gown we will walk him up and down the room for a while."

"But is that safe?" Mr. Weiss asked anxiously.

"Quite safe," I answered. "I will watch his pulse carefully. The danger is in the possibility, or rather certainty, of a relapse if he is not kept moving."

With obvious unwillingness and disapproval, Mr. Weiss produced a dressing gown and together we invested the patient in it. Then we dragged him, very limp, but not entirely unresisting, out of bed and stood him on his feet. He opened his eyes and blinked owlishly first at one and then at the other of us, and mumbled a few unintelligible words of protest; regardless of which, we thrust his feet into slippers and endeavored to make him walk. At first he seemed unable to stand, and we had to support him by his arms as we urged him forward; but presently his trailing legs began to make definite walking movements, and, after one or two turns up and down the room, he was not only able partly to support his weight, but showed evidence of reviving consciousness in more energetic protests.

At this point Mr. Weiss astonished me by transferring the arm that he held to the housekeeper.

"If you will excuse me, doctor," said he, "I will go now and attend to some rather important business that I have had to leave unfinished. Mrs. Schallibaum will be able to give you all the assistance that you require, and will order the carriage when you think it safe to leave the patient. In case I should not see you again I will say 'good night.' I hope you won't think me very unceremonious."

He shook hands with me and went out of the room, leaving me, as I have said, profoundly astonished that he should consider any business of more moment than the condition of his friend, whose life, even now, was but hanging by a thread. However, it was really no concern of mine. I could do without him, and the resuscitation of this unfortunate half-dead man gave me occupation enough to engross my whole attention.

The melancholy progress up and down the room re-commenced, and with it the mumbled protests from the patient. As we walked, and especially as we turned, I caught frequent glimpses of the housekeeper's face. But it was nearly always in profile. She appeared to avoid looking me in the face, though she did so once or twice; and on each of these occasions her eyes were directed at me in a normal manner without any sign of a squint. Nevertheless, I had the impression that when her face was turned away from me she squinted. The "swivel eye" — the left — was towards me as she held the patient's right arm, and it was almost continuously turned in my direction, whereas I felt convinced that she was really looking straight before her, though, of course, her right eye was invisible to me. It struck me, even at the time, as an odd affair, but I was too much concerned about my charge to give it much consideration.

Meanwhile the patient continued to revive apace. And the more he revived, the more energetically did he protest against this wearisome perambulation. But he was evidently a polite gentleman, for, muddled as his faculties were, he managed to clothe his objections in courteous and even gracious forms of speech singularly out of agreement with the character that Mr. Weiss had given him.

"I thangyou," he mumbled thickly. "Ver' good take s'much trouble. Think I will lie down now." He looked wistfully at the bed, but I wheeled him about and marched him once more down the room. He submitted unresistingly, but as we again approached the bed he reopened the matter.

"S'quite s'fficient, thang you. Gebback to bed now. Much 'bliged frall your kindness" — here I turned him round — "no, really; m'feeling rather tired. Sh'like to lie down now, f'you'd be s'good."

"You must walk about a little longer, Mr. Graves," I said. "It would be very bad for you to go to sleep again."

He looked at me with a curious, dull surprise, and reflected awhile as if in some perplexity. Then he looked at me again and said:

"Thing, sir, you are mistake — mistaken me — mist —"

Here Mrs. Schallibaum interrupted sharply:

"The doctor thinks it's good for you to walk about. You've been sleeping too much. He doesn't want you to sleep anymore just now."

"Don't wanter sleep; wanter lie down," said the patient.

"But you mustn't lie down for a little while. You must walk about for a few minutes more. And you'd better not talk. Just walk up and down."

"There's no harm in his talking," said I; "in fact it's good for him. It will help to keep him awake."

"I should think it would tire him," said Mrs. Schallibaum; "and it worries me to hear him asking to lie down when we can't let him."

She spoke sharply and in an unnecessarily high tone so that the patient could not fail to hear. Apparently he took in the very broad hint contained in the concluding sentence, for he trudged wearily and unsteadily up and down the room for some time without speaking, though he continued to look at me from time to time as if something in my appearance puzzled him exceedingly. At length his intolerable longing for repose overcame his politeness and he returned to the attack.

"Surely v' walked enough now. Feeling very tired. Am really. Would you be s'kind 's t'let me lie down few minutes?"

"Don't you think he might lie down for a little while?" Mrs. Schallibaum asked.

I felt his pulse, and decided that he was really becoming fatigued, and that it would be wiser not to overdo the exercise while he was so weak. Accordingly, I consented to his returning to bed, and turned him round in that direction; whereupon he tottered gleefully towards his resting-place like a tired horse heading for its stable.

As soon as he was tucked in, I gave him a full cup of coffee, which he drank with some avidity as if thirsty. Then I sat down by the bedside, and, with a view to keeping him awake, began once more to ply him with questions.

"Does your head ache, Mr. Graves?" I asked.

"The doctor says 'does your head ache?'" Mrs. Schallibaum squalled, so loudly that the patient started perceptibly.

"I heard him, m'dear girl," he answered with a faint smile. "Not deaf you know. Yes. Head aches a good deal. But I thing this gennleman mistakes —"

"He says you are to keep awake. You mustn't go to sleep again, and you are not to close your eyes."

"All ri' Pol'n. Keep'm open," and he proceeded forthwith to shut them with an air of infinite peacefulness. I grasped his hand and shook it gently, on which he opened his eyes and looked at me sleepily. The housekeeper stroked his head, keeping her face half-turned from me —

as she had done almost constantly, to conceal the squinting eye, as I assumed — and said:

"Need we keep you any longer, doctor? It is getting very late and you have a long way to go."

I looked doubtfully at the patient. I was loath to leave him, distrusting these people as I did. But I had my work to do on the morrow, with, perhaps, a night call or two in the interval, and the endurance even of a general practitioner has its linits.

"I think I heard the carriage some time ago," Mrs. Schallibaum added.

I rose hesitatingly and looked at my watch. It had turned half-past eleven.

"You understand," I said in a low voice, "that the danger is not over? If he is left now he will fall asleep, and in all human probability will never wake. You clearly understand that?"

"Yes, quite clearly. I promise you he shall not be allowed to fall asleep again."

As she spoke, she looked me full in the face for a few moments, and I noted that her eyes had a perfectly normal appearance, without any trace whatever of a squint.

"Very well," I said. "On that understanding I will go now; and I shall hope to find our friend quite recovered at my next visit."

I turned to the patient, who was already dozing, and shook his hand heartily.

"Good-bye, Mr. Graves!" I said. "I am sorry to have to disturb your repose so much; but you must keep awake, you know. Won't do to go to sleep."

"Ver' well," he replied drowsily. "Sorry t' give you all this trouble. L' keep awake. But I think you're mistak'n —"

"He says it's very important that you shouldn't go to sleep, and that I am to see that you don't. Do you understand?"

"Yes, I un'stan'. But why does this gennlem'n — ?"

"Now it's of no use for you to ask a lot of questions," Mrs. Schallibaum said playfully; "we'll talk to you tomorrow. Good night, doctor. I'll light you down the stairs, but I won't come down with you, or the patient will be falling asleep again."

Taking this definite dismissal, I retired, followed by a dreamily surprised glance from the sick man. The housekeeper held the candle over the balusters until I reached the bottom of the stairs, when I perceived through the open door along the passage a glimmer of light from the carriage lamps. The coachman was standing just outside, faintly illuminated by the very dim lamplight, and as I stepped into the carriage he remarked in his Scotch dialect that I "seemed to have been makin' a nicht of it." He did not wait for any reply — none being in fact needed — but shut the door and locked it.

I lit my little pocket-lamp and hung it on the back cushion. I even drew the board and notebook from my pocket. But it seemed rather unnecessary to take a fresh set of notes, and, to tell the truth, I rather shirked the labor, tired as I was after my late exertions; besides, I wanted to think over the events of the evening, while they were fresh in my memory. Accordingly I put away the notebook, filled and lighted my pipe, and settled myself to review the incidents attending my second visit to this rather uncanny house.

Considered in leisurely retrospect, that visit offered quite a number of problems that called for elucidation. There was the patient's condition, for instance. Any doubt as to the cause of his symptoms was set at rest by the effect of the antidotes. Mr. Graves was certainly under the influence of morphine, and the only doubtful question was how he had become so. That he had taken the poison himself was incredible. No morphinomaniac would take such a knock-down dose. It was practically certain that the poison had been administered by someone else, and, on Mr. Weiss's own showing, there was no one but himself and the housekeeper who could have administered it. And to this conclusion all the other very queer circumstances pointed.

What were these circumstances? They were, as I have said, numerous, though many of them seemed trivial. To begin with, Mr. Weiss's habit of appearing some time after my arrival and disappearing some time before my departure was decidedly odd. But still more odd was his sudden departure this evening on what looked like a mere pretext. That departure coincided in time with the sick man's recovery of the power of speech. Could it be that Mr. Weiss was afraid that the half-conscious man might say something compromising to him in my presence? It looked rather like it. And yet he had gone away and left me with the patient and the housekeeper.

But when I came to think about it I remembered that Mrs. Schallibaum had shown some anxiety to prevent the patient from talking. She had interrupted him more than once, and had on two occasions broken in when he seemed to be about to ask me some question. I was "mistaken" about something. What was that something that he wanted to tell me?

It had struck me as singular that there should be no coffee in the house, but a sufficiency of tea. Germans are not usually tea-drinkers and they do take coffee. But perhaps there was nothing in this. Rather more remarkable was the invisibility of the coachman. Why could he not be sent to fetch the coffee, and why did not he, rather than the housekeeper, come to take the place of Mr. Weiss when the latter had to go away.

There were other points, too. I recalled the word that sounded like "Pol'n," which Mr. Graves had used in speaking to the housekeeper. Apparently it was a Christian name of some kind; but why did Mr. Graves call the woman by her Christian name when Mr. Weiss addressed her formally as Mrs. Schallibaum? And, as to the woman herself: what was the meaning of that curious disappearing squint? Physically it presented no mystery. The woman had an ordinary divergent squint, and, like many people, who suffer from this displacement, could, by a strong muscular effort, bring the eyes temporarily into their normal parallel position. I had detected the displacement when she had tried to maintain the effort too long, and the muscular control had given way. But why had she done it? Was it only feminine vanity — mere sensitiveness respecting a slight personal disfigurement? It might be so; or there might be some further motive. It was impossible to say.

Turning this question over, I suddenly remembered the peculiarity of Mr. Weiss's spectacles. And here I met with a real poser. I had certainly seen through those spectacles as clearly as if they had been plain window-glass; and they had certainly given an inverted reflection of the candle-flame like that thrown from the surface of a concave lens. Now they obviously could not be both flat and concave; but yet they had the properties peculiar to both flatness and concavity. And there was a further difficulty. If I could see objects unaltered through them, so could Mr. Weiss. But the function of spectacles is to alter the appearances of objects, by magnification, reduction or compensating distortion. If they leave the appearances unchanged they are useless. I could make nothing of it. After puzzling over it for quite a long time, I had to give it up; which I did the less unwillingly inasmuch as the construction of Mr. Weiss's spectacles had no apparent bearing on the case.

On arriving home, I looked anxiously at the message-book, and was relieved to find that there were no further visits to be made. Having made up a mixture for Mr. Graves and handed it to the coachman, I raked the ashes of the surgery fire together and sat down to smoke a final pipe while I reflected once more on the singular and suspicious case in which I had become involved. But fatigue soon put an end to my meditations; and having come to the conclusion that the circumstances demanded a further consultation with Thorndyke, I turned down the gas to a microscopic blue spark and betook myself to bed.

Chapter IV

The Official View

I rose on the following morning still possessed by the determination
to make some oportunity during the day to call on Thorndyke and take
his advice on the now urgent question as to what I was to do. I use the
word "urgent" advisedly; for the incidents of the preceding evening had
left me with the firm conviction that poison was being administered
for some purpose to my mysterious patient, and that no time must be
lost if his life was to be saved. Last night he had escaped only by the
narrowest margin — assuming him to be still alive — and it was only my
unexpectedly firm attitude that had compelled Mr. Weiss to agree to
restorative measures.

That I should be sent for again I had not the slightest expectation.
If what I so strongly suspected was true, Weiss would call in some other
doctor, in the hope of better luck, and it was imperative that he should
be stopped before it was too late. This was my view, but I meant to have
Thorndyke's opinion, and act under his direction, but

> "The best laid plans of mice and men
> Gang aft agley."

When I came downstairs and took a preliminary glance at the rough
memorandum-book, kept by the bottle-boy, or, in his absence, by the
housemaid, I stood aghast. The morning's entries looked already like a
sample page of the Post Office directory. The new calls alone were more
than equal to an ordinary day's work, and the routine visits remained
to be added. Gloomily wondering whether the Black Death had made
a sudden reappearance in England, I hurried to the dining room and
made a hasty breakfast, interrupted at intervals by the apparition of the
bottle-boy to announce new messages.

The first two or three visits solved the mystery. An epidemic of influenza had descended on the neighborhood, and I was getting not only our own normal work but a certain amount of overflow from other practices. Further, it appeared that a strike in the building trade had been followed immediately by a widespread failure of health among the bricklayers who were members of a certain benefit club; which accounted for the remarkable suddenness of the outbreak.

Of course, my contemplated visit to Thorndyke was out of the question. I should have to act on my own responsibility. But in the hurry and rush and anxiety of the work — for some of the cases were severe and even critical — I had no opportunity to consider any course of action, nor time to carry it out. Even with the aid of a hansom which I chartered, as Stillbury kept no carriage, I had not finished my last visit until near on midnight, and was then so spent with fatigue that I fell asleep over my postponed supper.

As the next day opened with a further increase of work, I sent a telegram to Dr. Stillbury at Hastings, whither he had gone, like a wise man, to recruit after a slight illness. I asked for authority to engage an assistant, but the reply informed me that Stillbury himself was on his way to town; and to my relief, when I dropped in at the surgery for a cup of tea, I found him rubbing his hands over the open day-book.

"It's an ill wind that blows nobody good," he remarked cheerfully as we shook hands. "This will pay the expenses of my holiday, including you. By the way, you are not anxious to be off, I suppose?"

As a matter of fact, I was; for I had decided to accept Thorndyke's offer, and was now eager to take up my duties with him. But it would have been shabby to leave Stillbury to battle alone with this rush of work or to seek the services of a strange assistant.

"I should like to get off as soon as you can spare me," I replied, "but I'm not going to leave you in the lurch."

"That's a good fellow," said Stillbury. "I knew you wouldn't. Let us have some tea and divide up the work. Anything of interest going?"

There were one or two unusual cases on the list, and, as we marked off our respective patients, I gave him the histories in brief synopsis. And then I opened the subject of my mysterious experiences at the house of Mr. Weiss.

"There's another affair that I want to tell you about; rather an unpleasant business."

"Oh, dear!" exclaimed Stillbury. He put down his cup and regarded me with quite painful anxiety.

"It looks to me like an undoubted case of criminal poisoning," I continued.

Stillbury's face cleared instantly. "Oh, I'm glad it's nothing more than that," he said with an air of relief. "I was afraid, it was some confounded woman. There's always that danger, you know, when a locum is young and happens — if I may say so, Jervis — to be a good-looking fellow. Let us hear about this case."

I gave him a condensed narrative of my connection with the mysterious patient, omitting any reference to Thorndyke, and passing lightly over my efforts to fix the position of the house, and wound up with the remark that the facts ought certainly to be communicated to the police.

"Yes," he admitted reluctantly, "I suppose you're right. Deuced unpleasant though. Police cases don't do a practice any good. They waste a lot of time, too; keep you hanging about to give evidence. Still, you are quite right. We can't stand by and see the poor devil poisoned without making some effort. But I don't believe the police will do anything in the matter."

"Don't you really?"

"No, I don't. They like to have things pretty well cut and dried before they act. A prosecution is an expensive affair, so they don't care to prosecute unless they are fairly sure of a conviction. If they fail they get hauled over the coals."

"But don't you think they would get a conviction in this case?"

"Not on your evidence, Jervis. They might pick up something fresh, but, if they didn't they would fail. You haven't got enough hard-baked facts to upset a capable defense. Still, that isn't our affair. You want to put the responsibility on the police and I entirely agree with you."

"There ought not to be any delay," said I.

"There needn't be. I shall look in on Mrs. Wackford and you have to see the Rummel children; we shall pass the station on our way. Why shouldn't we drop in and see the inspector or superintendent?"

The suggestion met my views exactly. As soon as we had finished tea, we set forth, and in about ten minutes found ourselves in the bare and forbidding office attached to the station.

The presiding officer descended from a high stool, and, carefully laying down his pen, shook hands cordially.

"And what can I do for you gentlemen?" he asked, with an affable smile.

Stillbury proceeded to open our business.

"My friend here, Dr. Jervis, who has very kindly been looking after my work for a week or two, has had a most remarkable experience, and he wants to tell you about it."

"Something in my line of business?" the officer inquired.

"That," said I, "is for you to judge. I think it is, but you may think otherwise"; and hereupon, without further preamble, I plunged into the history of the case, giving him a condensed statement similar to that which I had already made to Stillbury.

He listened with close attention, jotting down from time to time a brief note on a sheet of paper; and, when I had finished, he wrote out in a black-covered notebook a short précis of my statement.

"I have written down here," he said, "the substance of what you have told me. I will read the deposition over to you, and, if it is correct, I will ask you to sign it."

He did so, and, when I had signed the document, I asked him what was likely to be done in the matter.

"I am afraid," he replied, "that we can't take any active measures. You have put us on our guard and we shall keep our eyes open. But I think that is all we can do, unless we hear something further."

"But," I exclaimed, "don't you think that it is a very suspicious affair?"

"I do," he replied. "A very fishy business indeed, and you were quite right to come and tell us about it."

"It seems a pity not to take some measures," I said. "While you are waiting to hear something further, they may give the poor wretch a fresh dose and kill him."

"In which case we should hear something further, unless some fool of a doctor were to give a death certificate."

"But that is very unsatisfactory. The man ought not to be allowed to die."

"I quite agree with you, sir. But we've no evidence that he is going to die. His friends sent for you, and you treated him skillfully and left him in a fair way to recovery. That's all that we really know about it. Yes, I know," the officer continued as I made signs of disagreement, "you think that a crime is possibly going to be committed and that we ought to prevent it. But you overrate our powers. We can only act on evidence that a crime has actually been committed or is actually being attempted. Now we have no such evidence. Look at your statement, and tell me what you can swear to."

"I think I could swear that Mr. Graves had taken a poisonous dose of morphine."

"And who gave him that poisonous dose?"

"I very strongly suspect —"

"That's no good, sir," interrupted the officer. "Suspicion isn't evidence. We should want you to swear an information and give us enough facts to make out a *primâ facie* case against some definite person. And you couldn't do it. Your information amounts to this: that a certain person has taken a poisonous dose of morphine and apparently recovered. That's all. You can't swear that the names given to you are real names, and you can't give us any address or even any locality."

"I took some compass bearings in the carriage," I said. "You could locate the house, I think, without much difficulty."

The officer smiled faintly and fixed an abstracted gaze on the clock. "*You* could, sir," he replied. "I have no doubt whatever that *you* could. *I* couldn't. But, in any case, we haven't enough to go upon. If you learn anything fresh, I hope you will let me know; and I am very much obliged to you for taking so much trouble in the matter. Good evening sir. Good evening, Dr. Stillbury."

He shook hands with us both genially, and, accepting perforce this very polite but unmistakable dismissal, we took our departure.

Outside the station, Stillbury heaved a comfortable sigh. He was evidently relieved to find that no upheavals were to take place in his domain.

"I thought that would be their attitude," he said, "and they are quite right, you know. The function of law is to prevent crime, it is true; but prophylaxis in the sense in which we understand it is not possible in legal practice."

I assented without enthusiasm. It was disappointing to find that no precautionary measures were to be taken. However, I had done all that I could in the matter. No further responsibility lay upon me, and, as it was practically certain that I had seen and heard the last of Mr. Graves and his mysterious household, I dismissed the case from my mind. At the next corner Stillbury and I parted to go our respective ways; and my attention was soon transferred from the romance of crime to the realities of epidemic influenza.

The plethora of work in Dr. Stillbury's practice continued longer than I had bargained for. Day after day went by and still found me tramping the dingy streets of Kennington or scrambling up and down narrow stairways; turning in at night dead tired, or turning out half awake to the hideous jangle of the night bell.

It was very provoking. For months I had resisted Thorndyke's persuasion to give up general practice and join him. Not from lack of inclination, but from a deep suspicion that he was thinking of my wants rather than his own; that his was a charitable rather than a business proposal. Now that I knew this not to be the case, I was impatient to join him; and, as I trudged through the dreary thoroughfares of this superannuated suburb, with its once rustic villas and its faded gardens, my thoughts would turn enviously to the quiet dignity of the Temple and my friend's chambers in King's Bench Walk.

The closed carriage appeared no more; nor did any whisper either of good or evil reach me in connection with the mysterious house from which it had come. Mr. Graves had apparently gone out of my life forever.

But if he had gone out of my life, he had not gone out of my memory. Often, as I walked my rounds, would the picture of that dimly-lit room rise unbidden. Often would I find myself looking once more into that ghastly face, so worn, so wasted and haggard, and yet so far from repellent. All the incidents of that last night would reconstitute themselves with a vividness that showed the intensity of the impression that they had made at the time. I would have gladly forgotten the whole affair, for every incident of it was fraught with discomfort. But it clung to my memory; it haunted me; and ever as it returned it bore with it the disquieting questions: Was Mr. Graves still alive? And, if he was not, was there really nothing which could have been done to save him?

Nearly a month passed before the practice began to show signs of returning to its normal condition. Then the daily lists became more and more contracted and the day's work proportionately shorter. And thus the term of my servitude came to an end. One evening, as we were writing up the day-book, Stillbury remarked:

"I almost think, Jervis, I could manage by myself now. I know you are only staying on for my sake."

"I am staying on to finish my engagement, but I shan't be sorry to clear out if you can do without me."

"I think I can. When would you like to be off?"

"As soon as possible. Say tomorrow morning, after I have made a few visits and transferred the patients to you."

"Very well," said Stillbury. "Then I will give you your check and settle up everything tonight, so that you shall be free to go off when you like tomorrow morning."

Thus ended my connection with Kennington Lane. On the following day at about noon, I found myself strolling across Waterloo Bridge with the sensations of a newly liberated convict and a check for twenty-five guineas in my pocket. My luggage was to follow when I sent for it. Now, unhampered even by a hand-bag, I joyfully descended the steps at the north end of the bridge and headed for King's Bench Walk by way of the Embankment and Middle Temple Lane.

Chapter V

Jeffrey Blackmore's Will

*M*y arrival at Thorndyke's chambers was not unexpected, having been heralded by a premonitory post-card. The "oak" was open and an application of the little brass knocker of the inner door immediately produced my colleague himself and a very hearty welcome.

"At last," said Thorndyke, "you have come forth from the house of bondage. I began to think that you had taken up your abode in Kennington for good."

"I was beginning, myself, to wonder when I should escape. But here I am; and I may say at once that I am ready to shake the dust of general practice off my feet forever — that is, if you are still willing to have me as your assistant."

"Willing!" exclaimed Thorndyke, "Barkis himself was not more willing than I. You will be invaluable to me. Let us settle the terms of our comradeship forthwith, and tomorrow we will take measures to enter you as a student of the Inner Temple. Shall we have our talk in the open air and the spring sunshine?"

I agreed readily to this proposal, for it was a bright, sunny day and warm for the time of year — the beginning of April. We descended to the Walk and thence slowly made our way to the quiet court behind the church, where poor old Oliver Goldsmith lies, as he would surely have wished to lie, in the midst of all that had been dear to him in his checkered life. I need not record the matter of our conversation. To Thorndyke's proposals I had no objections to offer but my own unworthiness and his excessive liberality. A few minutes saw our covenants fully agreed upon, and when Thorndyke had noted the points on a slip of paper, signed and dated it and handed it to me, the business was at an end.

"There," my colleague said with a smile as he put away his pocket-book, "if people would only settle their affairs in that way, a good part of the occupation of lawyers would be gone. Brevity is the soul of wit; and the fear of simplicity is the beginning of litigation."

"And now," I said, "I propose that we go and feed. I will invite you to lunch to celebrate our contract."

"My learned junior is premature," he replied. "I had already arranged a little festivity — or rather had modified one that was already arranged. You remember Mr. Marchmont, the solicitor?"

"Yes."

"He called this morning to ask me to lunch with him and a new client at the 'Cheshire Cheese.' I accepted and notified him that I should bring you."

"Why the 'Cheshire Cheese'?" I asked.

"Why not? Marchmont's reasons for the selection were, first, that his client has never seen an old-fashioned London tavern, and second, that this is Wednesday and he, Marchmont, has a gluttonous affection for a really fine beef-steak pudding. You don't object, I hope?"

"Oh, not at all. In fact, now that you mention it, my own sensations incline me to sympathize with Marchmont. I breakfasted rather early."

"Then come," said Thorndyke. "The assignation is for one o'clock, and, if we walk slowly, we shall just hit it off."

We sauntered up Inner Temple Lane, and, crossing Fleet Street, headed sedately for the tavern. As we entered the quaint old-world dining room, Thorndyke looked round and a gentleman, who was seated with a companion at a table in one of the little boxes or compartments, rose and saluted us.

"Let me introduce you to my friend Mr. Stephen Blackmore," he said as we approached. Then, turning to his companion, he introduced us by our respective names.

"I engaged this box," he continued, "so that we might be private if we wished to have a little preliminary chat; not that beef-steak pudding is a great help to conversation. But when people have a certain business in view, their talk is sure to drift towards it, sooner or later."

Thorndyke and I sat down opposite the lawyer and his client, and we mutually inspected one another. Marchmont I already knew; an elderly, professional-looking man, a typical solicitor of the old school; fresh-faced, precise, rather irascible, and conveying a not unpleasant impression of taking a reasonable interest in his diet. The other man was quite young, not more than five-and-twenty, and was a fine athletic-looking fellow with a healthy, out-of-door complexion and an intelligent and highly prepossessing face. I took a liking to him at the first glance, and so, I saw, did Thorndyke.

"You two gentlemen," said Blackmore, addressing us, "seem to be quite old acquaintances. I have heard so much about you from my friend, Reuben Hornby."

"Ah!" exclaimed Marchmont, "that was a queer case — 'The Case of the Red Thumb Mark,' as the papers called it. It was an eye-opener to old-fashioned lawyers like myself. We've had scientific witnesses before — and bullied 'em properly, by Jove! when they wouldn't give the evidence that we wanted. But the scientific lawyer is something new. His appearance in court made us all sit up, I can assure you."

"I hope we shall make you sit up again," said Thorndyke.

"You won't this time," said Marchmont. "The issues in this case of my friend Blackmore's are purely legal; or rather, there are no issues at all. There is nothing in dispute. I tried to prevent Blackmore from consulting you, but he wouldn't listen to reason. Here! Waiter! How much longer are we to be waiters? We shall die of old age before we get our victuals!"

The waiter smiled apologetically. "Yessir!" said he. "Coming now, sir." And at this very moment there was borne into the room a Gargantuan pudding in a great bucket of a basin, which being placed on a three-legged stool was forthwith attacked ferociously by the white-clothed, white-capped carver. We watched the process — as did everyone present — with an interest not entirely gluttonous, for it added a pleasant touch to the picturesque old room, with its sanded floor, its homely, pewlike boxes, its high-backed settles and the friendly portrait of the "great lexicographer" that beamed down on us from the wall.

"This is a very different affair from your great, glittering modern restaurant," Mr. Marchmont remarked.

"It is indeed," said Blackmore, "and if this is the way in which our ancestors lived, it would seem that they had a better idea of comfort than we have."

There was a short pause, during which Mr. Marchmont glared hungrily at the pudding; then Thorndyke said:

"So you refused to listen to reason, Mr. Blackmore?"

"Yes. You see, Mr. Marchmont and his partner had gone into the matter and decided that there was nothing to be done. Then I happened to mention the affair to Reuben Hornby, and he urged me to ask your advice on the case."

"Like his impudence," growled Marchmont, "to meddle with my client."

"On which," continued Blackmore, "I spoke to Mr. Marchmont and he agreed that it was worth while to take your opinion on the case, though he warned me to cherish no hopes, as the affair was not really within your specialty."

"So you understand," said Marchmont, "that we expect nothing. This is quite a forlorn hope. We are taking your opinion as a mere formality, to be able to say that we have left nothing untried."

"That is an encouraging start," Thorndyke remarked. "It leaves me unembarrassed by the possibility of failure. But meanwhile you are arousing in me a devouring curiosity as to the nature of the case. Is it highly confidential? Because if not, I would mention that Jervis has now joined me as my permanent colleague."

"It isn't confidential at all," said Marchmont. "The public are in full possession of the facts, and we should be only too happy to put them in still fuller possession, through the medium of the Probate Court, if we could find a reasonable pretext. But we can't."

Here the waiter charged our table with the fussy rapidity of the overdue.

"Sorry to keep you waiting, sir. Rather early, sir. Wouldn't like it underdone, sir."

Marchmont inspected his plate critically and remarked:

"I sometimes suspect these oysters of being mussels; and I'll swear the larks are sparrows."

"Let us hope so," said Thorndyke. "The lark is better employed 'at Heaven's gate singing' than garnishing a beef-steak pudding. But you were telling us about your case."

"So I was. Well it's just a matter of — ale or claret? Oh, claret, I know. You despise the good old British John Barleycorn."

"He that drinks beer thinks beer," retorted Thorndyke. "But you were saying that it is just a matter of — ?"

"A matter of a perverse testator and an ill-drawn will. A peculiarly irritating case, too, because the defective will replaces a perfectly sound one, and the intentions of the testator were — er — were — excellent ale, this. A little heady, perhaps, but sound. Better than your sour French wine, Thorndyke — were — er — were quite obvious. What he evidently desired was — mustard? Better have some mustard. No? Well, well! Even a Frenchman would take mustard. You can have no appreciation of flavor, Thorndyke, if you take your victuals in that crude, unseasoned state. And, talking of flavor, do you suppose that there is really any difference between that of a lark and that of a sparrow?"

Thorndyke smiled grimly. "I should suppose," said he, "that they were indistinguishable; but the question could easily be put to the test of experiment."

"That is true," agreed Marchmont, "and it would really be worth trying, for, as you say, sparrows are more easily obtainable than larks. But, about this will. I was saying — er — now, what was I saying?"

"I understood you to say," replied Thorndyke, "that the intentions of the testator were in some way connected with mustard. Isn't that so, Jervis?"

"That was what I gathered," said I.

Marchmont gazed at us for a moment with a surprised expression and then, laughing good-humoredly, fortified himself with a draft of ale.

"The moral of which is," Thorndyke added, "that testamentary dispositions should not be mixed up with beef-steak pudding."

"I believe you're right, Thorndyke," said the unabashed solicitor. "Business is business and eating is eating. We had better talk over our case in my office or your chambers after lunch."

"Yes," said Thorndyke, "come over to the Temple with me and I will give you a cup of coffee to clear your brain. Are there any documents?"

"I have all the papers here in my bag," replied Marchmont; and the conversation — such conversation as is possible "when beards wag all" over the festive board — drifted into other channels.

As soon as the meal was finished and the reckoning paid, we trooped out of Wine Office Court, and, insinuating ourselves through the line of empty hansoms that, in those days, crawled in a continuous procession on either side of Fleet Street, betook ourselves by way of Mitre Court to King's Bench Walk. There, when the coffee had been requisitioned and our chairs drawn up around the fire, Mr. Marchmont unloaded from his bag a portentous bundle of papers, and we addressed ourselves to the business in hand.

"Now," said Marchmont, "let me repeat what I said before. Legally speaking, we have no case — not the ghost of one. But my client wished to take your opinion, and I agreed on the bare chance that you might detect some point that we had overlooked. I don't think you will, for we have gone into the case very thoroughly, but still, there is the infinitesimal chance and we may as well take it. Would you like to read the two wills, or shall I first explain the circumstances?"

"I think," replied Thorndyke, "a narrative of the events in the order of their occurrence would be most helpful. I should like to know as much as possible about the testator before I examine the documents."

"Very well," said Marchmont. "Then I will begin with a recital of the circumstances, which, briefly stated, are these: My client, Stephen Blackmore, is the son of Mr. Edward Blackmore, deceased. Edward Blackmore had two brothers who survived him, John, the elder, and Jeffrey, the younger. Jeffrey is the testator in this case.

"Some two years ago, Jeffrey Blackmore executed a will by which he made his nephew Stephen his executor and sole legatee; and a few months later he added a codicil giving two hundred and fifty pounds to his brother John."

"What was the value of the estate?" Thorndyke asked.

"About three thousand five hundred pounds, all invested in Consols. The testator had a pension from the Foreign Office, on which he lived, leaving his capital untouched. Soon after having made his will, he left the rooms in Jermyn Street, where he had lived for some years, stored his furniture and went to Florence. From thence he moved on to Rome and then to Venice and other places in Italy, and so continued to travel about until the end of last September, when it appears that he returned to England, for at the beginning of October he took a set of chambers in New Inn, which he furnished with some of the things from his old rooms. As far as we can make out, he never communicated with any of his friends, excepting his brother, and the fact of his being in residence at New Inn or of his being in England at all became known to them only when he died."

"Was this quite in accordance with his ordinary habits?" Thorndyke asked.

"I should say not quite," Blackmore answered. "My uncle was a studious, solitary man, but he was not formerly a recluse. He was not much of a correspondent but he kept up some sort of communication with his friends. He used, for instance, to write to me sometimes, and, when I came down from Cambridge for the vacations, he had me to stay with him at his rooms."

"Is there anything known that accounts for the change in his habits?"

"Yes, there is," replied Marchmont. "We shall come to that presently. To proceed with the narrative: On the fifteenth of last March he was found dead in his chambers, and a more recent will was then discovered, dated the twelfth of November of last year. Now no change had taken place in the circumstances of the testator to account for the new will, nor was there any appreciable alteration in the disposition of the property. As far as we can make out, the new will was drawn with the idea of stating the intentions of the testator with greater exactness and for the sake of doing away with the codicil. The entire property, with the exception of two hundred and fifty pounds, was, as before, bequeathed to Stephen, but the separate items were specified, and the testator's brother, John Blackmore, was named as the executor and residuary legatee."

"I see," said Thorndyke. "So that your client's interest in the will would appear to be practically unaffected by the change."

"Yes. There it is," exclaimed the lawyer, slapping the table to add emphasis to his words. "That is the pity of it! If people who have no knowledge of law would only refrain from tinkering at their wills, what a world of trouble would be saved!"

"Oh, come!" said Thorndyke. "It is not for a lawyer to say that."

"No, I suppose not," Marchmont agreed. "Only, you see, we like the muddle to be made by the other side. But, in this case, the muddle is on our side. The change, as you say, seems to leave our friend Stephen's interests unaffected. That is, of course, what poor Jeffrey Blackmore thought. But he was mistaken. The effect of the change is absolutely disastrous."

"Indeed!"

"Yes. As I have said, no alteration in the testator's circumstances had taken place at the time the new will was executed. *But* only two days before his death, his sister, Mrs. Edmund Wilson, died; and on her will being proved it appeared that she had bequeathed to him her entire personalty, estimated at about thirty thousand pounds."

"Heigho!" exclaimed Thorndyke. "What an unfortunate affair!"

"You are right," said Mr. Marchmont; "it was a disaster. By the original will this great sum would have accrued to our friend Mr. Stephen, whereas now, of course, it goes to the residuary legatee, Mr. John Blackmore. And what makes it even more exasperating is the fact that this is obviously not in accordance with the wishes and intentions of Mr. Jeffrey, who clearly desired his nephew to inherit his property."

"Yes," said Thorndyke; "I think you are justified in assuming that. But do you know whether Mr. Jeffrey was aware of his sister's intentions?"

"We think not. Her will was executed as recently as the third of September last, and it seems that there had been no communication between her and Mr. Jeffrey since that date. Besides, if you consider Mr. Jeffrey's actions, you will see that they suggest no knowledge or expectation of this very important bequest. A man does not make elaborate dispositions in regard to three thousand pounds and then leave a sum of thirty thousand to be disposed of casually as the residue of the estate."

"No," Thorndyke agreed. "And, as you have said, the manifest intention of the testator was to leave the bulk of his property to Mr. Stephen. So we may take it as virtually certain that Mr. Jeffrey had no knowledge of the fact that he was a beneficiary under his sister's will."

"Yes," said Mr. Marchmont, "I think we may take that as nearly certain."

"With reference to the second will," said Thorndyke, "I suppose there is no need to ask whether the document itself has been examined; I mean as to its being a genuine document and perfectly regular?"

Mr. Marchmont shook his head sadly.

"No," he said, "I am sorry to say that there can be no possible doubt as to the authenticity and regularity of the document. The circumstances under which it was executed establish its genuineness beyond any question."

"What were those circumstances?" Thorndyke asked.

"They were these: On the morning of the twelfth of November last, Mr. Jeffrey came to the porter's lodge with a document in his hand. 'This,' he said, 'is my will. I want you to witness my signature. Would you mind doing so, and can you find another respectable person to act as the second witness?' Now it happened that a nephew of the porter's, a painter by trade, was at work in the Inn. The porter went out and fetched him into the lodge and the two men agreed to witness the signature. 'You had better read the will,' said Mr. Jeffrey. 'It is not actually necessary, but it is an additional safeguard and there is nothing of a private nature in the document.' The two men accordingly read the document, and, when Mr. Jeffrey had signed it in their presence, they affixed their signatures; and I may add that the painter left the recognizable impressions of three greasy fingers."

"And these witnesses have been examined?"

"Yes. They have both sworn to the document and to their own signatures, and the painter recognized his finger-marks."

"That," said Thorndyke, "seems to dispose pretty effectually of any question as to the genuineness of the will; and if, as I gather, Mr. Jeffrey came to the lodge alone, the question of undue influence is disposed of too."

"Yes," said Mr. Marchmont. "I think we must pass the will as absolutely flawless."

"It strikes me as rather odd," said Thorndyke, "that Jeffrey should have known so little about his sister's intentions. Can you explain it, Mr. Blackmore?"

"I don't think that it is very remarkable," Stephen replied. "I knew very little of my aunt's affairs and I don't think my uncle Jeffrey knew much more, for he was under the impression that she had only a life interest in her husband's property. And he may have been right. It is not clear what money this was that she left to my uncle. She was a very taciturn woman and made few confidences to anyone."

"So that it is possible," said Thorndyke, "that she, herself, may have acquired this money recently by some bequest?"

"It is quite possible," Stephen answered.

"She died, I understand," said Thorndyke, glancing at the notes that he had jotted down, "two days before Mr. Jeffrey. What date would that be?"

"Jeffrey died on the fourteenth of March," said Marchmont.

"So that Mrs. Wilson died on the twelfth of March?"

"That is so," Marchmont replied; and Thorndyke then asked:

"Did she die suddenly?"

"No," replied Stephen; "she died of cancer. I understand that it was cancer of the stomach."

"Do you happen to know," Thorndyke asked, "what sort of relations existed between Jeffrey and his brother John?"

"At one time," said Stephen, "I know they were not very cordial; but the breach may have been made up later, though I don't know that it actually was."

"I ask the question," said Thorndyke, "because, as I dare say you have noticed, there is, in the first will, some hint of improved relations. As it was originally drawn that will makes Mr. Stephen the sole legatee. Then, a little later, a codicil is added in favor of John, showing that Jeffrey had felt the necessity of making some recognition of his brother. This seems to point to some change in the relations, and the question arises: if such a change did actually occur, was it the beginning of a new and further improving state of feeling between the two brothers? Have you any facts bearing on that question?"

Marchmont pursed up his lips with the air of a man considering an unwelcome suggestion, and, after a few moments of reflection, answered:

"I think we must say 'yes' to that. There is the undeniable fact that, of all Jeffrey's friends, John Blackmore was the only one who knew that he was living in New Inn."

"Oh, John knew that, did he?"

"Yes, he certainly did; for it came out in the evidence that he had called on Jeffrey at his chambers more than once. There is no denying that. But, mark you!" Mr. Marchmont added emphatically, "that does not cover the inconsistency of the will. There is nothing in the second will to suggest that Jeffrey intended materially to increase the bequest to his brother."

"I quite agree with you, Marchmont. I think that is a perfectly sound position. You have, I suppose, fully considered the question as to whether it would be possible to set aside the second will on the ground that it fails to carry out the evident wishes and intentions of the testator?"

"Yes. My partner, Winwood, and I went into that question very carefully, and we also took counsel's opinion — Sir Horace Barnaby — and he was of the same opinion as ourselves; that the court would certainly uphold the will."

"I think that would be my own view," said Thorndyke, "especially after what you have told me. Do I understand that John Blackmore was the only person who knew that Jeffrey was in residence at New Inn?"

"The only one of his private friends. His bankers knew and so did the officials from whom he drew his pension."

"Of course he would have to notify his bankers of his change of address."

"Yes, of course. And à propos of the bank, I may mention that the manager tells me that, of late, they had noticed a slight change in the character of Jeffrey's signature — I think you will see the reason of the change when you hear the rest of his story. It was very trifling; not more than commonly occurs when a man begins to grow old, especially if there is some failure of eyesight."

"Was Mr. Jeffrey's eyesight failing?" asked Thorndyke.

"Yes, it was, undoubtedly," said Stephen. "He was practically blind in one eye and, in the very last letter that I ever had from him, he mentioned that there were signs of commencing cataract in the other."

"You spoke of his pension. He continued to draw that regularly?"

"Yes; he drew his allowance every month, or rather, his bankers drew it for him. They had been accustomed to do so when he was abroad, and the authorities seem to have allowed the practice to continue."

Thorndyke reflected a while, running his eye over the notes on the slips of paper in his hand, and Marchmont surveyed him with a malicious smile. Presently the latter remarked:

"Methinks the learned counsel is floored."

Thorndyke laughed. "It seems to me," he retorted, "that your proceedings are rather like those of the amiable individual who offered the bear a flint pebble, that he might crack it and extract the kernel. Your confounded will seems to offer no soft spot on which one could commence an attack. But we won't give up. We seem to have sucked the will dry. Let us now have a few facts respecting the parties concerned in it; and, as Jeffrey is the central figure, let us begin with him and the tragedy at New Inn that formed the starting-point of all this trouble."

Chapter VI

Jeffrey Blackmore, Deceased

*H*aving made the above proposition, Thorndyke placed a fresh slip of paper on the blotting pad on his knee and looked inquiringly at Mr. Marchmont; who, in his turn, sighed and looked at the bundle of documents on the table.

"What do you want to know?" he asked a little wearily.

"Everything," replied Thorndyke. "You have hinted at circumstances that would account for a change in Jeffrey's habits and that would explain an alteration in the character of his signature. Let us have those circumstances. And, if I might venture on a suggestion, it would be that we take the events in the order in which they occurred or in which they became known."

"That's the worst of you, Thorndyke," Marchmont grumbled. "When a case has been squeezed out to the last drop, in a legal sense, you want to begin all over again with the family history of everyone concerned and a list of his effects and household furniture. But I suppose you will have to be humored; and I imagine that the best way in which to give you the information you want will be to recite the circumstances surrounding the death of Jeffrey Blackmore. Will that suit you?"

"Perfectly," replied Thorndyke; and thereupon Marchmont began:

"The death of Jeffrey Blackmore was discovered at about eleven o'clock in the morning of the fifteenth of March. It seems that a builder's man was ascending a ladder to examine a gutter on number 31, New Inn, when, on passing a second-floor window that was open at the top, he looked in and perceived a gentleman lying on a bed. The gentleman was fully clothed and had apparently lain down on the bed to rest; at least so the builder thought at the time, for he was merely passing the window on his way up, and, very properly, did not make a minute examination. But when, some ten minutes later, he came down and saw that the gentleman was still in the same position, he looked at him more attentively; and this is what he noticed — but perhaps we had better have it in his own words as he told the story at the inquest.

"'When I came to look at the gentleman a bit more closely, it struck me that he looked rather queer. His face looked very white, or rather pale yellow, like parchment, and his mouth was open. He did not seem to be breathing. On the bed by his side was a brass object of some kind — I could not make out what it was — and he seemed to be holding some small metal object in his hand. I thought it rather a queer affair, so, when I came down I went across to the lodge and told the porter about it. The porter came out across the square with me and I showed him the window. Then he told me to go up the stairs to Mr. Blackmore's chambers on the second pair and knock and keep on knocking until I got an answer. I went up and knocked and kept on knocking as loud as I could, but, though I fetched everybody out of all the other chambers in the house, I couldn't get any answer from Mr. Blackmore. So I went downstairs again and then Mr. Walker, the porter, sent me for a police-man.

"'I went out and met a policeman just by Dane's Inn and told him about the affair, and he came back with me. He and the porter consulted together, and then they told me to go up the ladder and get in at the window and open the door of the chambers from the inside. So I went up; and as soon as I got in at the window I saw that the gentleman was dead. I went through the other room and opened the outer door and let in the porter and the policeman.'

"That," said Mr. Marchmont, laying down the paper containing the depositions, "is the way in which poor Jeffrey Blackmore's death came to be discovered.

"The constable reported to his inspector and the inspector sent for the divisional surgeon, whom he accompanied to New Inn. I need not go into the evidence given by the police officers, as the surgeon saw all that they saw and his statement covers everything that is known about Jeffrey's death. This is what he says, after describing how he was sent for and arrived at the Inn:

"'In the bedroom I found the body of a man between fifty and sixty years of age, which has since been identified in my presence as that of Mr. Jeffrey Blackmore. It was fully dressed and wore boots on which was a moderate amount of dry mud. It was lying on its back on the bed, which did not appear to have been slept in, and showed no sign of any struggle or disturbance. The right hand loosely grasped a hypodermic syringe containing a few drops of clear liquid which I have since analyzed and found to be a concentrated solution of strophanthin.

"'On the bed, close to the left side of the body, was a brass opium-pipe of a pattern which I believe is made in China. The bowl of the pipe contained a small quantity of charcoal, and a fragment of opium together with some ash, and there was on the bed a little ash which appeared to have dropped from the bowl when the pipe fell or was laid down. On the mantelshelf in the bedroom I found a small glass-stoppered jar containing about an ounce of solid opium, and another, larger jar containing wood charcoal broken up into small fragments. Also a bowl containing a quantity of ash with fragments of half-burned charcoal and a few minute particles of charred opium. By the side of the bowl were a knife, a kind of awl or pricker and a very small pair of tongs, which I believe to have been used for carrying a piece of lighted charcoal to the pipe.

"'On the dressing-table were two glass tubes labeled "Hypodermic Tabloids: Strophanthin $\frac{1}{500}$ grain," and a minute glass mortar and pestle, of which the former contained a few crystals which have since been analyzed by me and found to be strophanthin.

"'On examining the body, I found that it had been dead about twelve hours. There were no marks of violence or any abnormal condition excepting a single puncture in the right thigh, apparently made by the needle of the hypodermic syringe. The puncture was deep and vertical in direction as if the needle had been driven in through the clothing.

"'I made a post-mortem examination of the body and found that death was due to poisoning by strophanthin, which appeared to have been injected into the thigh. The two tubes which I found on the dressing-table would each have contained, if full, twenty tabloids, each tabloid representing one five-hundredth of a grain of strophanthin. Assuming that the whole of this quantity was injected the amount taken would be forty five-hundredths, or about one twelfth of a grain. The ordinary medicinal dose of strophanthin is one five-hundredth of a grain.

"'I also found in the body appreciable traces of morphine — the principal alkaloid of opium — from which I infer that the deceased was a confirmed opium-smoker. This inference was supported by the general condition of the body, which was ill-nourished and emaciated and presented all the appearances usually met with in the bodies of persons addicted to the habitual use of opium.'

"That is the evidence of the surgeon. He was recalled later, as we shall see, but, meanwhile, I think you will agree with me that the facts testified to by him fully account, not only for the change in Jeffrey's habits — his solitary and secretive mode of life — but also for the alteration in his handwriting."

"Yes," agreed Thorndyke, "that seems to be so. By the way, what did the change in the handwriting amount to?"

"Very little," replied Marchmont. "It was hardly perceptible. Just a slight loss of firmness and distinctness; such a trifling change as you would expect to find in the handwriting of a man who had taken to drink or drugs, or anything that might impair the steadiness of his hand. I should not have noticed it, myself, but, of course, the people at the bank are experts, constantly scrutinizing signatures and scrutinizing them with a very critical eye."

"Is there any other evidence that bears on the case?" Thorndyke asked.

Marchmont turned over the bundle of papers and smiled grimly.

"My dear Thorndyke," he said, "none of this evidence has the slightest bearing on the case. It is all perfectly irrelevant as far as the will is concerned. But I know your little peculiarities and I am indulging you, as you see, to the top of your bent. The next evidence is that of the chief porter, a very worthy and intelligent man named Walker. This is what he says, after the usual preliminaries.

"'I have viewed the body which forms the subject of this inquiry. It is that of Mr. Jeffrey Blackmore, the tenant of a set of chambers on the second floor of number thirty-one, New Inn. I have known the deceased nearly six months, and during that time have seen and conversed with him frequently. He took the chambers on the second of last October and came into residence at once. Tenants at New Inn have to furnish two references. The references that the deceased gave were his bankers and his brother, Mr. John Blackmore. I may say that the deceased was very well known to me. He was a quiet, pleasant-mannered gentleman, and it was his habit to drop in occasionally at the lodge and have a chat with me. I went into his chambers with him once or twice on some small matters of business and I noticed that there were always a number of books and papers on the table. I understood from him that he spent most of his time indoors engaged in study and writing. I know very little about his way of living. He had no laundress to look after his rooms, so I suppose he did his own house-work and cooking; but he told me that he took most of his meals outside, at restaurants or his club.

"'Deceased impressed me as a rather melancholy, low-spirited gentleman. He was very much troubled about his eyesight and mentioned the matter to me on several occasions. He told me that he was practically blind in one eye and that the sight of the other was failing rapidly. He said that this afflicted him greatly, because his only pleasure in life was in the reading of books, and that if he could not read he should not wish to live. On another occasion he said that "to a blind man life was not worth living."'

"'On the twelfth of last November he came to the lodge with a paper in his hand which he said was his will' — But I needn't read that," said Marchmont, turning over the leaf, "I've told you how the will was signed and witnessed. We will pass on to the day of poor Jeffrey's death.

"'On the fourteenth of March,' the porter says, 'at about half-past six in the evening, the deceased came to the Inn in a four-wheeled cab. That was the day of the great fog. I do not know if there was anyone in the cab with the deceased, but I think not, because he came to the lodge just before eight o'clock and had a little talk with me. He said that he had been overtaken by the fog and could not see at all. He was quite blind and had been obliged to ask a stranger to call a cab for him as he could not find his way through the streets. He then gave me a check for the rent. I reminded him that the rent was not due until the twenty-fifth, but he said he wished to pay it now. He also gave me some money to pay one or two small bills that were owing to some of the tradespeople — a milk-man, a baker and a stationer.

"'This struck me as very strange, because he had always managed his business and paid the tradespeople himself. He told me that the fog had irritated his eye so that he could hardly read, and he was afraid he should soon be quite blind. He was very depressed; so much so that I felt quite uneasy about him. When he left the lodge, he went back across the square as if returning to his chambers. There was then no gate open excepting the main gate where the lodge is situated. That was the last time that I saw the deceased alive.'"

Mr. Marchmont laid the paper on the table. "That is the porter's evidence. The remaining depositions are those of Noble, the night porter, John Blackmore and our friend here, Mr. Stephen. The night porter had not much to tell. This is the substance of his evidence:

"'I have viewed the body of the deceased and identify it as that of Mr. Jeffrey Blackmore. I knew the deceased well by sight and occasionally had a few words with him. I know nothing of his habits excepting that he used to sit up rather late. It is one of my duties to go round the Inn at night and call out the hours until one o'clock in the morning. When calling out "one o'clock" I often saw a light in the sitting room of the deceased's chambers. On the night of the fourteenth instant, the light was burning until past one o'clock, but it was in the bedroom. The light in the sitting room was out by ten o'clock.'

"We now come to John Blackmore's evidence. He says:

"'I have viewed the body of the deceased and recognize it as that of my brother Jeffrey. I last saw him alive on the twenty-third of February, when I called at his chambers. He then seemed in a very despondent state of mind and told me that his eyesight was fast failing. I was aware that he occasionally smoked opium, but I did not know that it was a confirmed habit. I urged him, on several occasions, to abandon the practice. I have no reason to believe that his affairs were in any way embarrassed or that he had any reason for making away with himself other than his failing eyesight; but, having regard to his state of mind when I last saw him, I am not surprised at what has happened.'

"That is the substance of John Blackmore's evidence, and, as to Mr. Stephen, his statement merely sets forth the fact that he had identified the body as that of his uncle Jeffrey. And now I think you have all the facts. Is there anything more that you want to ask me before I go, for I must really run away now?"

"I should like," said Thorndyke, "to know a little more about the parties concerned in this affair. But perhaps Mr. Stephen can give me the information."

"I expect he can," said Marchmont; "at any rate, he knows more about them than I do; so I will be off. If you should happen to think of any way," he continued, with a sly smile, "of upsetting that will, just let me know, and I will lose no time in entering a caveat. Good-bye! Don't trouble to let me out."

As soon as he was gone, Thorndyke turned to Stephen Blackmore.

"I am going," he said, "to ask you a few questions which may appear rather trifling, but you must remember that my methods of inquiry concern themselves with persons and things rather than with documents. For instance, I have not gathered very completely what sort of person your uncle Jeffrey was. Could you tell me a little more about him?"

"What shall I tell you?" Stephen asked with a slightly embarrassed air.

"Well, begin with his personal appearance."

"That is rather difficult to describe," said Stephen. "He was a medium-sized man and about five feet seven — fair, slightly grey, clean-shaved, rather spare and slight, had grey eyes, wore spectacles and stooped a little as he walked. He was quiet and gentle in manner, rather yielding and irresolute in character, and his health was not at all robust though he had no infirmity or disease excepting his bad eyesight. His age was about fifty-five."

"How came he to be a civil-service pensioner at fifty-five?" asked Thorndyke.

"Oh, that was through an accident. He had a nasty fall from a horse, and, being a rather nervous man, the shock was very severe. For some time after he was a complete wreck. But the failure of his eyesight was the actual cause of his retirement. It seems that the fall damaged his eyes in some way; in fact he practically lost the sight of one — the right — from that moment; and, as that had been his good eye, the accident left his vision very much impaired. So that he was at first given sick leave and then allowed to retire on a pension."

Thorndyke noted these particulars and then said:

"Your uncle has been more than once referred to as a man of studious habits. Does that mean that he pursued any particular branch of learning?"

"Yes. He was an enthusiastic Oriental scholar. His official duties had taken him at one time to Yokohama and Tokyo and at another to Baghdad, and while at those places he gave a good deal of attention to the languages, literature and arts of the countries. He was also greatly interested in Babylonian and Assyrian archaeology, and I believe he assisted for some time in the excavations at Birs Nimroud."

"Indeed!" said Thorndyke. "This is very interesting. I had no idea that he was a man of such considerable attainments. The facts mentioned by Mr. Marchmont would hardly have led one to think of him as what he seems to have been: a scholar of some distinction."

"I don't know that Mr. Marchmont realized the fact himself," said Stephen; "or that he would have considered it of any moment if he had. Nor, as far as that goes, do I. But, of course, I have no experience of legal matters."

"You can never tell beforehand," said Thorndyke, "what facts may turn out to be of moment, so that it is best to collect all you can get. By the way, were you aware that your uncle was an opium-smoker?"

"No, I was not. I knew that he had an opium-pipe which he brought with him when he came home from Japan; but I thought it was only a curio. I remember him telling me that he once tried a few puffs at an opium-pipe and found it rather pleasant, though it gave him a headache. But I had no idea he had contracted the habit; in fact, I may say that I was utterly astonished when the fact came out at the inquest."

Thorndyke made a note of this answer, too, and said:

"I think that is all I have to ask you about your uncle Jeffrey. And now as to Mr. John Blackmore. What sort of man is he?"

"I am afraid I can't tell you very much about him. Until I saw him at the inquest, I had not met him since I was a boy. But he is a very different kind of man from Uncle Jeffrey; different in appearance and different in character."

"You would say that the two brothers were physically quite unlike, then?"

"Well," said Stephen, "I don't know that I ought to say that. Perhaps I am exaggerating the difference. I am thinking of Uncle Jeffrey as he was when I saw him last and of uncle John as he appeared at the inquest. They were very different then. Jeffrey was thin, pale, clean shaven, wore spectacles and walked with a stoop. John is a shade taller, a shade greyer, has good eyesight, a healthy, florid complexion, a brisk, upright carriage, is distinctly stout and wears a beard and moustache which are black and only very slightly streaked with grey. To me they looked as unlike as two men could, though their features were really of the same type; indeed, I have heard it said that, as young men, they were rather alike, and they both resembled their mother. But there is no doubt as to their difference in character. Jeffrey was quiet, serious and studious, whereas John rather inclined to what is called a fast life; he used to frequent race meetings, and, I think, gambled a good deal at times."

"What is his profession?"

"That would be difficult to tell; he has so many; he is so very versatile. I believe he began life as an articled pupil in the laboratory of a large brewery, but he soon left that and went on the stage. He seems to have remained in 'the profession' for some years, touring about this country and making occasional visits to America. The life seemed to suit him and I believe he was decidedly successful as an actor. But suddenly he left the stage and blossomed out in connection with a bucket-shop in London."

"And what is he doing now?"

"At the inquest he described himself as a stockbroker, so I presume he is still connected with the bucket-shop."

Thorndyke rose, and taking down from the reference shelves a list of members of the Stock Exchange, turned over the leaves.

"Yes," he said, replacing the volume, "he must be an outside broker. His name is not in the list of members of 'the House.' From what you tell me, it is easy to understand that there should have been no great intimacy between the two brothers, without assuming any kind of ill-feeling. They simply had very little in common. Do you know of anything more?"

"No. I have never heard of any actual quarrel or disagreement. My impression that they did not get on very well may have been, I think, due to the terms of the will, especially the first will. And they certainly did not seek one another's society."

"That is not very conclusive," said Thorndyke. "As to the will, a thrifty man is not usually much inclined to bequeath his savings to a gentleman who may probably employ them in a merry little flutter on the turf or the Stock Exchange. And then there was yourself; clearly a more suitable subject for a legacy, as your life is all before you. But this is mere speculation and the matter is not of much importance, as far as we can see. And now, tell me what John Blackmore's relations were with Mrs. Wilson. I gather that she left the bulk of her property to Jeffrey, her younger brother. Is that so?"

"Yes. She left nothing to John. The fact is that they were hardly on speaking terms. I believe John had treated her rather badly, or, at any rate, she thought he had. Mr. Wilson, her late husband, dropped some money over an investment in connection with the bucket-shop that I spoke of, and I think she suspected John of having let him in. She may have been mistaken, but you know what ladies are when they get an idea into their heads."

"Did you know your aunt well?"

"No; very slightly. She lived down in Devonshire and saw very little of any of us. She was a taciturn, strong-minded woman; quite unlike her brothers. She seems to have resembled her father's family."

"You might give me her full name."

"Julia Elizabeth Wilson. Her husband's name was Edmund Wilson."

"Thank you. There is just one more point. What has happened to your uncle's chambers in New Inn since his death?"

"They have remained shut up. As all his effects were left to me, I have taken over the tenancy for the present to avoid having them disturbed. I thought of keeping them for my own use, but I don't think I could live in them after what I have seen."

"You have inspected them, then?"

"Yes; I have just looked through them. I went there on the day of the inquest."

"Now tell me: as you looked through those rooms, what kind of impression did they convey to you as to your uncle's habits and mode of life?"

Stephen smiled apologetically. "I am afraid," said he, "that they did not convey any particular impression in that respect. I looked into the sitting room and saw all his old familiar household gods, and then I went into the bedroom and saw the impression on the bed where his corpse had lain; and that gave me such a sensation of horror that I came away at once."

"But the appearance of the rooms must have conveyed something to your mind," Thorndyke urged.

"I am afraid it did not. You see, I have not your analytical eye. But perhaps you would like to look through them yourself? If you would, pray do so. They are my chambers now."

"I think I should like to glance round them," Thorndyke replied.

"Very well," said Stephen. "I will give you my card now, and I will look in at the lodge presently and tell the porter to hand you the key whenever you like to look over the rooms."

He took a card from his case, and, having written a few lines on it, handed it to Thorndyke.

"It is very good of you," he said, "to take so much trouble. Like Mr. Marchmont, I have no expectation of any result from your efforts, but I am very grateful to you, all the same, for going into the case so thoroughly. I suppose you don't see any possibility of upsetting that will — if I may ask the question?"

"At present," replied Thorndyke, "I do not. But until I have carefully weighed every fact connected with the case — whether it seems to have any bearing or not — I shall refrain from expressing, or even entertaining, an opinion either way."

Stephen Blackmore now took his leave; and Thorndyke, having collected the papers containing his notes, neatly punched a couple of holes in their margins and inserted them into a small file, which he slipped into his pocket.

"That," said he, "is the nucleus of the body of data on which our investigations must be based; and I very much fear that it will not receive any great additions. What do you think, Jervis?"

"The case looks about as hopeless as a case could look," I replied.

"That is what I think," said he; "and for that reason I am more than ordinarily keen on making something of it. I have not much more hope than Marchmont has; but I shall squeeze the case as dry as a bone before I let go. What are you going to do? I have to attend a meeting of the board of directors of the Griffin Life Office."

"Shall I walk down with you?"

"It is very good of you to offer, Jervis, but I think I will go alone. I want to run over these notes and get the facts of the case arranged in my mind. When I have done that, I shall be ready to pick up new matter. Knowledge is of no use unless it is actually in your mind, so that it can be produced at a moment's notice. So you had better get a book and your pipe and spend a quiet hour by the fire while I assimilate the miscellaneous mental feast that we have just enjoyed. And you might do a little rumination yourself."

With this, Thorndyke took his departure; and I, adopting his advice, drew my chair closer to the fire and filled my pipe. But I did not discover any inclination to read. The curious history that I had just heard, and Thorndyke's evident determination to elucidate it further, disposed me to meditation. Moreover, as his subordinate, it was my business to occupy myself with his affairs. Wherefore, having stirred the fire and got my pipe well alight, I abandoned myself to the renewed consideration of the facts relating to Jeffrey Blackmore's will.

Chapter VII

The Cuneiform Inscription

*T*he surprise which Thorndyke's proceedings usually occasioned, especially to lawyers, was principally due, I think, to my friend's habit of viewing occurrences from an unusual standpoint. He did not look at things quite as other men looked at them. He had no prejudices and he knew no conventions. When other men were cocksure, Thorndyke was doubtful. When other men despaired, he entertained hopes; and thus it happened that he would often undertake cases that had been rejected contemptuously by experienced lawyers, and, what is more, would bring them to a successful issue.

Thus it had been in the only other case in which I had been personally associated with him – the so-called "Red Thumb Mark" case. There he was presented with an apparent impossibility; but he had given it careful consideration. Then, from the category of the impossible he had brought it to that of the possible; from the merely possible to the actually probable; from the probable to the certain; and in the end had won the case triumphantly.

Was it conceivable that he could make anything of the present case? He had not declined it. He had certainly entertained it and was probably thinking it over at this moment. Yet could anything be more impossible? Here was the case of a man making his own will, probably writing it out himself, bringing it voluntarily to a certain place and executing it in the presence of competent witnesses. There was no suggestion of any compulsion or even influence or persuasion. The testator was admittedly sane and responsible; and if the will did not give effect to his wishes – which, however, could not be proved – that was due to his own carelessness in drafting the will and not to any unusual circumstances. And the problem – which Thorndyke seemed to be considering – was how to set aside that will.

I reviewed the statements that I had heard, but turn them about as I would, I could get nothing out of them but confirmation of Mr. Marchmont's estimate of the case. One fact that I had noted with some curiosity I again considered; that was Thorndyke's evident desire to inspect Jeffrey Blackmore's chambers. He had, it is true, shown no eagerness, but I had seen at the time that the questions which he put to Stephen were put, not with any expectation of eliciting information but for the purpose of getting an opportunity to look over the rooms himself.

I was still cogitating on the subject when my colleague returned, followed by the watchful Polton with the tea-tray, and I attacked him forthwith.

"Well, Thorndyke," I said, "I have been thinking about this Blackmore case while you have been gadding about."

"And may I take it that the problem is solved?"

"No, I'm hanged if you may. I can make nothing of it."

"Then you are in much the same position as I am."

"But, if you can make nothing of it, why did you undertake it?"

"I only undertook to think about it," said Thorndyke. "I never reject a case off-hand unless it is obviously fishy. It is surprising how difficulties, and even impossibilities, dwindle if you look at them attentively. My experience has taught me that the most unlikely case is, at least, worth thinking over."

"By the way, why do you want to look over Jeffrey's chambers? What do you expect to find there?"

"I have no expectations at all. I am simply looking for stray facts."

"And all those questions that you asked Stephen Blackmore; had you nothing in your mind — no definite purpose?"

"No purpose beyond getting to know as much about the case as I can."

"But," I exclaimed, "do you mean that you are going to examine those rooms without any definite object at all?"

"I wouldn't say that," replied Thorndyke. "This is a legal case. Let me put an analogous medical case as being more within your present sphere. Supposing that a man should consult you, say, about a progressive loss of weight. He can give no explanation. He has no pain, no discomfort, no symptoms of any kind; in short, he feels perfectly well in every respect; *but* he is losing weight continuously. What would you do?"

"I should overhaul him thoroughly," I answered.

"Why? What would you expect to find?"

"I don't know that I should start by expecting to find anything in particular. But I should overhaul him organ by organ and function by function, and if I could find nothing abnormal I should have to give it up."

"Exactly," said Thorndyke. "And that is just my position and my line of action. Here is a case which is perfectly regular and straightforward excepting in one respect. It has a single abnormal feature. And for that abnormality there is nothing to account.

"Jeffrey Blackmore made a will. It was a well-drawn will and it apparently gave full effect to his intentions. Then he revoked that will and made another. No change had occurred in his circumstances or in his intentions. The provisions of the new will were believed by him to be identical with those of the old one. The new will differed from the old one only in having a defect in the drafting from which the first will was free, and of which he must have been unaware. Now why did he revoke the first will and replace it with another which he believed to be identical in its provisions? There is no answer to that question. It is an abnormal feature in the case. There must be some explanation of that abnormality and it is my business to discover it. But the facts in my possession yield no such explanation. Therefore it is my purpose to search for new facts which may give me a starting-point for an investigation."

This exposition of Thorndyke's proposed conduct of the case, reasonable as it was, did not impress me as very convincing. I found myself coming back to Marchmont's position, that there was really nothing in dispute. But other matters claimed our attention at the moment, and it was not until after dinner that my colleague reverted to the subject.

"How should you like to take a turn round to New Inn this evening?" he asked.

"I should have thought," said I, "that it would be better to go by daylight. Those old chambers are not usually very well illuminated."

"That is well thought of," said Thorndyke. "We had better take a lamp with us. Let us go up to the laboratory and get one from Polton."

"There is no need to do that," said I. "The pocket-lamp that you lent me is in my overcoat pocket. I put it there to return it to you."

"Did you have occasion to use it?" he asked.

"Yes. I paid another visit to the mysterious house and carried out your plan. I must tell you about it later."

"Do. I shall be keenly interested to hear all about your adventures. Is there plenty of candle left in the lamp?"

"Oh yes. I only used it for about an hour."

"Then let us be off," said Thorndyke; and we accordingly set forth on our quest; and, as we went, I reflected once more on the apparent vagueness of our proceedings. Presently I reopened the subject with Thorndyke.

"I can't imagine," said I, "that you have absolutely nothing in view. That you are going to this place with no defined purpose whatever."

"I did not say exactly that," replied Thorndyke. "I said that I was not going to look for any particular thing or fact. I am going in the hope that I may observe something that may start a new train of speculation. But that is not all. You know that an investigation follows a certain logical course. It begins with the observation of the conspicuous facts. We have done that. The facts were supplied by Marchmont. The next stage is to propose to oneself one or more provisional explanations or hypotheses. We have done that, too — or, at least I have, and I suppose you have."

"I haven't," said I. "There is Jeffrey's will, but why he should have made the change I cannot form the foggiest idea. But I should like to hear your provisional theories on the subject."

"You won't hear them at present. They are mere wild conjectures. But to resume: what do we do next?"

"Go to New Inn and rake over the deceased gentleman's apartments."

Thorndyke smilingly ignored my answer and continued —

"We examine each explanation in turn and see what follows from it; whether it agrees with all the facts and leads to the discovery of new ones, or, on the other hand, disagrees with some facts or leads us to an absurdity. Let us take a simple example.

"Suppose we find scattered over a field a number of largish masses of stone, which are entirely different in character from the rocks found in the neighborhood. The question arises, how did those stones get into that field? Three explanations are proposed. One: that they are the products of former volcanic action; two: that they were brought from a distance by human agency; three: that they were carried thither from some distant country by icebergs. Now each of those explanations involves certain consequences. If the stones are volcanic, then they were once in a state of fusion. But we find that they are unaltered limestone and contain fossils. Then they are not volcanic. If they were borne by icebergs, then they were once part of a glacier and some of them will probably show the flat surfaces with parallel scratches which are found on glacier-borne stones. We examine them and find the characteristic scratched surfaces. Then they have probably been brought to this place by icebergs. But this does not exclude human agency, for they might have been brought by men to this place from some other where the icebergs had deposited them. A further comparison with other facts would be needed.

"So we proceed in cases like this present one. Of the facts that are known to us we invent certain explanations. From each of those explanations we deduce consequences; and if those consequences agree with new facts, they confirm the explanation, whereas if they disagree they tend to disprove it. But here we are at our destination."

We turned out of Wych Street into the arched passage leading into New Inn, and, halting at the half-door of the lodge, perceived a stout, purple-faced man crouching over the fire, coughing violently. He held up his hand to intimate that he was fully occupied for the moment, and we accordingly waited for his paroxysm to subside. At length he turned towards us, wiping his eyes, and inquired our business.

"Mr. Stephen Blackmore," said Thorndyke, "has given me permission to look over his chambers. He said that he would mention the matter to you."

"So he has, sir," said the porter; "but he has just taken the key himself to go to the chambers. If you walk across the Inn you'll find him there; it's on the farther side; number thirty-one, second floor."

We made our way across to the house indicated, the ground floor of which was occupied by a solicitor's offices and was distinguished by a good-sized brass plate. Although it had now been dark some time there was no light on the lower stairs, but we encountered on the first-floor landing a man who had just lit the lamp there. Thorndyke halted to address him.

"Can you tell me who occupies the chambers on the third floor?"

"The third floor has been empty about three months," was the reply.

"We are going up to look at the chambers on the second floor," said Thorndyke. "Are they pretty quiet?"

"Quiet!" exclaimed the man. "Lord bless you the place is like a cemetery for the deaf and dumb. There's the solicitors on the ground floor and the architects on the first floor. They both clear out about six, and when they're gone the house is as empty as a blown hegg. I don't wonder poor Mr. Blackmore made away with his-self. Livin' up there all alone, it must have been like Robinson Crusoe without no man Friday and not even a blooming goat to talk to. Quiet! It's quiet enough, if that's what you want. Wouldn't be no good to *me.*"

With a contemptuous shake of the head, he turned and retired down the next flight, and, as the echoes of his footsteps died away we resumed our ascent.

"So it would appear," Thorndyke commented, "that when Jeffrey Blackmore came home that last evening, the house was empty."

Arrived on the second-floor landing, we were confronted by a solid-looking door on the lintel of which the deceased man's name was painted in white lettering which still looked new and fresh. Thorndyke knocked at the door, which was at once opened by Stephen Blackmore.

"I haven't wasted any time before taking advantage of your permission, you see," my colleague said as we entered.

"No, indeed," said Stephen; "you are very prompt. I have been rather wondering what kind of information you expect to gather from an inspection of these rooms."

Thorndyke smiled genially, amused, no doubt, by the similarity of Stephen's remarks to those of mine which he had so recently criticized.

"A man of science, Mr. Blackmore," he said, "expects nothing. He collects facts and keeps an open mind. As to me, I am a mere legal Autolycus, a snapper-up of unconsidered trifles of evidence. When I have accumulated a few facts, I arrange them, compare them and think about them. Sometimes the comparison yields new matter and sometimes it doesn't; but in any case, believe me, it is a capital error to decide beforehand what data are to be sought for."

"Yes, I suppose that is so," said Stephen; "though, to me, it almost looks as if Mr. Marchmont was right; that there is nothing to investigate."

"You should have thought of that before you consulted me," laughed Thorndyke. "As it is, I am engaged to look into the case and I shall do so; and, as I have said, I shall keep an open mind until I have all the facts in my possession."

He glanced round the sitting room, which we had now entered, and continued:

"These are fine, dignified old rooms. It seems a sin to have covered up all this oak paneling and that carved cornice and mantel with paint. Think what it must have been like when the beautiful figured wood was exposed."

"It would be very dark," Stephen observed.

"Yes," Thorndyke agreed, "and I suppose we care more for light and less for beauty than our ancestors did. But now, tell me; looking round these rooms, do they convey to you a similar impression to that which the old rooms did? Have they the same general character?"

"Not quite, I think. Of course the rooms in Jermyn Street were in a different kind of house, but beyond that, I seem to feel a certain difference; which is rather odd, seeing that the furniture is the same. But the old rooms were more cozy, more homelike. I find something rather bare and cheerless, I was almost going to say squalid, in the look of these chambers."

"That is rather what I should have expected," said Thorndyke. "The opium habit alters a man's character profoundly; and, somehow, apart from the mere furnishing, a room reflects in some subtle way, but very distinctly, the personality of its occupant, especially when that occupant lives a solitary life. Do you see any evidences of the activities that used to occupy your uncle?"

"Not very much," replied Stephen. "But the place may not be quite as he left it. I found one or two of his books on the table and put them back in the shelves, but I found no manuscript or notes such as he used to make. I noticed, too, that his ink-slab which he used to keep so scrupulously clean is covered with dry smears and that the stick of ink is all cracked at the end, as if he had not used it for months. It seems to point to a great change in his habits."

"What used he to do with Chinese ink?" Thorndyke asked.

"He corresponded with some of his native friends in Japan, and he used to write in the Japanese character even if they understood English. That was what he chiefly used the Chinese ink for. But he also used to copy the inscriptions from these things." Here Stephen lifted from the mantelpiece what looked like a fossil Bath bun, but was actually a clay tablet covered with minute indented writing.

"Your uncle could read the cuneiform character, then?"

"Yes; he was something of an expert. These tablets are, I believe, leases and other legal documents from Eridu and other Babylonian cities. He used to copy the inscriptions in the cuneiform writing and then translate them into English. But I mustn't stay here any longer as I have an engagement for this evening. I just dropped in to get these two volumes — *Thornton's History of Babylonia,* which he once advised me to read. Shall I give you the key? You'd better have it and leave it with the porter as you go out."

He shook hands with us and we walked out with him to the landing and stood watching him as he ran down the stairs. Glancing at Thorndyke by the light of the gas lamp on the landing, I thought I detected in his impassive face that almost imperceptible change of expression to which I have already alluded as indicating pleasure or satisfaction.

"You are looking quite pleased with yourself," I remarked.

"I am not displeased," he replied calmly. "Autolycus has picked up a few crumbs; very small ones, but still crumbs. No doubt his learned junior has picked up a few likewise?"

I shook my head — and inwardly suspected it of being rather a thick head.

"I did not perceive anything in the least degree significant in what Stephen was telling you," said I. "It was all very interesting, but it did not seem to have any bearing on his uncle's will."

"I was not referring only to what Stephen has told us, although that was, as you say, very interesting. While he was talking I was looking about the room, and I have seen a very strange thing. Let me show it to you."

He linked his arm in mine and, walking me back into the room, halted opposite the fireplace.

"There," said he, "look at that. It is a most remarkable object."

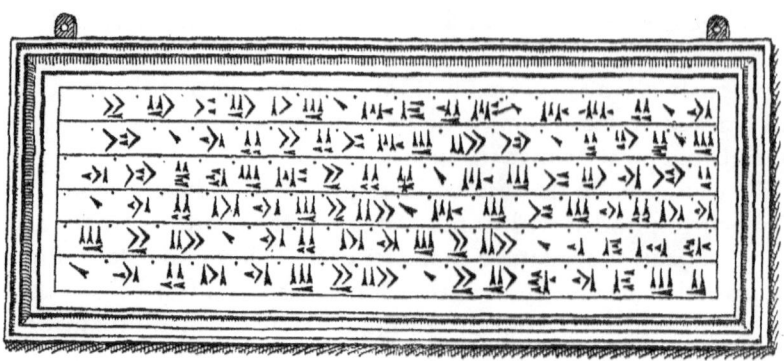

The Inverted Inscription

I followed the direction of his gaze and saw an oblong frame enclosing a large photograph of an inscription in the weird and cabalistic arrow-head character. I looked at it in silence for some seconds and then, somewhat disappointed, remarked:

"I don't see anything very remarkable in it, under the circumstances. In any ordinary room it would be, I admit; but Stephen has just told us that his uncle was something of an expert in cuneiform writing."

"Exactly," said Thorndyke. "That is my point. That is what makes it so remarkable."

"I don't follow you at all," said I. "That a man should hang upon his wall an inscription that is legible to him does not seem to me at all out of the way. It would be much more singular if he should hang up an inscription that he could *not* read."

"No doubt," replied Thorndyke. "But you will agree with me that it would be still more singular if a man should hang upon his wall an inscription that he *could* read — and hang it upside down."

I stared at Thorndyke in amazement.

"Do you mean to tell me," I exclaimed, "that that photograph is really upside down?"

"I do indeed," he replied.

"But how do you know? Have we here yet another Oriental scholar?"

Thorndyke chuckled. "Some fool," he replied, "has said that 'a little knowledge is a dangerous thing.' Compared with much knowledge, it may be; but it is a vast deal better than no knowledge. Here is a case in point. I have read with very keen interest the wonderful history of the decipherment of the cuneiform writing, and I happen to recollect one or two of the main facts that seemed to me to be worth remembering. This particular inscription is in the Persian cuneiform, a much more simple and open form of the script than the Babylonian or Assyrian; in fact, I suspect that this is the famous inscription from the gateway at Persepolis — the first to be deciphered; which would account for its presence here in a frame. Now this script consists, as you see, of two kinds of characters; the small, solid, acutely pointed characters which are known as wedges, and the larger, more obtuse characters, somewhat like our government broad arrows, and called arrow-heads. The names are rather unfortunate, as both forms are wedgelike and both resemble arrow-heads. The script reads from left to right, like our own writing, and unlike that of the Semitic peoples and the primitive Greeks; and the rule for the placing of the characters is that all the 'wedges' point to the right or downwards and the arrow-head forms are open towards the right. But if you look at this photograph you will see that all the wedges point upwards to the left and that the arrow-head characters are open towards the left. Obviously the photograph is upside down."

"But," I exclaimed, "this is really most mysterious. What do you suppose can be the explanation?"

"I think," replied Thorndyke, "that we may perhaps get a suggestion from the back of the frame. Let us see."

He disengaged the frame from the two nails on which it hung, and, turning it round, glanced at the back; which he then presented for my inspection. A label on the backing paper bore the words, "J. Budge, Frame-maker and Gilder, 16, Gt. Anne Street, W.C."

"Well?" I said, when I had read the label without gathering from it anything fresh.

"The label, you observe, is the right way up as it hangs on the wall."

"So it is," I rejoined hastily, a little annoyed that I had not been quicker to observe so obvious a fact. "I see your point. You mean that the frame-maker hung the thing upside down and Jeffrey never noticed the mistake?"

"That is a perfectly sound explanation," said Thorndyke. "But I think there is something more. You will notice that the label is an old one; it must have been on some years, to judge by its dingy appearance, whereas the two mirror-plates look to me comparatively new. But we can soon put that matter to the test, for the label was evidently stuck on when the frame was new, and if the plates were screwed on at the same time, the wood that they cover will be clean and new-looking."

He drew from his pocket a "combination" knife containing, among other implements, a screw-driver, with which he carefully extracted the screws from one of the little brass plates by which the frame had been suspended from the nails.

"You see," he said, when he had removed the plate and carried the photograph over to the gas jet, "the wood covered by the plate is as dirty and time-stained as the rest of the frame. The plates have been put on recently."

"And what are we to infer from that?"

"Well, since there are no other marks of plates or rings upon the frame, we may safely infer that the photograph was never hung up until it came to these rooms."

"Yes, I suppose we may. But what then? What inference does that lead to?"

Thorndyke reflected for a few moments and I continued:

"It is evident that this photograph suggests more to you than it does to me. I should like to hear your exposition of its bearing on the case, if it has any."

"Whether or no it has any real bearing on the case," Thorndyke answered, "it is impossible for me to say at this stage. I told you that I had proposed to myself one or two hypotheses to account for and explain Jeffrey Blackmore's will, and I may say that the curious misplacement of this photograph fits more than one of them. I won't say more than that, because I think it would be profitable to you to work at this case independently. You have all the facts that I have and you shall have a copy of my notes of Marchmont's statement of the case. With this material you ought to be able to reach some conclusion. Of course neither of us may be able to make anything of the case — it doesn't look very hopeful at present — but whatever happens, we can compare notes after the event and you will be the richer by so much experience of actual investigation. But I will start you off with one hint, which is this: that neither you nor Marchmont seem to appreciate in the least the very extraordinary nature of the facts that he communicated to us."

"I thought Marchmont seemed pretty much alive to the fact that it was a very queer will."

"So he did," agreed Thorndyke. "But that is not quite what I mean. The whole set of circumstances, taken together and in relation to one another, impressed me as most remarkable; and that is why I am giving so much attention to what looks at first sight like such a very unpromising case. Copy out my notes, Jervis, and examine the facts critically. I think you will see what I mean. And now let us proceed."

He replaced the brass plate and having reinserted the screws, hung up the frame, and proceeded to browse slowly round the room, stopping now and again to inspect the Japanese color-prints and framed photographs of buildings and other objects of archaeological interest that formed the only attempts at wall-decoration. To one of the former he drew my attention.

"These things are of some value," he remarked. "Here is one by Utamaro — that little circle with the mark over it is his signature — and you notice that the paper is becoming spotted in places with mildew. The fact is worth noting in more than one connection."

I accordingly made a mental note and the perambulation continued.

"You observe that Jeffrey used a gas-stove, instead of a coal fire, no doubt to economize work, but perhaps for other reasons. Presumably he cooked by gas, too; let us see."

We wandered into the little cupboardlike kitchen and glanced round. A ring-burner on a shelf, a kettle, a frying-pan and a few pieces of crockery were its sole appointments. Apparently the porter was correct in his statement as to Jeffrey's habits.

Returning to the sitting room, Thorndyke resumed his inspection, pulling out the table drawers, peering inquisitively into cupboards and bestowing a passing glance on each of the comparatively few objects that the comfortless room contained.

"I have never seen a more characterless apartment," was his final comment. "There is nothing that seems to suggest any kind of habitual activity on the part of the occupant. Let us look at the bedroom."

We passed through into the chamber of tragic memories, and, when Thorndyke had lit the gas, we stood awhile looking about us in silence. It was a bare, comfortless room, dirty, neglected and squalid. The bed appeared not to have been remade since the catastrophe, for an indentation still marked the place where the corpse had lain, and even a slight powdering of ash could still be seen on the shabby counterpane. It looked to me a typical opium-smoker's bedroom.

"Well," Thorndyke remarked at length, "there is character enough here — of a kind. Jeffrey Blackmore would seem to have been a man of few needs. One could hardly imagine a bedroom in which less attention seemed to have been given to the comfort of the occupant."

He looked about him keenly and continued: "The syringe and the rest of the lethal appliances and material have been taken away, I see. Probably the analyst did not return them. But there are the opium-pipe and the jar and the ash-bowl, and I presume those are the clothes that the undertakers removed from the body. Shall we look them over?"

He took up the clothes which lay, roughly folded, on a chair and held them up, garment by garment.

"These are evidently the trousers," he remarked, spreading them out on the bed. "Here is a little white spot on the middle of the thigh which looks like a patch of small crystals from a drop of the solution. Just light the lamp, Jervis, and let us examine it with a lens."

I lit the lamp, and when we had examined the spot minutely and identified it as a mass of minute crystals, Thorndyke asked:

"What do you make of those creases? You see there is one on each leg."

"It looks as if the trousers had been turned up. But if they have been they must have been turned up about seven inches. Poor Jeffrey couldn't have had much regard for appearances, for they would have been right above his socks. But perhaps the creases were made in undressing the body."

"That is possible," said Thorndyke: "though I don't quite see how it would have happened. I notice that his pockets seem to have been emptied — no, wait; here is something in the waistcoat pocket."

He drew out a shabby, pigskin card-case and a stump of lead pencil, at which latter he looked with what seemed to me much more interest than was deserved by so commonplace an object.

"The cards, you observe," said he, "are printed from type, not from a plate. I would note that fact. And tell me what you make of that."

He handed me the pencil, which I examined with concentrated attention, helping myself even with the lamp and my pocket lens. But even with these aids I failed to discover anything unusual in its appearance. Thorndyke watched me with a mischievous smile, and, when I had finished, inquired:

"Well; what is it?"

"Confound you!" I exclaimed. "It's a pencil. Any fool can see that, and this particular fool can't see anymore. It's a wretched stump of a pencil, villainously cut to an abominably bad point. It is colored dark red on the outside and was stamped with some name that began with C – O – Co-operative Stores, perhaps."

"Now, my dear Jervis," Thorndyke protested, "don't begin by confusing speculation with fact. The letters which remain are C – O. Note that fact and find out what pencils there are which have inscriptions beginning with those letters. I am not going to help you, because you can easily do this for yourself. And it will be good discipline even if the fact turns out to mean nothing."

At this moment he stepped back suddenly, and, looking down at the floor, said:

"Give me the lamp, Jervis, I've trodden on something that felt like glass."

I brought the lamp to the place where he had been standing, close by the bed, and we both knelt on the floor, throwing the light of the lamp on the bare and dusty boards. Under the bed, just within reach of the foot of a person standing close by, was a little patch of fragments of glass. Thorndyke produced a piece of paper from his pocket and delicately swept the little fragments on to it, remarking:

"By the look of things, I am not the first person who has trodden on that object, whatever it is. Do you mind holding the lamp while I inspect the remains?"

I took the lamp and held it over the paper while he examined the little heap of glass through his lens.

"Well," I asked. "What have you found?"

"That is what I am asking myself," he replied. "As far as I can judge by the appearance of these fragments, they appear to be portions of a small watch-glass. I wish there were some larger pieces."

"Perhaps there are," said I. "Let us look about the floor under the bed."

We resumed our groping about the dirty floor, throwing the light of the lamp on one spot after another. Presently, as we moved the lamp about, its light fell on a small glass bead, which I instantly picked up and exhibited to Thorndyke.

"Is this of any interest to you?" I asked.

Thorndyke took the bead and examined it curiously.

"It is certainly," he said, "a very odd thing to find in the bedroom of an old bachelor like Jeffrey, especially as we know that he employed no woman to look after his rooms. Of course, it may be a relic of the last tenant. Let us see if there are anymore."

We renewed our search, crawling under the bed and throwing the light of the lamp in all directions over the floor. The result was the discovery of three more beads, one entire bugle and the crushed remains of another, which had apparently been trodden on. All of these, including the fragments of the bugle that had been crushed, Thorndyke placed carefully on the paper, which he laid on the dressing-table the more conveniently to examine our find.

"I am sorry," said he, "that there are no more fragments of the watch-glass, or whatever it was. The broken pieces were evidently picked up, with the exception of the one that I trod on, which was an isolated fragment that had been overlooked. As to the beads, judging by their number and the position in which we found some of them — that crushed bugle, for instance — they must have been dropped during Jeffrey's tenancy and probably quite recently."

"What sort of garment do you suppose they came from?" I asked.

"They may have been part of a beaded veil or the trimming of a dress, but the grouping rather suggests to me a tag of bead fringe. The color is rather unusual."

"I thought they looked like black beads."

"So they do by this light, but I think that by daylight we shall find them to be a dark, reddish-brown. You can see the color now if you look at the smaller fragments of the one that is crushed."

He handed me his lens, and, when I had verified his statement, he produced from his pocket a small tin box with a closely-fitting lid in which he deposited the paper, having first folded it up into a small parcel.

"We will put the pencil in too," said he; and, as he returned the box to his pocket he added: "you had better get one of these little boxes from Polton. If is often useful to have a safe receptacle for small and fragile articles."

He folded up and replaced the dead man's clothes as we had found them. Then, observing a pair of shoes standing by the wall, he picked them up and looked them over thoughtfully, paying special attention to the backs of the soles and the fronts of the heels.

"I suppose we may take it," said he, "that these are the shoes that poor Jeffrey wore on the night of his death. At any rate there seem to be no others. He seems to have been a fairly clean walker. The streets were shockingly dirty that day, as I remember most distinctly. Do you see any slippers? I haven't noticed any."

He opened and peeped into a cupboard in which an overcoat sur-mounted by a felt hat hung from a peg like an attenuated suicide; he looked in all the corners and into the sitting room, but no slippers were to be seen.

"Our friend seems to have had surprisingly little regard for comfort," Thorndyke remarked. "Think of spending the winter evenings in damp boots by a gas fire!"

"Perhaps the opium-pipe compensated," said I; "or he may have gone to bed early."

"But he did not. The night porter used to see the light in his rooms at one o'clock in the morning. In the sitting room, too, you remember. But he seems to have been in the habit of reading in bed — or perhaps smoking — for here is a candlestick with the remains of a whole dynasty of candles in it. As there is gas in the room, he couldn't have wanted the candle to undress by. He used stearine candles, too; not the common paraffin variety. I wonder why he went to that expense."

"Perhaps the smell of the paraffin candle spoiled the aroma of the opium," I suggested; to which Thorndyke made no reply but continued his inspection of the room, pulling out the drawer of the washstand — which contained a single, worn-out nail-brush — and even picking up and examining the dry and cracked cake of soap in the dish.

"He seems to have had a fair amount of clothing," said Thorndyke, who was now going through the chest of drawers, "though, by the look of it, he didn't change very often, and the shirts have a rather yellow and faded appearance. I wonder how he managed about his washing. Why, here are a couple of pairs of boots in the drawer with his clothes!

And here is his stock of candles. Quite a large box — though nearly empty now — of stearine candles, six to the pound."

He closed the drawer and cast another inquiring look round the room.

"I think we have seen all now, Jervis," he said, "unless there is anything more that you would like to look into?"

"No," I replied. "I have seen all that I wanted to see and more than I am able to attach any meaning to. So we may as well go."

I blew out the lamp and put it in my overcoat pocket, and, when we had turned out the gas in both rooms, we took our departure.

As we approached the lodge, we found our stout friend in the act of retiring in favor of the night porter. Thorndyke handed him the key of the chambers, and, after a few sympathetic inquiries, about his health — which was obviously very indifferent — said:

"Let me see; you were one of the witnesses to Mr. Blackmore's will, I think?"

"I was, sir," replied the porter.

"And I believe you read the document through before you witnessed the signature?"

"I did, sir."

"Did you read it aloud?"

"Aloud, sir! Lor' bless you, no, sir! Why should I? The other witness read it, and, of course, Mr. Blackmore knew what was in it, seeing that it was in his own handwriting. What should I want to read it aloud for?"

"No, of course you wouldn't want to. By the way, I have been wondering how Mr. Blackmore managed about his washing."

The porter evidently regarded this question with some disfavor, for he replied only with an interrogative grunt. It was, in fact, rather an odd question.

"Did you get it done for him," Thorndyke pursued.

"No, certainly not, sir. He got it done for himself. The laundry people used to deliver the basket here at the lodge, and Mr. Blackmore used to take it in with him when he happened to be passing."

"It was not delivered at his chambers, then?"

"No, sir. Mr. Blackmore was a very studious gentleman and he didn't like to be disturbed. A studious gentleman would naturally not like to be disturbed."

Thorndyke cordially agreed with these very proper sentiments and finally wished the porter "good night." We passed out through the gateway into Wych Street, and, turning our faces eastward towards the Temple, set forth in silence, each thinking his own thoughts. What Thorndyke's were I cannot tell, though I have no doubt that he was busily engaged in piecing together all that he had seen and heard and considering its possible application to the case in hand.

As to me, my mind was in a whirl of confusion. All this searching and examining seemed to be the mere flogging of a dead horse. The will was obviously a perfectly valid and regular will and there was an end of the matter. At least, so it seemed to me. But clearly that was not Thorndyke's view. His investigations were certainly not purposeless; and, as I walked by his side trying to conceive some purpose in his actions, I only became more and more mystified as I recalled them one by one, and perhaps most of all by the cryptic questions that I had just heard him address to the equally mystified porter.

Chapter VIII

The Track Chart

*A*s Thorndyke and I arrived at the main gateway of the Temple and he swung round into the narrow lane, it was suddenly borne in on me that I had made no arrangements for the night. Events had followed one another so continuously and each had been so engrossing that I had lost sight of what I may call my domestic affairs.

"We seem to be heading for your chambers, Thorndyke," I ventured to remark. "It is a little late to think of it, but I have not yet settled where I am to put up tonight."

"My dear fellow," he replied, "you are going to put up in your own bedroom which has been waiting in readiness for you ever since you left it. Polton went up and inspected it as soon as you arrived. I take it that you will consider my chambers yours until such time as you may join the Benedictine majority and set up a home for yourself."

"That is very handsome of you," said I. "You didn't mention that the billet you offered was a resident appointment."

"Rooms and commons included," said Thorndyke; and when I protested that I should at least contribute to the costs of living he impatiently waved the suggestion away. We were still arguing the question when we reached our chambers — as I will now call them — and a diversion was occasioned by my taking the lamp from my pocket and placing it on the table.

"Ah," my colleague remarked, "that is a little reminder. We will put it on the mantelpiece for Polton to collect and you shall give me a full account of your further adventures in the wilds of Kennington. That was a very odd affair. I have often wondered how it ended."

He drew our two armchairs up to the fire, put on some more coal, placed the tobacco jar on the table exactly equidistant from the two chairs, and settled himself with the air of a man who is anticipating an agreeable entertainment.

I filled my pipe, and, taking up the thread of the story where I had broken off on the last occasion, began to outline my later experiences. But he brought me up short.

"Don't be sketchy, Jervis. To be sketchy is to be vague. Detail, my child, detail is the soul of induction. Let us have all the facts. We can sort them out afterwards."

I began afresh in a vein of the extremest circumstantiality. With deliberate malice I loaded a prolix narrative with every triviality that a fairly retentive memory could rake out of the half-forgotten past. I cudgeled my brains for irrelevant incidents. I described with the minutest accuracy things that had not the faintest significance. I drew a vivid picture of the carriage inside and out; I painted a lifelike portrait of the horse, even going into particulars of the harness — which I was surprised to find that I had noticed. I described the furniture of the dining room and the cobwebs that had hung from the ceiling; the auction-ticket on the chest of drawers, the rickety table and the melancholy chairs. I gave the number per minute of the patient's respirations and the exact quantity of coffee consumed on each occasion, with an exhaustive description of the cup from which it was taken; and I left no personal details unconsidered, from the patient's fingernails to the roseate pimples on Mr. Weiss's nose.

But my tactics of studied prolixity were a complete failure. The attempt to fatigue Thorndyke's brain with superabundant detail was like trying to surfeit a pelican with whitebait. He consumed it all with calm enjoyment and asked for more; and when, at last, I did really begin to think that I had bored him a little, he staggered me by reading over his notes and starting a brisk cross-examination to elicit fresh facts! And the most surprising thing of all was that when I had finished I seemed to know a great deal more about the case than I had ever known before.

"It was a very remarkable affair," he observed, when the cross-examination was over — leaving me somewhat in the condition of a cider-apple that has just been removed from a hydraulic press — "a very suspicious affair with a highly unsatisfactory end. I am not sure that I entirely agree with your police officer. Nor do I fancy that some of my acquaintances at Scotland Yard would have agreed with him."

"Do you think I ought to have taken any further measures?" I asked uneasily.

"No; I don't see how you could. You did all that was possible under the circumstances. You gave information, which is all that a private individual can do, especially if he is an overworked general practitioner. But still, an actual crime is the affair of every good citizen. I think we ought to take some action."

"You think there really was a crime, then?"

"What else can one think? What do you think about it yourself?"

"I don't like to think about it at all. The recollection of that corpselike figure in that gloomy bedroom has haunted me ever since I left the house. What do you suppose has happened?"

Thorndyke did not answer for a few seconds. At length he said gravely:

"I am afraid, Jervis, that the answer to that question can be given in one word."

"Murder?" I asked with a slight shudder.

He nodded, and we were both silent for a while.

"The probability," he resumed after a pause, "that Mr. Graves is alive at this moment seems to me infinitesimal. There was evidently a conspiracy to murder him, and the deliberate, persistent manner in which that object was being pursued points to a very strong and definite motive. Then the tactics adopted point to considerable forethought and judgment. They are not the tactics of a fool or an ignoramus. We may criticize the closed carriage as a tactical mistake, calculated to arouse suspicion, but we have to weigh it against its alternative."

"What is that?"

"Well, consider the circumstances. Suppose Weiss had called you in in the ordinary way. You would still have detected the use of poison. But now you could have located your man and made inquiries about him in the neighborhood. You would probably have given the police a hint and they would almost certainly have taken action, as they would have had the means of identifying the parties. The result would have been fatal to Weiss. The closed carriage invited suspicion, but it was a great safeguard. Weiss's method's were not so unsound after all. He is a cautious man, but cunning and very persistent. And he could be bold on occasion. The use of the blinded carriage was a decidedly audacious proceeding. I should put him down as a gambler of a very discreet, courageous and resourceful type."

"Which all leads to the probability that he has pursued his scheme and brought it to a successful issue."

"I am afraid it does. But — have you got your notes of the compass-bearings?"

"The book is in my overcoat pocket with the board. I will fetch them."

I went into the office, where our coats hung, and brought back the notebook with the little board to which it was still attached by the rubber band. Thorndyke took them from me, and, opening the book, ran his eye quickly down one page after another. Suddenly he glanced at the clock.

"It is a little late to begin," said he, "but these notes look rather alluring. I am inclined to plot them out at once. I fancy, from their appearance, that they will enable us to locate the house without much difficulty. But don't let me keep you up if you are tired. I can work them out by myself."

"You won't do anything of the kind," I exclaimed. "I am as keen on plotting them as you are, and, besides, I want to see how it is done. It seems to be a rather useful accomplishment."

"It is," said Thorndyke. "In our work, the ability to make a rough but reliable sketch survey is often of great value. Have you ever looked over these notes?"

"No. I put the book away when I came in and have never looked at it since."

"It is a quaint document. You seem to be rich in railway bridges in those parts, and the route was certainly none of the most direct, as you noticed at the time. However, we will plot it out and then we shall see exactly what it looks like and whither it leads us."

He retired to the laboratory and presently returned with a T-square, a military protractor, a pair of dividers and a large drawing-board on which was pinned a sheet of cartridge paper.

"Now," said he, seating himself at the table with the board before him, "as to the method. You started from a known position and you arrived at a place the position of which is at present unknown. We shall fix the position of that spot by applying two factors, the distance that you traveled and the direction in which you were moving. The direction is given by the compass; and, as the horse seems to have kept up a remarkably even pace, we can take time as representing distance. You seem to have been traveling at about eight miles an hour, that is, roughly, a seventh of a mile in one minute. So if, on our chart, we take one inch as representing one minute, we shall be working with a scale of about seven inches to the mile."

"That doesn't sound very exact as to distance," I objected.

"It isn't. But that doesn't matter much. We have certain landmarks, such as these railway arches that you have noted, by which the actual distance can be settled after the route is plotted. You had better read out the entries, and, opposite each, write a number for reference, so that we need not confuse the chart by writing details on it. I shall start near the middle of the board, as neither you nor I seem to have the slightest notion what your general direction was."

I laid the open notebook before me and read out the first entry:

"'Eight fifty-eight. West by South. Start from home. Horse thirteen hands.'"

"You turned round at once, I understand," said Thorndyke, "so we draw no line in that direction. The next is — ?"

"'Eight fifty-eight minutes, thirty seconds, East by North'; and the next is 'Eight fifty-nine, Northeast.'"

"Then you traveled east by north about a fifteenth of a mile and we shall put down half an inch on the chart. Then you turned northeast. How long did you go on?"

"Exactly a minute. The next entry is 'Nine. West northwest.'"

"Then you traveled about the seventh of a mile in a northeasterly direction and we draw a line an inch long at an angle of forty-five degrees to the right of the north and south line. From the end of that we carry a line at an angle of fifty-six and a quarter degrees to the left of the north and south line, and so on. The method is perfectly simple, you see."

"Perfectly; I quite understand it now."

I went back to my chair and continued to read out the entries from the notebook while Thorndyke laid off the lines of direction with the protractor, taking out the distances with the dividers from a scale of equal parts on the back of the instrument. As the work proceeded, I noticed, from time to time, a smile of quiet amusement spread over my colleague's keen, attentive face, and at each new reference to a railway bridge he chuckled softly.

"What, again!" he laughed, as I recorded the passage of the fifth or sixth bridge. "It's like a game of croquet. Go on. What is the next?"

I went on reading out the notes until I came to the final one:

"'Nine twenty-four. Southeast. In covered way. Stop. Wooden gates closed.'"

Thorndyke ruled off the last line, remarking: "Then your covered way is on the south side of a street which bears northeast. So we complete our chart. Just look at your route, Jervis."

He held up the board with a quizzical smile and I stared in astonishment at the chart. The single line, which represented the route of the carriage, zigzagged in the most amazing manner, turning, re-turning and crossing itself repeatedly, evidently passing more than once down the same thoroughfares and terminating at a comparatively short distance from its commencement.

"Why!" I exclaimed, the "rascal must have lived quite near to Stillbury's house!"

Thorndyke measured with the dividers the distance between the starting and arriving points of the route and took it off from the scale.

"Five-eighths of a mile, roughly," he said. "You could have walked it in less than ten minutes. And now let us get out the ordnance map and see if we can give to each of those marvelously erratic lines 'a local habitation and a name.'"

He spread the map out on the table and placed our chart by its side.

"I think," said he, "you started from Lower Kennington Lane?"

"Yes, from this point," I replied, indicating the spot with a pencil.

"Then," said Thorndyke, "if we swing the chart round twenty degrees to correct the deviation of the compass, we can compare it with the ordnance map."

He set off with the protractor an angle of twenty degrees from the north and south line and turned the chart round to that extent. After closely scrutinizing the map and the chart and comparing the one with the other, he said:

"By mere inspection it seems fairly easy to identify the thoroughfares that correspond to the lines of the chart. Take the part that is near your destination. At nine twenty-one you passed under a bridge, going westward. That would seem to be Glasshouse Street. Then you turned south, apparently along the Albert Embankment, where you heard the tug's whistle. Then you heard a passenger train start on your left; that would be Vauxhall Station. Next you turned round due east and passed under a large railway bridge, which suggests the bridge that carries the Station over Upper Kennington Lane. If that is so, your house should be on the south side of Upper Kennington Lane, some three hundred yards from the bridge. But we may as well test our inferences by one or two measurements."

"How can you do that if you don't know the exact scale of the chart?"

"I will show you," said Thorndyke. "We shall establish the true scale and that will form part of the proof."

He rapidly constructed on the upper blank part of the paper, a proportional diagram consisting of two intersecting lines with a single cross-line.

"This long line," he explained, "is the distance from Stillbury's house to the Vauxhall railway bridge as it appears on the chart; the shorter cross-line is the same distance taken from the ordnance map. If our inference is correct and the chart is reasonably accurate, all the other distances will show a similar proportion. Let us try some of them. Take the distance from Vauxhall bridge to the Glasshouse Street bridge."

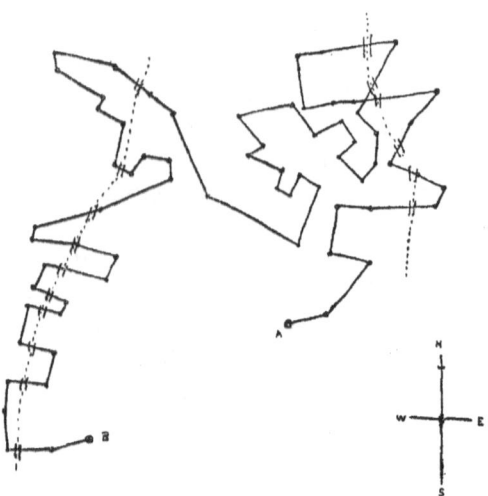

The Track Chart, Showing the Route
Followed by Weiss's Carriage.

A. — Starting-point in Lower Kennington Lane.
B. — Position of Mr. Weiss's house. The dotted lines connecting the
bridges indicate probable railway lines.

He made the two measurements carefully, and, as the point of the dividers came down almost precisely in the correct place on the diagram, he looked up at me.

"Considering the roughness of the method by which the chart was made, I think that is pretty conclusive, though, if you look at the various arches that you passed under and see how nearly they appear to follow the position of the Southwestern Railway line, you hardly need further proof. But I will take a few more proportional measurements for the satisfaction of proving the case by scientific methods before we proceed to verify our conclusions by a visit to the spot."

He took off one or two more distances, and on comparing them with the proportional distances on the ordnance map, found them in every case as nearly correct as could be expected.

"Yes," said Thorndyke, laying down the dividers, "I think we have narrowed down the locality of Mr. Weiss's house to a few yards in a known street. We shall get further help from your note of nine twenty-three thirty, when records a patch of newly laid macadam extending up to the house."

"That new macadam will be pretty well smoothed down by now," I objected.

"Not so very completely," answered Thorndyke. "It is only a little over a month ago, and there has been very little wet weather since. It may be smooth, but it will be easily distinguishable from the old."

"And do I understand that you propose to go and explore the neighborhood?"

"Undoubtedly I do. That is to say, I intend to convert the locality of this house into a definite address; which, I think, will now be perfectly easy, unless we should have the bad luck to find more than one covered way. Even then, the difficulty would be trifling."

"And when you have ascertained where Mr. Weiss lives? What then?"

"That will depend on circumstances. I think we shall probably call at Scotland Yard and have a little talk with our friend Mr. Superintendent Miller; unless, for any reason, it seems better to look into the case ourselves."

"When is this voyage of exploration to take place?"

Thorndyke considered this question, and, taking out his pocketbook, glanced through his engagements.

"It seems to me," he said, "that tomorrow is a fairly free day. We could take the morning without neglecting other business. I suggest that we start immediately after breakfast. How will that suit my learned friend?"

"My time is yours," I replied; "and if you choose to waste it on matters that don't concern you, that's your affair."

"Then we will consider the arrangement to stand for tomorrow morning, or rather, for this morning, as I see that it is past twelve."

With this Thorndyke gathered up the chart and instruments and we separated for the night.

Chapter IX

The House of Mystery

*H*alf-past nine on the following morning found us spinning along the Albert Embankment in a hansom to the pleasant tinkle of the horse's bell. Thorndyke appeared to be in high spirits, though the full enjoyment of the matutinal pipe precluded fluent conversation. As a precaution, he had put my notebook in his pocket before starting, and once or twice he took it out and looked over its pages; but he made no reference to the object of our quest, and the few remarks that he uttered would have indicated that his thoughts were occupied with other matters.

Arrived at Vauxhall Station, we alighted and forthwith made our way to the bridge that spans Upper Kennington Lane near its junction with Harleyford Road.

"Here is our starting point," said Thorndyke. "From this place to the house is about three hundred yards — say four hundred and twenty paces — and at about two hundred paces we ought to reach our patch of new road-metal. Now, are you ready? If we keep step we shall average our stride."

We started together at a good pace, stepping out with military regularity and counting aloud as we went. As we told out the hundred and ninety-fourth pace I observed Thorndyke nod towards the roadway a little ahead, and, looking at it attentively as we approached, it was easy to see by the regularity of surface and lighter color, that it had recently been re-metalled.

Having counted out the four hundred and twenty paces, we halted, and Thorndyke turned to me with a smile of triumph.

"Not a bad estimate, Jervis," said he. "That will be your house if I am not much mistaken. There is no other mews or private roadway in sight."

He pointed to a narrow turning some dozen yards ahead, apparently the entrance to a mews or yard and closed by a pair of massive wooden gates.

"Yes," I answered, "there can be no doubt that this is the place; but, by Jove!" I added, as we drew nearer, "the nest is empty! Do you see?"

I pointed to a bill that was stuck on the gate, bearing, as I could see at this distance, the inscription "To Let."

"Here is a new and startling, if not altogether unexpected, development," said Thorndyke, as we stood gazing at the bill; which set forth that "these premises, including stabling and workshops," were "to be let on lease or otherwise," and referred inquiries to Messrs. Ryebody Brothers, house-agents and valuers, Upper Kennington Lane. "The question is, should we make a few inquiries of the agent, or should we get the keys and have a look at the inside of the house? I am inclined to do both, and the latter first, if Messrs. Ryebody Brothers will trust us with the keys."

We proceeded up the lane to the address given, and, entering the office, Thorndyke made his request — somewhat to the surprise of the clerk; for Thorndyke was not quite the kind of person whom one naturally associates with stabling and workshops. However, there was no difficulty, but as the clerk sorted out the keys from a bunch hanging from a hook, he remarked:

"I expect you will find the place in a rather dirty and neglected condition. The house has not been cleaned yet; it is just as it was left when the brokers took away the furniture."

"Was the last tenant sold up, then?" Thorndyke asked.

"Oh, no. He had to leave rather unexpectedly to take up some business in Germany."

"I hope he paid his rent," said Thorndyke.

"Oh, yes. Trust us for that. But I should say that Mr. Weiss — that was his name — was a man of some means. He seemed to have plenty of money, though he always paid in notes. I don't fancy he had a banking account in this country. He hadn't been here more than about six or seven months and I imagine he didn't know many people in England, as he paid us a cash deposit in lieu of references when he first came."

"I think you said his name was Weiss. It wouldn't be H. Weiss by any chance?"

"I believe it was. But I can soon tell you." He opened a drawer and consulted what looked like a book of receipt forms. "Yes; H Weiss. Do you know him, sir?"

"I knew a Mr. H. Weiss some years ago. He came from Bremen, I remember."

"This Mr. Weiss has gone back to Hamburg," the clerk observed.

"Ah," said Thorndyke, "then it would seem not to be the same. My acquaintance was a fair man with a beard and a decidedly red nose and he wore spectacles."

"That's the man. You've described him exactly," said the clerk, who was apparently rather easily satisfied in the matter of description.

"Dear me," said Thorndyke; "what a small world it is. Do you happen to have a note of his address in Hamburg?"

"I haven't," the clerk replied. "You see we've done with him, having got the rent, though the house is not actually surrendered yet. Mr. Weiss's housekeeper still has the front-door key. She doesn't start for Hamburg for a week or so, and meanwhile she keeps the key so that she can call every day and see if there are any letters."

"Indeed," said Thorndyke. "I wonder if he still has the same housekeeper."

"This lady is a German," replied the clerk, "with a regular jaw-twisting name. Sounded like Shallybang."

"Schallibaum. That is the lady. A fair woman with hardly any eyebrows and a pronounced cast in the left eye."

"Now that's very curious, sir," said the clerk. "It's the same name, and this is a fair woman with remarkably thin eyebrows, I remember, now that you mention it But it can't be the same person. I have only seen her a few times and then only just for a minute or so; but I'm quite certain she had no cast in her eye. So, you see, sir, she can't be the same person. You can dye your hair or you can wear a wig or you can paint your face; but a squint is a squint. There's no faking a swivel eye."

Thorndyke laughed softly. "I suppose not; unless, perhaps, someone might invent an adjustable glass eye. Are these the keys?"

"Yes, sir. The large one belongs to the wicket in the front gate. The other is the latchkey belonging to the side door. Mrs. Shallybang has the key of the front door."

"Thank you," said Thorndyke. He took the keys, to which a wooden label was attached, and we made our way back towards the house of mystery, discussing the clerk's statements as we went.

"A very communicable young gentleman, that," Thorndyke remarked. "He seemed quite pleased to relieve the monotony of office work with a little conversation. And I am sure I was very delighted to indulge him."

"He hadn't much to tell, all the same," said I.

Thorndyke looked at me in surprise. "I don't know what you would have, Jervis, unless you expect casual strangers to present you with a ready-made body of evidence, fully classified, with all the inferences and implications stated. It seemed to me that he was a highly instructive young man."

"What did you learn from him?" I asked.

"Oh, come, Jervis," he protested; "is that a fair question, under our present arrangement? However, I will mention a few points. We learn that about six or seven months ago, Mr. H. Weiss dropped from the clouds into Kennington Lane and that he has now ascended from Kennington Lane into the clouds. That is a useful piece of information. Then we learn that Mrs. Schallibaum has remained in England; which might be of little importance if it were not for a very interesting corollary that it suggests."

"What is that?"

"I must leave you to consider the facts at your leisure; but you will have noticed the ostensible reason for her remaining behind. She is engaged in puttying up the one gaping joint in their armor. One of them has been indiscreet enough to give this address to some correspondent — probably a foreign correspondent. Now, as they obviously wish to leave no tracks, they cannot give their new address to the Post Office to have their letters forwarded, and, on the other hand, a letter left in the box might establish such a connection as would enable them to be traced. Moreover, the letter might be of a kind that they would not wish to fall into the wrong hands. They would not have given this address excepting under some peculiar circumstances."

"No, I should think not, if they took this house for the express purpose of committing a crime in it."

"Exactly. And then there is one other fact that you may have gathered from our young friend's remarks."

"What is that?"

"That a controllable squint is a very valuable asset to a person who wishes to avoid identification."

"Yes, I did note that. The fellow seemed to think that it was absolutely conclusive."

"And so would most people; especially in the case of a squint of that kind. We can all squint towards our noses, but no normal person can turn his eyes away from one another. My impression is that the presence or absence, as the case might be, of a divergent squint would be accepted as absolute disproof of identity. But here we are."

He inserted the key into the wicket of the large gate, and, when we had stepped through into the covered way, he locked it from the inside.

"Why have you locked us in?" I asked, seeing that the wicket had a latch.

"Because," he replied, "if we now hear anyone on the premises we shall know who it is. Only one person besides ourselves has a key."

His reply startled me somewhat. I stopped and looked at him.

"That is a quaint situation, Thorndyke. I hadn't thought of it. Why she may actually come to the house while we are here; in fact, she may be in the house at this moment."

"I hope not," said he. "We don't particularly want Mr. Weiss to be put on his guard, for I take it, he is a pretty wide-awake gentleman under any circumstances. If she does come, we had better keep out of sight. I think we will look over the house first. That is of the most interest to us. If the lady does happen to come while we are here, she may stay to show us over the place and keep an eye on us. So we will leave the stables to the last."

We walked down the entry to the side door at which I had been admitted by Mrs. Schallibaum on the occasion of my previous visits. Thorndyke inserted the latchkey, and, as soon as we were inside, shut the door and walked quickly through into the hall, whither I followed him. He made straight for the front door, where, having slipped up the catch of the lock, he began very attentively to examine the letterbox. It was a somewhat massive wooden box, fitted with a lock of good quality and furnished with a wire grille through which one could inspect the interior.

"We are in luck, Jervis," Thorndyke remarked. "Our visit has been most happily timed. There is a letter in the box."

"Well," I said, "we can't get it out; and if we could, it would be hardly justifiable."

"I don't know," he replied, "that I am prepared to assent off-hand to either of those propositions; but I would rather not tamper with another person's letter, even if that person should happen to be a murderer. Perhaps we can get the information we want from the outside of the envelope."

He produced from his pocket a little electric lamp fitted with a bull's-eye, and, pressing the button, threw a beam of light in through the grille. The letter was lying on the bottom of the box face upwards, so that the address could easily be read.

"Herrn Dr. H. Weiss," Thorndyke read aloud. "German stamp, postmark apparently Darmstadt. You notice that the 'Herrn Dr.' is printed and the rest written. What do you make of that?"

"I don't quite know. Do you think he is really a medical man?"

"Perhaps we had better finish our investigation, in case we are disturbed, and discuss the bearings of the facts afterwards. The name of the sender may be on the flap of the envelope. If it is not, I shall pick the lock and take out the letter. Have you got a probe about you?"

"Yes; by force of habit I am still carrying my pocket case."

I took the little case from my pocket and extracting from it a jointed probe of thickish silver wire, screwed the two halves together and handed the completed instrument to Thorndyke; who passed the slender rod through the grille and adroitly turned the letter over.

"Ha!" he exclaimed with deep satisfaction, as the light fell on the reverse of the envelope, "we are saved from the necessity of theft — or rather, unauthorized borrowing — 'Johann Schnitzler, Darmstadt.' That is all that we actually want. The German police can do the rest if necessary."

He handed me back my probe, pocketed his lamp, released the catch of the lock on the door, and turned away along the dark, musty-smelling hall.

"Do you happen to know the name of Johann Schnitzler?" he asked.

I replied that I had no recollection of ever having heard the name before.

"Neither have I," said he; "but I think we may form a pretty shrewd guess as to his avocation. As you saw, the words 'Herrn Dr.' were printed on the envelope, leaving the rest of the address to be written by hand. The plain inference is that he is a person who habitually addresses letters to medical men, and as the style of the envelope and the lettering — which is printed, not embossed — is commercial, we may assume that he is engaged in some sort of trade. Now, what is a likely trade?"

"He might be an instrument maker or a drug manufacturer; more probably the latter, as there is an extensive drug and chemical industry in Germany, and as Mr. Weiss seemed to have more use for drugs than instruments."

"Yes, I think you are right; but we will look him up when we get home. And now we had better take a glance at the bedroom; that is, if you can remember which room it was."

"It was on the first floor," said I, "and the door by which I entered was just at the head of the stairs."

We ascended the two flights, and, as we reached the landing, I halted.

"This was the door," I said, and was about to turn the handle when Thorndyke caught me by the arm.

"One moment, Jervis," said he. "What do you make of this?"

He pointed to a spot near the bottom of the door where, on close inspection, four good-sized screw-holes were distinguishable. They had been neatly stopped with putty and covered with knotting, and were so nearly the color of the grained and varnished woodwork as to be hardly visible.

"Evidently," I answered, "there has been a bolt there, though it seems a queer place to fix one."

"Not at all," replied Thorndyke. "If you look up you will see that there was another at the top of the door, and, as the lock is in the middle, they must have been highly effective. But there are one or two other points that strike one. First, you will notice that the bolts have been fixed on quite recently, for the paint that they covered is of the same grimy tint as that on the rest of the door. Next, they have been taken off, which, seeing that they could hardly have been worth the trouble of removal, seems to suggest that the person who fixed them considered that their presence might appear remarkable, while the screw-holes, which have been so skillfully and carefully stopped, would be less conspicuous.

"Then, they are on the outside of the door — an unusual situation for bedroom bolts — and were of considerable size. They were long and thick."

"I can see, by the position of the screw-holes, that they were long; but how do you arrive at their thickness?"

"By the size of the counter-holes in the jamb of the door. These holes have been very carefully filled with wooden plugs covered with knotting; but you can make out their diameter, which is that of the bolts, and which is decidedly out of proportion for an ordinary bedroom door. Let me show you a light."

He flashed his lamp into the dark corner, and I was able to see distinctly the portentously large holes into which the bolts had fitted, and also to note the remarkable neatness with which they had been plugged.

"There was a second door, I remember," said I. "Let us see if that was guarded in a similar manner."

We strode through the empty room, awakening dismal echoes as we trod the bare boards, and flung open the other door. At top and bottom, similar groups of screw-holes showed that this also had been made secure, and that these bolts had been of the same very substantial character as the others.

Thorndyke turned away from the door with a slight frown.

"If we had any doubts," said he, "as to what has been going on in this house, these traces of massive fastenings would be almost enough to settle them."

"They might have been there before Weiss came," I suggested. "He only came about seven months ago and there is no date on the screw-holes."

"That is quite true. But when, with their recent fixture, you couple the facts that they have been removed, that very careful measures have been taken to obliterate the traces of their presence, and that they would have been indispensable for the commission of the crime that we are almost certain was being committed here, it looks like an excess of caution to seek other explanations."

"But," I objected, "if the man, Graves, was really imprisoned, could not he have smashed the window and called for help?"

"The window looks out on the yard, as you see; but I expect it was secured too."

He drew the massive, old-fashioned shutters out of their recess and closed them.

"Yes, here we are." He pointed to four groups of screw-holes at the corners of the shutters, and, once more producing his lamp, narrowly examined the insides of the recesses into which the shutters folded.

"The nature of the fastening is quite evident," said he. "An iron bar passed right across at the top and bottom and was secured by a staple and padlock. You can see the mark the bar made in the recess when the shutters were folded. When these bars were fixed and padlocked and the bolts were shot, this room was as secure, for a prisoner unprovided with tools, as a cell in Newgate."

We looked at one another for awhile without speaking; and I fancy that if Mr. H. Weiss could have seen our faces he might have thought it desirable to seek some retreat even more remote than Hamburg.

"It was a diabolical affair, Jervis," Thorndyke said at length, in an ominously quiet and even gentle tone. "A sordid, callous, cold-blooded crime of a type that is to me utterly unforgivable and incapable of extenuation. Of course, it may have failed. Mr. Graves may even now be alive. I shall make it my very especial business to ascertain whether he is or not. And if he is not, I shall take it to myself as a sacred duty to lay my hand on the man who has compassed his death."

I looked at Thorndyke with something akin to awe. In the quiet unemotional tone of his voice, in his unruffled manner and the stony calm of his face, there was something much more impressive, more fateful, than there could have been in the fiercest threats or the most passionate denunciations. I felt that in those softly spoken words he had pronounced the doom of the fugitive villain.

He turned away from the window and glanced round the empty room. It seemed that our discovery of the fastenings had exhausted the information that it had to offer.

"It is a thousand pities," I remarked, "that we were unable to look round before they moved out the furniture. We might have found some clue to the scoundrel's identity."

"Yes," replied Thorndyke; "there isn't much information to be gathered here, I am afraid. I see they have swept up the small litter from the floor and poked it under the grate. We will turn that over, as there seems to be nothing else, and then look at the other rooms."

He raked out the little heap of rubbish with his stick and spread it out on the hearth. It certainly looked unpromising enough, being just such a rubbish heap as may be swept up in any untidy room during a move. But Thorndyke went through it systematically, examining each item attentively, even to the local tradesmen's bills and empty paper bags, before laying them aside. Another rake of his stick scattered the bulky masses of crumpled paper and brought into view an object which he picked up with some eagerness. It was a portion of a pair of spectacles, which had apparently been trodden on, for the side-bar was twisted and bent and the glass was shattered into fragments.

"This ought to give us a hint," said he. "It will probably have belonged either to Weiss or Graves, as Mrs. Schallibaum apparently did not wear glasses. Let us see if we can find the remainder."

We both groped carefully with our sticks amongst the rubbish, spreading it out on the hearth and removing the numerous pieces of crumpled paper. Our search was rewarded by the discovery of the second eye-piece of the spectacles, of which the glass was badly cracked but less shattered than the other. I also picked up two tiny sticks at which Thorndyke looked with deep interest before laying them on the mantelshelf.

"We will consider them presently," said he. "Let us finish with the spectacles first. You see that the left eye-glass is a concave cylindrical lens of some sort. We can make out that much from the fragments that remain, and we can measure the curvature when we get them home, although that will be easier if we can collect some more fragments and stick them together. The right eye is plain glass; that is quite evident. Then these will have belonged to your patient, Jervis. You said that the tremulous iris was in the right eye, I think?"

"Yes," I replied. "These will be his spectacles, without doubt."

"They are peculiar frames," he continued. "If they were made in this country, we might be able to discover the maker. But we must collect as many fragments of glass as we can."

Once more we searched amongst the rubbish and succeeded, eventually, in recovering some seven or eight small fragments of the broken spectacle-glasses, which Thorndyke laid on the mantelshelf beside the little sticks.

"By the way, Thorndyke," I said, taking up the latter to examine them afresh, "what are these things? Can you make anything of them?"

He looked at them thoughtfully for a few moments and then replied:

"I don't think I will tell you what they are. You should find that out for yourself, and it will be well worth your while to do so. They are rather suggestive objects under the circumstances. But notice their peculiarities carefully. Both are portions of some smooth, stout reed.

There is a long, thin stick — about six inches long — and a thicker piece only three inches in length. The longer piece has a little scrap of red paper stuck on at the end; apparently a portion of a label of some kind with an ornamental border. The other end of the stick has been broken off. The shorter, stouter stick has had its central cavity artificially enlarged so that it fits over the other to form a cap or sheath. Make a careful note of those facts and try to think what they probably mean; what would be the most likely use for an object of this kind. When you have ascertained that, you will have learned something new about this case. And now, to resume our investigations. Here is a very suggestive thing." He picked up a small, wide-mouthed bottle and, holding it up for my inspection, continued: "Observe the fly sticking to the inside, and the name on the label, 'Fox, Russell Street, Covent Garden.'"

"I don't know Mr. Fox."

"Then I will inform you that he is a dealer in the materials for 'make-up,' theatrical or otherwise, and will leave you to consider the bearing of this bottle on our present investigation. There doesn't seem to be anything else of interest in this El Dorado excepting that screw, which you notice is about the size of those with which the bolts were fastened on the doors. I don't think it is worth while to unstop any of the holes to try it; we should learn nothing fresh."

He rose, and, having kicked the discarded rubbish back under the grate, gathered up his gleanings from the mantelpiece, carefully bestowing the spectacles and the fragments of glass in the tin box that he appeared always to carry in his pocket, and wrapping the larger objects in his handkerchief.

"A poor collection," was his comment, as he returned the box and handkerchief to his pocket, "and yet not so poor as I had feared. Perhaps, if we question them closely enough, these unconsidered trifles may be made to tell us something worth learning after all. Shall we go into the other room?"

We passed out on to the landing and into the front room, where, guided by experience, we made straight for the fireplace. But the little heap of rubbish there contained nothing that even Thorndyke's inquisitive eye could view with interest. We wandered disconsolately round the room, peering into the empty cupboards and scanning the floor and the corners by the skirting, without discovering a single object or relic of the late occupants. In the course of my perambulations I halted by the window and was looking down into the street when Thorndyke called to me sharply:

"Come away from the window, Jervis! Have you forgotten that Mrs. Schallibaum may be in the neighborhood at this moment?"

As a matter of fact I had entirely forgotten the matter, nor did it now strike me as anything but the remotest of possibilities. I replied to that effect.

"I don't agree with you," Thorndyke rejoined. "We have heard that she comes here to look for letters. Probably she comes every day, or even oftener. There is a good deal at stake, remember, and they cannot feel quite as secure as they would wish. Weiss must have seen what view you took of the case and must have had some uneasy moments thinking of what you might do. In fact, we may take it that the fear of you drove them out of the neighborhood, and that they are mighty anxious to get that letter and cut the last link that binds them to this house."

"I suppose that is so," I agreed; "and if the lady should happen to pass this way and should see me at the window and recognize me, she would certainly smell a rat."

"A rat!" exclaimed Thorndyke. "She would smell a whole pack of foxes, and Mr. H. Weiss would be more on his guard than ever. Let us have a look at the other rooms; there is nothing here."

We went up to the next floor and found traces of recent occupation in one room only. The garrets had evidently been unused, and the kitchen and ground-floor rooms offered nothing that appeared to Thorndyke worth noting. Then we went out by the side door and down the covered way into the yard at the back. The workshops were fastened with rusty padlocks that looked as if they had not been disturbed for months. The stables were empty and had been tentatively cleaned out, the coach-house was vacant, and presented no traces of recent use excepting a half-bald spoke-brush. We returned up the covered way and I was about to close the side door, which Thorndyke had left ajar, when he stopped me.

"We'll have another look at the hall before we go," said he; and, walking softly before me, he made his way to the front door, where, producing his lamp, he threw a beam of light into the letterbox.

"Anymore letters?" I asked.

"Anymore!" he repeated. "Look for yourself."

I stooped and peered through the grille into the lighted interior; and then I uttered an exclamation.

The box was empty.

Thorndyke regarded me with a grim smile. "We have been caught on the hop, Jervis, I suspect," said he.

"It is queer," I replied. "I didn't hear any sound of the opening or closing of the door; did you?"

"No; I didn't hear any sound; which makes me suspect that she did. She would have heard our voices and she is probably keeping a sharp look-out at this very moment. I wonder if she saw you at the window.

But whether she did or not, we must go very warily. Neither of us must return to the Temple direct, and we had better separate when we have returned the keys and I will watch you out of sight and see if anyone is following you. What are you going to do?"

"If you don't want me, I shall run over to Kensington and drop in to lunch at the Hornbys'. I said I would call as soon as I had an hour or so free."

"Very well. Do so; and keep a look-out in case you are followed. I have to go down to Guildford this afternoon. Under the circumstances, I shall not go back home, but send Polton a telegram and take a train at Vauxhall and change at some small station where I can watch the platform. Be as careful as you can. Remember that what you have to avoid is being followed to anyplace where you are known, and, above all, revealing your connection with number Five A, King's Bench Walk."

Having thus considered our immediate movements, we emerged together from the wicket, and locking it behind us, walked quickly to the house-agents', where an opportune office-boy received the keys without remark. As we came out of the office, I halted irresolutely and we both looked up and down the lane.

"There is no suspicious looking person in sight at present," Thorndyke said, and then asked: "Which way do you think of going?"

"It seems to me," I replied, "that my best plan would be to take a cab or an omnibus so as to get out of the neighborhood as quickly as possible. If I go through Ravensden Street into Kennington Park Road, I can pick up an omnibus that will take me to the Mansion House, where I can change for Kensington. I shall go on the top so that I can keep a look-out for any other omnibus or cab that may be following."

"Yes," said Thorndyke, "that seems a good plan. I will walk with you and see that you get a fair start."

We walked briskly along the lane and through Ravensden Street to the Kennington Park Road. An omnibus was approaching from the south at a steady jog-trot and we halted at the corner to wait for it. Several people passed us in different directions, but none seemed to take any particular notice of us, though we observed them rather narrowly, especially the women. Then the omnibus crawled up. I sprang on the foot-board and ascended to the roof, where I seated myself and surveyed the prospect to the rear. No one else got on the omnibus — which had not stopped — and no cab or other passenger vehicle was in sight. I continued to watch Thorndyke as he stood sentinel at the corner, and noted that no one appeared to be making any effort to overtake the omnibus. Presently my colleague waved his hand to me and turned back towards Vauxhall, and I, having satisfied myself once more that no pursuing cab or hurrying foot-passenger was in sight, decided that our precautions had been unnecessary and settled myself in a rather more comfortable position.

Chapter X

The Hunter Hunted

*T*he omnibus of those days was a leisurely vehicle. Its ordinary pace was a rather sluggish trot, and in a thickly populated thoroughfare its speed was further reduced by frequent stoppages. Bearing these facts in mind, I gave an occasional backward glance as we jogged northward, though my attention soon began to wander from the rather remote possibility of pursuit to the incidents of our late exploration.

It had not been difficult to see that Thorndyke was very well pleased with the results of our search, but excepting the letter — which undoubtedly opened up a channel for further inquiry and possible identification — I could not perceive that any of the traces that we had found justified his satisfaction. There were the spectacles, for instance. They were almost certainly the pair worn by Mr. Graves. But what then? It was exceedingly improbable that we should be able to discover the maker of them, and if we were, it was still more improbable that he would be able to give us any information that would help us. Spectacle-makers are not usually on confidential terms with their customers.

As to the other objects, I could make nothing of them. The little sticks of reed evidently had some use that was known to Thorndyke and furnished, by inference, some kind of information about Weiss, Graves, or Mrs. Schallibaum. But I had never seen anything like them before and they conveyed nothing whatever to me. Then the bottle that had seemed so significant to Thorndyke was to me quite uninforming. It did, indeed, suggest that some member of the household might be connected with the stage, but it gave no hint as to which one. Certainly that person was not Mr. Weiss, whose appearance was as remote from that of an actor as could well be imagined. At any rate, the bottle and its label gave me no more useful hint than it might be worth while to call on Mr. Fox and make inquiries; and something told me very emphatically that this was not what it had conveyed to Thorndyke.

These reflections occupied me until the omnibus, having rumbled over London Bridge and up King William Street, joined the converging streams of traffic at the Mansion House. Here I got down and changed to an omnibus bound for Kensington; on which I traveled westward pleasantly enough, looking down into the teeming streets and whiling away the time by meditating upon the very agreeable afternoon that I promised myself, and considering how far my new arrangement with Thorndyke would justify me in entering into certain domestic engagements of a highly interesting kind.

What might have happened under other circumstances it is impossible to tell and useless to speculate; the fact is that my journey ended in a disappointment. I arrived, all agog, at the familiar house in Endsley Gardens only to be told by a sympathetic housemaid that the family was out; that Mrs. Hornby had gone into the country and would not be home until night, and — which mattered a good deal more to me — that her niece, Miss Juliet Gibson, had accompanied her.

Now a man who drops into lunch without announcing his intention or previously ascertaining those of his friends has no right to quarrel with fate if he finds an empty house. Thus philosophically I reflected as I turned away from the house in profound discontent, demanding of the universe in general why Mrs. Hornby need have perversely chosen my first free day to go gadding into the country, and above all, why she must needs spirit away the fair Juliet. This was the crowning misfortune (for I could have endured the absence of the elder lady with commendable fortitude), and since I could not immediately return to the Temple it left me a mere waif and stray for the time being.

Instinct — of the kind that manifests itself especially about one o'clock in the afternoon — impelled me in the direction of Brompton Road, and finally landed me at a table in a large restaurant apparently adjusted to the needs of ladies who had come from a distance to engage in the feminine sport of shopping. Here, while waiting for my lunch, I sat idly scanning the morning paper and wondering what I should do with the rest of the day; and presently it chanced that my eye caught the announcement of a matinée at the theater in Sloane Square. It was quite a long time since I had been at a theater, and, as the play — light comedy — seemed likely to satisfy my not very critical taste, I decided to devote the afternoon to reviving my acquaintance with the drama. Accordingly as soon as my lunch was finished, I walked down the Brompton Road, stepped on to an omnibus, and was duly deposited at the door of the theater. A couple of minutes later I found myself occupying an excellent seat in the second row of the pit, oblivious alike of my recent disappointment and of Thorndyke's words of warning.

I am not an enthusiastic play-goer. To dramatic performances I am disposed to assign nothing further than the modest function of furnishing entertainment. I do not go to a theater to be instructed or to have my moral outlook elevated. But, by way of compensation, I am not difficult to please. To a simple play, adjusted to my primitive taste, I can bring a certain bucolic appreciation that enables me to extract from the performance the maximum of enjoyment; and when, on this occasion, the final curtain fell and the audience rose, I rescued my hat from its insecure resting-place and turned to go with the feeling that I had spent a highly agreeable afternoon.

Emerging from the theater, borne on the outgoing stream, I presently found myself opposite the door of a tea-shop. Instinct — the five o'clock instinct this time — guided me in; for we are creatures of habit, especially of the tea habit. The unoccupied table to which I drifted was in a shady corner not very far from the pay-desk; and here I had been seated less than a minute when a lady passed me on her way to the farther table. The glimpse that I caught of her as she approached — it was but a glimpse, since she passed behind me — showed that she was dressed in black, that she wore a beaded veil and hat, and in addition to the glass of milk and the bun that she carried, she was encumbered by an umbrella and a small basket, apparently containing some kind of needlework. I must confess that I gave her very little attention at the time, being occupied in anxious speculation as to how long it would be before the fact of my presence would impinge on the consciousness of the waitress.

The exact time by the clock on the wall was three minutes and a quarter, at the expiration of which an anemic young woman sauntered up to the table and bestowed on me a glance of sullen interrogation, as if mutely demanding what the devil I wanted. I humbly requested that I might be provided with a pot of tea; whereupon she turned on her heel (which was a good deal worn down on the offside) and reported my conduct to a lady behind a marble-topped counter.

It seemed that the counter lady took a lenient view of the case, for in less than four minutes the waitress returned and gloomily deposited on the table before me a teapot, a milk-jug, a cup and saucer, a jug of hot water, and a small pool of milk. Then she once more departed in dudgeon.

I had just given the tea in the pot a preliminary stir and was about to pour out the first cup when I felt someone bump lightly against my chair and heard something rattle on the floor. I turned quickly and perceived the lady, whom I had seen enter, stooping just behind my chair. It seemed that having finished her frugal meal she was on her way out when she had dropped the little basket that I had noticed hanging from her wrist; which basket had promptly disgorged its entire contents on the floor.

Now everyone must have noticed the demon of agility that seems to enter into an inanimate object when it is dropped, and the apparently intelligent malice with which it discovers, and rolls into, the most inaccessible places. Here was a case in point. This particular basket had contained materials for Oriental bead-work; and no sooner had it reached the floor than each item of its contents appeared to become possessed of a separate and particular devil impelling it to travel at headlong speed to some remote and unapproachable corner as distant as possible from its fellows.

As the only man — and almost the only person — near, the duty of salvage-agent manifestly devolved upon me; and down I went, accordingly, on my hands and knees, regardless of a nearly new pair of trousers, to grope under tables, chairs and settles in reach of the scattered treasure. A ball of the thick thread or twine I recovered from a dark and dirty corner after a brief interview with the sharp corner of a settle, and a multitude of the large beads with which this infernal industry is carried on I gathered from all parts of the compass, coming forth at length (quadrupedally) with a double handful of the treasure-trove and a very lively appreciation of the resistant qualities of a cast-iron table-stand when applied to the human cranium.

The owner of the lost and found property was greatly distressed by the accident and the trouble it had caused me; in fact she was quite needlessly agitated about it. The hand which held the basket into which I poured the rescued trash trembled visibly, and the brief glance that I bestowed on her as she murmured her thanks and apologies — with a very slight foreign accent — showed me that she was excessively pale. That much I could see plainly in spite of the rather dim light in this part of the shop and the beaded veil that covered her face; and I could also see that she was a rather remarkable looking woman, with a great mass of harsh, black hair and very broad black eyebrows that nearly met above her nose and contrasted strikingly with the dead white of her skin. But, of course, I did not look at her intently. Having returned her property and received her acknowledgments, I resumed my seat and left her to go on her way.

I had once more grasped the handle of the teapot when I made a rather curious discovery. At the bottom of the teacup lay a single lump of sugar. To the majority of persons it would have meant nothing. They would have assumed that they had dropped it in and forgotten it and would have proceeded to pour out the tea. But it happened that, at this time, I did not take sugar in my tea; whence it followed that the lump had not been put in by me. Assuming, therefore, that it had been carelessly dropped in by the waitress, I turned it out on the table, filled the cup, added the milk, and took a tentative draft to test the temperature.

The cup was yet at my lips when I chanced to look into the mirror that faced my table. Of course it reflected the part of the shop that was behind me, including the cashier's desk; at which the owner of the basket now stood paying for her refreshment. Between her and me was a gas chandelier which cast its light on my back but full on her face; and her veil notwithstanding, I could see that she was looking at me steadily; was, in fact, watching me intently and with a very curious expression — an expression of expectancy mingled with alarm. But this was not all. As I returned her intent look — which I could do unobserved, since my face, reflected in the mirror, was in deep shadow — I suddenly perceived that that steady gaze engaged her right eye only; the other eye was looking sharply towards her left shoulder. In short, she had a divergent squint of the left eye.

I put down my cup with a thrill of amazement and a sudden surging up of suspicion and alarm. An instant's reflection reminded me that when she had spoken to me a few moments before, both her eyes had looked into mine without the slightest trace of a squint. My thoughts flew back to the lump of sugar, to the unguarded milk-jug and the draft of tea that I had already swallowed; and, hardly knowing what I intended, I started to my feet and turned to confront her. But as I rose, she snatched up her change and darted from the shop. Through the glass door, I saw her spring on to the foot-board of a passing hansom and give the driver some direction. I saw the man whip up his horse, and, by the time I reached the door, the cab was moving off swiftly towards Sloane Street.

I stood irresolute. I had not paid and could not run out of the shop without making a fuss, and my hat and stick were still on the rail opposite my seat. The woman ought to be followed, but I had no fancy for the task. If the tea that I had swallowed was innocuous, no harm was done and I was rid of my pursuer. So far as I was concerned, the incident was closed. I went back to my seat, and picking up the lump of sugar which still lay on the table where I had dropped it, put it carefully in my pocket. But my appetite for tea was satisfied for the present. Moreover it was hardly advisable to stay in the shop lest some fresh spy should come to see how I fared. Accordingly I obtained my check, handed it in at the cashier's desk and took my departure.

All this time, it will be observed, I had been taking it for granted that the lady in black had followed me from Kensington to this shop; that, in fact, she was none other than Mrs. Schallibaum. And, indeed, the circumstances had rendered the conclusion inevitable. In the very in-

stant when I had perceived the displacement of the left eye, complete
recognition had come upon me. When I had stood facing the woman,
the brief glance at her face had conveyed to me something dimly
reminiscent of which I had been but half conscious and had instantly
forgotten. But the sight of that characteristic squint had at once revived
and explained it. That the woman was Mrs. Schallibaum I now felt no
doubt whatever.

Nevertheless, the whole affair was profoundly mysterious. As to the
change in the woman's appearance, there was little in that. The coarse,
black hair might be her own, dyed, or it might be a wig. The eyebrows
were made-up; it was a simple enough proceeding and made still more
simple by the beaded veil. But how did she come to be there at all? How
did she happen to be made-up in this fashion at this particular time?
And, above all, how came she to be provided with a lump of what I had
little doubt was poisoned sugar?

I turned over the events of the day, and the more I considered them
the less comprehensible they appeared. No one had followed the omnibus either on foot or in a vehicle, as far as I could see; and I had kept
a careful look-out, not only at starting but for some considerable time
after. Yet, all the time, Mrs. Schallibaum must have been following. But
how? If she had known that I was intending to travel by the omnibus
she might have gone to meet it and entered before I did. But she could
not have known: and moreover she did not meet the omnibus, for we
watched its approach from some considerable distance. I considered
whether she might not have been concealed in the house and overheard
me mention my destination to Thorndyke. But this failed to explain
the mystery, since I had mentioned no address beyond "Kensington." I
had, indeed, mentioned the name of Mrs. Hornby, but the supposition
that my friends might be known by name to Mrs. Schallibaum, or even
that she might have looked the name up in the directory, presented a
probability too remote to be worth entertaining.

But, if I reached no satisfactory conclusion, my cogitations had one
useful effect; they occupied my mind to the exclusion of that unfortunate draft of tea. Not that I had been seriously uneasy after the first
shock. The quantity that I had swallowed was not large — the tea being
hotter than I cared for — and I remembered that, when I had thrown
out the lump of sugar, I had turned the cup upside down on the table;
so there could have been nothing solid left in it. And the lump of sugar
was in itself reassuring, for it certainly would not have been used in
conjunction with any less conspicuous but more incriminating form of
poison. That lump of sugar was now in my pocket, reserved for careful
examination at my leisure; and I reflected with a faint grin that it would

be a little disconcerting if it should turn out to contain nothing but sugar after all.

On leaving the tea-shop, I walked up Sloane Street with the intention of doing what I ought to have done earlier in the day. I was going to make perfectly sure that no spy was dogging my footsteps. But for my ridiculous confidence I could have done so quite easily before going to Endsley Gardens; and now, made wiser by a startling experience, I proceeded with systematic care. It was still broad daylight — for the lamps in the tea-shop had been rendered necessary only by the faulty construction of the premises and the dullness of the afternoon — and in an open space I could see far enough for complete safety. Arriving at the top of Sloane Street, I crossed Knightsbridge, and, entering Hyde Park, struck out towards the Serpentine. Passing along the eastern shore, I entered one of the long paths that lead towards the Marble Arch and strode along it at such a pace as would make it necessary for any pursuer to hurry in order to keep me in sight. Halfway across the great stretch of turf, I halted for a few moments and noted the few people who were coming in my direction. Then I turned sharply to the left and headed straight for the Victoria Gate, but again, halfway, I turned off among a clump of trees, and, standing behind the trunk of one of them, took a fresh survey of the people who were moving along the paths. All were at a considerable distance and none appeared to be coming my way.

I now moved cautiously from one tree to another and passed through the wooded region to the south, crossed the Serpentine bridge at a rapid walk and hurrying along the south shore left the Park by Apsley House. From hence I walked at the same rapid pace along Piccadilly, insinuating myself among the crowd with the skill born of long acquaintance with the London streets, crossed amidst the seething traffic at the Circus, darted up Windmill Street and began to zigzag amongst the narrow streets and courts of Soho. Crossing the Seven Dials and Drury Lane I passed through the multitudinous back-streets and alleys that then filled the area south of Lincoln's Inn, came out by Newcastle Street, Holywell Street and Half-Moon Alley into the Strand, which I crossed immediately, ultimately entering the Temple by Devereux Court.

Even then I did not relax my precautions. From one court to another I passed quickly, loitering in those dark entries and unexpected passages that are known to so few but the regular Templars, and coming out into the open only at the last where the wide passage of King's Bench Walk admits of no evasion. Halfway up the stairs, I stood for some time in the shadow, watching the approaches from the staircase window; and when, at length, I felt satisfied that I had taken every precaution that was possible, I inserted my key and let myself into our chambers.

Thorndyke had already arrived, and, as I entered, he rose to greet me with an expression of evident relief.

"I am glad to see you, Jervis," he said. "I have been rather anxious about you."

"Why?" I asked.

"For several reasons. One is that you are the sole danger that threatens these people — as far as they know. Another is that we made a most ridiculous mistake. We overlooked a fact that ought to have struck us instantly. But how have you fared?"

"Better than I deserved. That good lady stuck to me like a burr — at least I believe she did."

"I have no doubt she did. We have been caught napping finely, Jervis."

"How?"

"We'll go into that presently. Let us hear about your adventures first."

I gave him a full account of my movements from the time when we parted to that of my arrival home, omitting no incident that I was able to remember and, as far as I could, reconstituting my exceedingly devious homeward route.

"Your retreat was masterly," he remarked with a broad smile. "I should think that it would have utterly defeated any pursuer; and the only pity is that it was probably wasted on the desert air. Your pursuer had by that time become a fugitive. But you were wise to take these precautions, for, of course, Weiss might have followed you."

"But I thought he was in Hamburg?"

"Did you? You are a very confiding young gentleman, for a budding medical jurist. Of course we don't know that he is not; but the fact that he has given Hamburg as his present whereabouts establishes a strong presumption that he is somewhere else. I only hope that he has not located you, and, from what you tell me of your later methods, I fancy that you would have shaken him off even if he had started to follow you from the tea-shop."

"I hope so too. But how did that woman manage to stick to me in that way? What was the mistake we made?"

Thorndyke laughed grimly. "It was a perfectly asinine mistake, Jervis. You started up Kennington Park Road on a leisurely, jog-trotting omnibus, and neither you nor I remembered what there is underneath Kennington Park Road."

"Underneath!" I exclaimed, completely puzzled for the moment. Then, suddenly realizing what he meant, "Of course!" I exclaimed. "Idiot that I am! You mean the electric railway?"

"Yes. That explains everything. Mrs. Schallibaum must have watched us from some shop and quietly followed us up the lane. There were a good many women about and several were walking in our direction.

There was nothing to distinguish her from the others unless you had recognized her, which you would hardly have been able to do if she had worn a veil and kept at a fair distance. At least I think not."

"No," I agreed, "I certainly should not. I had only seen her in a half-dark room. In outdoor clothes and with a veil, I should never have been able to identify her without very close inspection. Besides there was the disguise or make-up."

"Not at that time. She would hardly come disguised to her own house, for it might have led to her being challenged and asked who she was. I think we may take it that there was no actual disguise, although she would probably wear a shady hat and a veil; which would have prevented either of us from picking her out from the other women in the street."

"And what do you think happened next?"

"I think that she simply walked past us — probably on the other side of the road — as we stood waiting for the omnibus, and turned up Kennington Park Road. She probably guessed that we were waiting for the omnibus and walked up the road in the direction in which it was going. Presently the omnibus would pass her, and there were you in full view on top keeping a vigilant look-out in the wrong direction. Then she would quicken her pace a little and in a minute or two would arrive at the Kennington Station of the South London Railway. In a minute or two more she would be in one of the electric trains whirling along under the street on which your omnibus was crawling. She would get out at the Borough Station, or she might take a more risky chance and go on to the Monument; but in any case she would wait for your omnibus, hail it and get inside. I suppose you took up some passengers on the way?"

"Oh dear, yes. We were stopping every two or three minutes to take up or set down passengers; and most of them were women."

"Very well; then we may take it that when you arrived at the Mansion House, Mrs. Schallibaum was one of your inside passengers. It was a rather quaint situation, I think."

"Yes, confound her! What a couple of noodles she must have thought us!"

"No doubt. And that is the one consoling feature in the case. She will have taken us for a pair of absolute greenhorns. But to continue. Of course she traveled in your omnibus to Kensington — you ought to have gone inside on both occasions, so that you could see everyone who entered and examine the inside passengers; she will have followed you to Endsley Gardens and probably noted the house you went to. Thence she will have followed you to the restaurant and may even have lunched there."

"It is quite possible," said I. "There were two rooms and they were filled principally with women."

"Then she will have followed you to Sloane Street, and, as you persisted in riding outside, she could easily take an inside place in your omnibus. As to the theater, she must have taken it as a veritable gift of the gods; an arrangement made by you for her special convenience."

"Why?"

"My dear fellow! consider. She had only to follow you in and see you safely into your seat and there you were, left till called for. She could then go home, make up for her part; draw out a plan of action, with the help, perhaps, of Mr. Weiss, provide herself with the necessary means and appliances and, at the appointed time, call and collect you."

"That is assuming a good deal," I objected. "It is assuming, for instance, that she lives within a moderate distance of Sloane Square. Otherwise it would have been impossible."

"Exactly. That is why I assume it. You don't suppose that she goes about habitually with lumps of prepared sugar in her pocket. And if not, then she must have got that lump from somewhere. Then the beads suggest a carefully prepared plan, and, as I said just now, she can hardly have been made-up when she met us in Kennington Lane. From all of which it seems likely that her present abode is not very far from Sloane Square."

"At any rate," said I, "it was taking a considerable risk. I might have left the theater before she came back."

"Yes," Thorndyke agreed. "But it is like a woman to take chances. A man would probably have stuck to you when once he had got you off your guard. But she was ready to take chances. She chanced the railway, and it came off; she chanced your remaining in the theater, and that came off too. She calculated on the probability of your getting tea when you came out, and she hit it off again. And then she took one chance too many; she assumed that you probably took sugar in your tea, and she was wrong."

"We are taking it for granted that the sugar was prepared," I remarked.

"Yes. Our explanation is entirely hypothetical and may be entirely wrong. But it all hangs together, and if we find any poisonous matter in the sugar, it will be reasonable to assume that we are right. The sugar is the Experimentum Crucis. If you will hand it over to me, we will go up to the laboratory and make a preliminary test or two."

I took the lump of sugar from my pocket and gave it to him, and he carried it to the gas-burner, by the light of which he examined it with a lens.

"I don't see any foreign crystals on the surface," said he; "but we had better make a solution and go to work systematically. If it contains any poison we may assume that it will be some alkaloid, though I will test for arsenic too. But a man of Weiss's type would almost certainly use an alkaloid, on account of its smaller bulk and more ready solubility. You ought not to have carried this loose in your pocket. For legal purposes that would seriously interfere with its value as evidence. Bodies that are suspected of containing poison should be carefully isolated and preserved from contact with anything that might lead to doubt in the analysis. It doesn't matter much to us, as this analysis is only for our own information and we can satisfy ourselves as to the state of your pocket. But bear the rule in mind another time."

We now ascended to the laboratory, where Thorndyke proceeded at once to dissolve the lump of sugar in a measured quantity of distilled water by the aid of gentle heat.

"Before we add any acid," said he, "or introduce any fresh matter, we will adopt the simple preliminary measure of tasting the solution. The sugar is a disturbing factor, but some of the alkaloids and most mineral poisons excepting arsenic have a very characteristic taste."

He dipped a glass rod in the warm solution and applied it gingerly to his tongue.

"Ha!" he exclaimed, as he carefully wiped his mouth with his hand-kerchief, "simple methods are often very valuable. There isn't much doubt as to what is in that sugar. Let me recommend my learned brother to try the flavor. But be careful. A little of this will go a long way."

He took a fresh rod from the rack, and, dipping it in the solution, handed it to me. I cautiously applied it to the tip of my tongue and was immediately aware of a peculiar tingling sensation accompanied by a feeling of numbness.

"Well," said Thorndyke; "what is it?"

"Aconite," I replied without hesitation.

"Yes," he agreed; "aconite it is, or more probably aconitine. And that, I think, gives us all the information we want. We need not trouble now to make a complete analysis, though I shall have a quantitative examination made later. You note the intensity of the taste and you see what the strength of the solution is. Evidently that lump of sugar contained a very large dose of the poison. If the sugar had been dissolved in your tea, the quantity that you drank would have contained enough aconitine to lay you out within a few minutes; which would account for Mrs. Schallibaum's anxiety to get clear of the premises. She saw you drink from the cup, but I imagine she had not seen you turn the sugar out."

"No, I should say not, to judge by her expression. She looked terrified. She is not as hardened as her rascally companion."

"Which is fortunate for you, Jervis. If she had not been in such a fluster, she would have waited until you had poured out your tea, which was what she probably meant to do, or have dropped the sugar into the milk-jug. In either case you would have got a poisonous dose before you noticed anything amiss."

"They are a pretty pair, Thorndyke," I exclaimed. "A human life seems to be no more to them than the life of a fly or a beetle."

"No; that is so. They are typical poisoners of the worst kind; of the intelligent, cautious, resourceful kind. They are a standing menace to society. As long as they are at large, human lives are in danger, and it is our business to see that they do not remain at large a moment longer than is unavoidable. And that brings us to another point. You had better keep indoors for the next few days."

"Oh, nonsense," I protested. "I can take care of myself."

"I won't dispute that," said Thorndyke, "although I might. But the matter is of vital importance and we can't be too careful. Yours is the only evidence that could convict these people. They know that and will stick at nothing to get rid of you — for by this time they will almost certainly have ascertained that the tea-shop plan has failed. Now your life is of some value to you and to another person whom I could mention; but apart from that, you are the indispensable instrument for ridding society of these dangerous vermin. Moreover, if you were seen abroad and connected with these chambers, they would get the information that their case was really being investigated in a businesslike manner. If Weiss has not already left the country he would do so immediately, and if he has, Mrs. Schallibaum would join him at once, and we might never be able to lay hands on them. You must stay indoors, out of sight, and you had better write to Miss Gibson and ask her to warn the servants to give no information about you to anyone."

"And how long," I asked, "am I to be held on parole?"

"Not long, I think. We have a very promising start. If I have any luck, I shall be able to collect all the evidence I want in about a week. But there is an element of chance in some of it which prevents me from giving a date. And it is just possible that I may have started on a false track. But that I shall be able to tell you better in a day or two."

"And I suppose," I said gloomily, "I shall be out of the hunt altogether?"

"Not at all," he replied. "You have got the Blackmore case to attend to. I shall hand you over all the documents and get you to make an orderly digest of the evidence. You will then have all the facts and can work out the case for yourself. Also I shall ask you to help Polton in some little operations which are designed to throw light into dark places and which you will find both entertaining and instructive."

"Supposing Mrs. Hornby should propose to call and take tea with us in the gardens?" I suggested.

"And bring Miss Gibson with her?" Thorndyke added dryly. "No, Jervis, it would never do. You must make that quite clear to her. It is more probable than not that Mrs. Schallibaum made a careful note of the house in Endsley Gardens, and as that would be the one place actually known to her, she and Weiss — if he is in England — would almost certainly keep a watch on it. If they should succeed in connecting that house with these chambers, a few inquiries would show them the exact state of the case. No; we must keep them in the dark if we possibly can. We have shown too much of our hand already. It is hard on you, but it cannot be helped."

"Oh, don't think I am complaining," I exclaimed. "If it is a matter of business, I am as keen as you are. I thought at first that you were merely considering the safety of my vile body. When shall I start on my job?"

"Tomorrow morning. I shall give you my notes on the Blackmore case and the copies of the will and the depositions, from which you had better draw up a digest of the evidence with remarks as to the conclusions that it suggests. Then there are our gleanings from New Inn to be looked over and considered; and with regard to this case, we have the fragments of a pair of spectacles which had better be put together into a rather more intelligible form in case we have to produce them in evidence. That will keep you occupied for a day or two, together with some work appertaining to other cases. And now let us dismiss professional topics. You have not dined and neither have I, but I dare say Polton has made arrangements for some sort of meal. We will go down and see."

We descended to the lower floor, where Thorndyke's anticipations were justified by a neatly laid table to which Polton was giving the finishing touches.

Chapter XI

The Blackmore Case Reviewed

One of the conditions of medical practice is the capability of transferring one's attention at a moment's notice from one set of circumstances to another equally important but entirely unrelated. At each visit on his round, the practitioner finds himself concerned with a particular, self-contained group of phenomena which he must consider at the moment with the utmost concentration, but which he must instantly dismiss from his mind as he moves on to the next case. It is a difficult habit to acquire; for an important, distressing or obscure case is apt to take possession of the consciousness and hinder the exercise of attention that succeeding cases demand; but experience shows the faculty to be indispensable, and the practitioner learns in time to forget everything but the patient with whose condition he is occupied at the moment.

My first morning's work on the Blackmore case showed me that the same faculty is demanded in legal practice; and it also showed me that I had yet to acquire it. For, as I looked over the depositions and the copy of the will, memories of the mysterious house in Kennington Lane continually intruded into my reflections, and the figure of Mrs. Schallibaum, white-faced, terrified, expectant, haunted me continually.

In truth, my interest in the Blackmore case was little more than academic, whereas in the Kennington case I was one of the parties and was personally concerned. To me, John Blackmore was but a name, Jeffrey but a shadowy figure to which I could assign no definite personality, and Stephen himself but a casual stranger. Mr. Graves, on the other hand, was a real person. I had seen him amidst the tragic circumstances that had probably heralded his death, and had brought away with me, not only a lively recollection of him, but a feeling of profound pity and concern as to his fate. The villain Weiss, too, and the terrible woman who aided, abetted and, perhaps, even directed him, lived in my memory as vivid and dreadful realities. Although I had uttered no hint to Thorndyke, I lamented inwardly that I had not been given some work — if there was any to do — connected with this case, in which I was so deeply interested, rather than with the dry, purely legal and utterly bewildering case of Jeffrey Blackmore's will.

Nevertheless, I stuck loyally to my task. I read through the depositions and the will — without getting a single glimmer of fresh light on the case — and I made a careful digest of all the facts. I compared my digest with Thorndyke's notes — of which I also made a copy — and found that, brief as they were, they contained several matters that I had overlooked. I also drew up a brief account of our visit to New Inn, with a list of the objects that we had observed or collected. And then I addressed myself to the second part of my task, the statement of my conclusions from the facts set forth.

It was only when I came to make the attempt that I realized how completely I was at sea. In spite of Thorndyke's recommendation to study Marchmont's statement as it was summarized in those notes which I had copied, and of his hint that I should find in that statement something highly significant, I was borne irresistibly to one conclusion, and one only — and the wrong one at that, as I suspected: that Jeffrey Blackmore's will was a perfectly regular, sound and valid document.

I tried to attack the validity of the will from various directions, and failed every time. As to its genuineness, that was obviously not in question. There seemed to me only two conceivable respects in which any objection could be raised, viz. the competency of Jeffrey to execute a will and the possibility of undue influence having been brought to bear on him.

With reference to the first, there was the undoubted fact that Jeffrey was addicted to the opium habit, and this might, under some circumstances, interfere with a testator's competency to make a will. But had any such circumstances existed in this case? Had the drug habit produced such mental changes in the deceased as would destroy or weaken his judgment? There was not a particle of evidence in favor of any such belief. Up to the very end he had managed his own affairs, and, if his habits of life had undergone a change, they were still the habits of a perfectly sane and responsible man.

The question of undue influence was more difficult. If it applied to any person in particular, that person could be none other than John Blackmore. Now it was an undoubted fact that, of all Jeffrey's acquaintance, his brother John was the only one who knew that he was in residence at New Inn. Moreover John had visited him there more than once. It was therefore possible that influence might have been brought to bear on the deceased. But there was no evidence that it had. The fact that the deceased man's only brother should be the one person who knew where he was living was not a remarkable one, and it had been satisfactorily explained by the necessity of Jeffrey's finding a reference on applying for the chambers. And against the theory of undue influence was the fact that the testator had voluntarily brought his will to the lodge and executed it in the presence of entirely disinterested witnesses.

In the end I had to give up the problem in despair, and, abandoning the documents, turned my attention to the facts elicited by our visit to New Inn.

What had we learned from our exploration? It was clear that Thorndyke had picked up some facts that had appeared to him important. But important in what respect? The only possible issue that could be raised was the validity or otherwise of Jeffrey Blackmore's will; and since the validity of that will was supported by positive evidence of the most incontestable kind, it seemed that nothing that we had observed could have any real bearing on the case at all.

But this, of course, could not be. Thorndyke was no dreamer nor was he addicted to wild speculation. If the facts observed by us seemed to him to be relevant to the case, I was prepared to assume that they were relevant, although I could not see their connection with it. And, on this assumption, I proceeded to examine them afresh.

Now, whatever Thorndyke might have observed on his own account, I had brought away from the dead man's chambers only a single fact; and a very extraordinary fact it was. The cuneiform inscription was upside down. That was the sum of the evidence that I had collected; and the question was, What did it prove? To Thorndyke it conveyed some deep significance. What could that significance be?

The inverted position was not a mere temporary accident, as it might have been if the frame had been stood on a shelf or support. It was hung on the wall, and the plates screwed on the frame showed that its position was permanent and that it had never hung in any other. That it could have been hung up by Jeffrey himself was clearly inconceivable. But allowing that it had been fixed in its present position by some workman when the new tenant moved in, the fact remained that there it had hung, presumably for months, and that Jeffrey Blackmore, with his expert knowledge of the cuneiform character, had never noticed that it was upside down; or, if he had noticed it, that he had never taken the trouble to have it altered.

What could this mean? If he had noticed the error but had not troubled to correct it, that would point to a very singular state of mind, an inertness and indifference remarkable even in an opium-smoker. But assuming such a state of mind, I could not see that it had any bearing on the will, excepting that it was rather inconsistent with the tendency to make fussy and needless alterations which the testator had actually shown. On the other hand, if he had not noticed the inverted position of the photograph he must have been nearly blind or quite idiotic; for the photograph was over two feet long and the characters large enough to be read easily by a person of ordinary eyesight at a distance of forty or fifty feet. Now he obviously was not in a state of dementia, whereas his eyesight was admittedly bad; and it seemed to me that the only conclusion deducible from the photograph was that it furnished a measure of the badness of the deceased man's vision – that it proved him to have been verging on total blindness.

But there was nothing startling new in this. He had, himself, declared that he was fast losing his sight. And again, what was the bearing of his partial blindness on the will? A totally blind man cannot draw up his will at all. But if he has eyesight sufficient to enable him to write out and sign a will, mere defective vision will not lead him to muddle the provisions. Yet something of this kind seemed to be in Thorndyke's mind, for now I recalled the question that he had put to the porter: "When you read the will over in Mr. Blackmore's presence, did you read it aloud?" That question could have but one significance. It implied a doubt as to whether the testator was fully aware of the exact nature of the document that he was signing. Yet, if he was able to write and sign it, surely he was able also to read it through, to say nothing of the fact that, unless he was demented, he must have remembered what he had written.

Thus, once more, my reasoning only led me into a blind alley at the end of which was the will, regular and valid and fulfilling all the requirements that the law imposed. Once again I had to confess myself beaten and in full agreement with Mr. Marchmont that "there was no case"; that "there was nothing in dispute." Nevertheless, I carefully fixed in the pocket file that Thorndyke had given me the copy that I had made of his notes, together with the notes on our visit to New Inn, and the few and unsatisfactory conclusions at which I had arrived; and this brought me to the end of my first morning in my new capacity.

"And how," Thorndyke asked as we sat at lunch, "has my learned friend progressed? Does he propose that we advise Mr. Marchmont to enter a caveat?"

"I've read all the documents and boiled all the evidence down to a stiff jelly; and I am in a worse fog than ever."

"There seems to be a slight mixture of metaphors in my learned friend's remarks. But never mind the fog, Jervis. There is a certain virtue in fog. It serves, like a picture frame, to surround the essential with a neutral zone that separates it from the irrelevant."

"That is a very profound observation, Thorndyke," I remarked ironically.

"I was just thinking so myself," he rejoined.

"And if you could contrive to explain what it means —"

"Oh, but that is unreasonable. When one throws off a subtly philosophic obiter dictum one looks to the discerning critic to supply the meaning. By the way, I am going to introduce you to the gentle art of photography this afternoon. I am getting the loan of all the checks that were drawn by Jeffrey Blackmore during his residence at New Inn — there are only twenty-three of them, all told — and I am going to photograph them."

"I shouldn't have thought the bank people would have let them go out of their possession."

"They are not going to. One of the partners, a Mr. Britton, is bringing them here himself and will be present while the photographs are being taken; so they will not go out of his custody. But, all the same, it is a great concession, and I should not have obtained it but for the fact that I have done a good deal of work for the bank and that Mr. Britton is more or less a personal friend."

"By the way, how comes it that the checks are at the bank? Why were they not returned to Jeffrey with the pass-book in the usual way?"

"I understand from Britton," replied Thorndyke, "that all Jeffrey's checks were retained by the bank at his request. When he was traveling he used to leave his investment securities and other valuable documents in his bankers' custody, and, as he has never applied to have them returned, the bankers still have them and are retaining them until the will is proved, when they will, of course, hand over everything to the executors."

"What is the object of photographing these checks?" I asked.

"There are several objects. First, since a good photograph is practically as good as the original, when we have the photographs we practically have the checks for reference. Then, since a photograph can be duplicated indefinitely, it is possible to perform experiments on it which involve its destruction; which would, of course, be impossible in the case of original checks."

"But the ultimate object, I mean. What are you going to prove?"

"You are incorrigible, Jervis," he exclaimed. "How should I know what I am going to prove? This is an investigation. If I knew the result beforehand, I shouldn't want to perform the experiment."

He looked at his watch, and, as we rose from the table, he said:

"If we have finished, we had better go up to the laboratory and see that the apparatus is ready. Mr. Britton is a busy man, and, as he is doing us a great service, we mustn't keep him waiting when he comes."

We ascended to the laboratory, where Polton was already busy inspecting the massively built copying camera which — with the long, steel guides on which the easel or copy-holder traveled — took up the whole length of the room on the side opposite to that occupied by the chemical bench. As I was to be inducted into the photographic art, I looked at it with more attention than I had ever done before.

"We've made some improvements since you were here last, sir," said Polton, who was delicately lubricating the steel guides. "We've fitted these steel runners instead of the blackleaded wooden ones that we used to have. And we've made two scales instead of one. Hallo! That's the downstairs bell. Shall I go sir?"

"Perhaps you'd better," said Thorndyke. "It may not be Mr. Britton, and I don't want to be caught and delayed just now."

However, it was Mr. Britton; a breezy alert-looking middle-aged man, who came in escorted by Polton and shook our hands cordially, having been previously warned of my presence. He carried a small but solid hand-bag, to which he clung tenaciously up to the very moment when its contents were required for use.

"So that is the camera," said he, running an inquisitive eye over the instrument. "Very fine one, too; I am a bit of a photographer myself. What is that graduation on the side-bar?"

"Those are the scales," replied Thorndyke, "that shows the degree of magnification or reduction. The pointer is fixed to the easel and travels with it, of course, showing the exact size of the photograph. When the pointer is opposite o the photograph will be identical in size with the object photographed; when it points to, say, × 6, the photograph will be six times as long as the object, or magnified thirty-six times superficially, whereas if the pointer is at ÷ 6, the photograph will be a sixth of the length of the object, or one thirty-sixth superficial."

"Why are there two scales?" Mr. Britton asked.

"There is a separate scale for each of the two lenses that we principally use. For great magnification or reduction a lens of comparatively short focus must be used, but, as a long-focus lens gives a more perfect image, we use one of very long focus — thirty-six inches — for copying the same size or for slight magnification or reduction."

"Are you going to magnify these checks?" Mr. Britton asked.

"Not in the first place," replied Thorndyke. "For convenience and speed I am going to photograph them half-size, so that six checks will go on one whole plate. Afterwards we can enlarge from the negatives as much as we like. But we should probably enlarge only the signatures in any case."

The precious bag was now opened and the twenty-three checks brought out and laid on the bench in a consecutive series in the order of their dates. They were then fixed by tapes — to avoid making pin-holes in them — in batches of six to small drawing boards, each batch being so arranged that the signatures were towards the middle. The first board was clamped to the easel, the latter was slid along its guides until the pointer stood at ÷ 2 on the long-focus scale and Thorndyke proceeded to focus the camera with the aid of a little microscope that Polton had made for the purpose. When Mr. Britton and I had inspected the exquisitely sharp image on the focusing-screen through the microscope, Polton introduced the plate and made the first exposure, carrying the dark-slide off to develop the plate while the next batch of checks was being fixed in position.

In his photographic technique, as in everything else, Polton followed as closely as he could the methods of his principal and instructor; methods characterized by that unhurried precision that leads to perfect accomplishment. When the first negative was brought forth, dripping, from the dark-room, it was without spot or stain, scratch or pin-hole; uniform in color and of exactly the required density. The six checks shown on it — ridiculously small in appearance, though only reduced to half-length — looked as clear and sharp as fine etchings; though, to be sure, my opportunity for examining them was rather limited, for Polton was uncommonly careful to keep the wet plate out of reach and so safe from injury.

"Well," said Mr. Britton, when, at the end of the séance, he returned his treasures to the bag, "you have now got twenty-three of our checks, to all intents and purposes. I hope you are not going to make any unlawful use of them — must tell our cashiers to keep a bright look-out; and" — here he lowered his voice impressively and addressed himself to me and Polton — "you understand that this is a private matter between Dr. Thorndyke and me. Of course, as Mr. Blackmore is dead, there is no reason why his checks should not be photographed for legal purposes; but we don't want it talked about; nor, I think, does Dr. Thorndyke."

"Certainly not," Thorndyke agreed emphatically; "but you need not be uneasy, Mr. Britton. We are very uncommunicative people in this establishment."

As my colleague and I escorted our visitor down the stairs, he returned to the subject of the checks.

"I don't understand what you want them for," he remarked. "There is no question turning on signatures in the case of Blackmore deceased, is there?"

"I should say not," Thorndyke replied rather evasively.

"I should say very decidedly not," said Mr. Britton, "if I understood Marchmont aright. And, even if there were, let me tell you, these signatures that you have got wouldn't help you. I have looked them over very closely — and I have seen a few signatures in my time, you know. Marchmont asked me to glance over them as a matter of form, but I don't believe in matters of form; I examined them very carefully. There is an appreciable amount of variation; a very appreciable amount. *But* under the variation one can trace the personal character (which is what matters); the subtle, indescribable quality that makes it recognizable to the expert eye as Jeffrey Blackmore's writing. You understand me. There is such a quality, which remains when the coarser characteristics vary; just as a man may grow old, or fat, or bald, or may take to drink, and become quite changed; and yet, through it all, he preserves a certain something which makes him recognizable as a member of a particular family. Well, I find that quality in all those signatures, and so will you, if you have had enough experience of handwriting. I thought it best to mention it in case you might be giving yourself unnecessary trouble."

"It is very good of you," said Thorndyke, "and I need not say that the information is of great value, coming from such a highly expert source. As a matter of fact, your hint will be of great value to me."

He shook hands with Mr. Britton, and, as the latter disappeared down the stairs, he turned into the sitting room and remarked:

"There is a very weighty and significant observation, Jervis. I advise you to consider it attentively in all its bearings."

"You mean the fact that these signatures are undoubtedly genuine?"

"I meant, rather, the very interesting general truth that is contained in Britton's statement; that physiognomy is not a mere matter of facial character. A man carries his personal trademark, not in his face only, but in his nervous system and muscles — giving rise to characteristic movements and gait; in his larynx — producing an individual voice; and even in his mouth, as shown by individual peculiarities of speech and accent. And the individual nervous system, by means of these characteristic movements, transfers its peculiarities to inanimate objects that are the products of such movements; as we see in pictures, in carving, in musical execution and in handwriting. No one has ever painted quite like Reynolds or Romney; no one has ever played exactly like Liszt or Paganini; the pictures or the sounds produced by them, were, so to speak, an extension of the physiognomy of the artist. And so with handwriting.

A particular specimen is the product of a particular set of motor centers in an individual brain."

"These are very interesting considerations, Thorndyke," I remarked; "but I don't quite see their present application. Do you mean them to bear in any special way on the Blackmore case?"

"I think they do bear on it very directly. I thought so while Mr. Britton was making his very illuminating remarks."

"I don't see how. In fact I cannot see why you are going into the question of the signatures at all. The signature on the will is admittedly genuine, and that seems to me to dispose of the whole affair."

"My dear Jervis," said he, "you and Marchmont are allowing yourselves to be obsessed by a particular fact — a very striking and weighty fact, I will admit, but still, only an isolated fact. Jeffrey Blackmore executed his will in a regular manner, complying with all the necessary formalities and conditions. In the face of that single circumstance you and Marchmont would 'chuck up the sponge,' as the old pugilists expressed it. Now that is a great mistake. You should never allow yourself to be bullied and browbeaten by a single fact."

"But, my dear Thorndyke!" I protested, "this fact seems to be final. It covers all possibilities — -unless you can suggest any other that would cancel it."

"I could suggest a dozen," he replied. "Let us take an instance. Supposing Jeffrey executed this will for a wager; that he immediately revoked it and made a fresh will, that he placed the latter in the custody of some person and that that person has suppressed it."

"Surely you do not make this suggestion seriously!" I exclaimed.

"Certainly I do not," he replied with a smile. "I merely give it as an instance to show that your final and absolute fact is really only conditional on there being no other fact that cancels it."

"Do you think he might have made a third will?"

"It is obviously possible. A man who makes two wills may make three or more; but I may say that I see no present reason for assuming the existence of another will. What I want to impress on you is the necessity of considering all the facts instead of bumping heavily against the most conspicuous one and forgetting all the rest. By the way, here is a little problem for you. What was the object of which these are the parts?"

He pushed across the table a little cardboard box, having first removed the lid. In it were a number of very small pieces of broken glass, some of which had been cemented together by their edges.

"These, I suppose," said I, looking with considerable curiosity at the little collection, "are the pieces of glass that we picked up in poor Blackmore's bedroom?"

"Yes. You see that Polton has been endeavoring to reconstitute the object, whatever it was; but he has not been very successful, for the fragments were too small and irregular and the collection too incomplete. However, here is a specimen, built up of six small pieces, which exhibits the general character of the object fairly well."

He picked out the little irregularly shaped object and handed it to me; and I could not but admire the neatness with which Polton had joined the tiny fragments together.

I took the little "restoration," and, holding it up before my eyes, moved it to and fro as I looked through it at the window.

"It was not a lens," I pronounced eventually.

"No," Thorndyke agreed, "it was not a lens."

"And so cannot have been a spectacle-glass. But the surface was curved — one side convex and the other concave — and the little piece that remains of the original edge seems to have been ground to fit a bezel or frame. I should say that these are portions of a watch-glass."

"That is Polton's opinion," said Thorndyke, "and I think you are both wrong."

"What do you say to the glass of a miniature or locket?"

"That is rather more probable, but it is not my view."

"What do you think it is?" I asked. But Thorndyke was not to be drawn.

"I am submitting the problem for solution by my learned friend," he replied with an exasperating smile, and then added: "I don't say that you and Polton are wrong; only that I don't agree with you. Perhaps you had better make a note of the properties of this object, and consider it at your leisure when you are ruminating on the other data referring to the Blackmore case."

"My ruminations," I said, "always lead me back to the same point."

"But you mustn't let them," he replied. "Shuffle your data about. Invent hypotheses. Never mind if they seem rather wild. Don't put them aside on that account. Take the first hypothesis that you can invent and test it thoroughly with your facts. You will probably have to reject it, but you will be certain to have learned something new. Then try again with a fresh one. You remember what I told you of my methods when I began this branch of practice and had plenty of time on my hands?"

"I am not sure that I do."

"Well, I used to occupy my leisure in constructing imaginary cases, mostly criminal, for the purpose of study and for the acquirement of experience. For instance, I would devise an ingenious fraud and would plan it in detail, taking every precaution that I could think of against failure or detection, considering, and elaborately providing for, every imaginable contingency. For the time being, my entire attention was concentrated on it, making it as perfect and secure and undetectable as I could with the knowledge and ingenuity at my command. I behaved exactly as if I were proposing actually to carry it out, and my life or liberty depended on its success — excepting that I made full notes of every detail of the scheme. Then when my plans were as complete as I could make them, and I could think of no way in which to improve them, I changed sides and considered the case from the standpoint of detection. I analyzed the case, I picked out its inherent and unavoidable weaknesses, and, especially, I noted the respects in which a fraudulent proceeding of a particular kind differed from the *bona fide* proceeding that it simulated. The exercise was invaluable to me. I acquired as much experience from those imaginary cases as I should from real ones, and in addition, I learned a method which is the one that I practice to this day."

"Do you mean that you still invent imaginary cases as mental exercises?"

"No; I mean that, when I have a problem of any intricacy, I invent a case which fits the facts and the assumed motives of one of the parties. Then I work at that case until I find whether it leads to elucidation or to some fundamental disagreement. In the latter case I reject it and begin the process over again."

"Doesn't that method sometimes involve a good deal of wasted time and energy?" I asked.

"No; because each time that you fail to establish a given case, you exclude a particular explanation of the facts and narrow down the field of inquiry. By repeating the process, you are bound, in the end, to arrive at an imaginary case which fits all the facts. Then your imaginary case is the real case and the problem is solved. Let me recommend you to give the method a trial."

I promised to do so, though with no very lively expectations as to the result, and with this, the subject was allowed, for the present, to drop.

Chapter XII

The Portrait

The state of mind which Thorndyke had advised me to cultivate was one that did not come easily. However much I endeavored to shuffle the facts of the Blackmore case, there was one which inevitably turned up on the top of the pack. The circumstances surrounding the execution of Jeffrey Blackmore's will intruded into all my cogitations on the subject with hopeless persistency. That scene in the porter's lodge was to me what King Charles's head was to poor Mr. Dick. In the midst of my praiseworthy efforts to construct some intelligible scheme of the case, it would make its appearance and reduce my mind to instant chaos.

For the next few days, Thorndyke was very much occupied with one or two civil cases, which kept him in court during the whole of the sitting; and when he came home, he seemed indisposed to talk on professional topics. Meanwhile, Polton worked steadily at the photographs of the signatures, and, with a view to gaining experience, I assisted him and watched his methods.

In the present case, the signatures were enlarged from their original dimensions — rather less than an inch and a half in length — to a length of four and a half inches; which rendered all the little peculiarities of the handwriting surprisingly distinct and conspicuous. Each signature was eventually mounted on a slip of card bearing a number and the date of the check from which it was taken, so that it was possible to place any two signatures together for comparison. I looked over the whole series and very carefully compared those which showed any differences, but without discovering anything more than might have been expected in view of Mr. Britton's statement. There were some trifling variations, but they were all very much alike, and no one could doubt, on looking at them, that they were all written by the same hand.

As this, however, was apparently not in dispute, it furnished no new information. Thorndyke's object — for I felt certain that he had something definite in his mind — must be to test something apart from the genuineness of the signatures. But what could that something be? I dared not ask him, for questions of that kind were anathema, so there was nothing for it but to lie low and see what he would do with the photographs.

The whole series was finished on the fourth morning after my adventure at Sloane Square, and the pack of cards was duly delivered by Polton when he brought in the breakfast tray. Thorndyke took up the pack somewhat with the air of a whist player, and, as he ran through them, I noticed that the number had increased from twenty-three to twenty-four.

"The additional one," Thorndyke explained, "is the signature to the first will, which was in Marchmont's possession. I have added it to the collection as it carries us back to an earlier date. The signature of the second will presumably resembles those of the checks drawn about the same date. But that is not material, or, if it should become so, we could claim to examine the second will."

He laid the cards out on the table in the order of their dates and slowly ran his eye down the series. I watched him closely and ventured presently to ask:

"Do you agree with Mr. Britton as to the general identity of character in the whole set of signatures?"

"Yes," he replied. "I should certainly have put them down as being all the signatures of one person. The variations are very slight. The later signatures are a little stiffer, a little more shaky and indistinct, and the B's and k's are both appreciably different from those in the earlier ones. But there is another fact which emerges when the whole series is seen together, and it is so striking and significant a fact, that I am astonished at its not having been remarked on by Mr. Britton."

"Indeed!" said I, stooping to examine the photographs with fresh interest; "what is that?"

"It is a very simple fact and very obvious, but yet, as I have said, very significant. Look carefully at number one, which is the signature of the first will, dated three years ago, and compare it with number three, dated the eighteenth of September last year."

"They look to me identical," said I, after a careful comparison.

"So they do to me," said Thorndyke. "Neither of them shows the change that occurred later. But if you look at number two, dated the sixteenth of September, you will see that it is in the later style. So is number four, dated the twenty-third of September; but numbers five and six, both at the beginning of October, are in the earlier style, like the signature of the will. Thereafter all the signatures are in the new style; but, if you compare number two, dated the sixteenth of September with number twenty-four, dated the fourteenth of March of this year — the day of Jeffrey's death — you see that they exhibit no difference. Both are in the 'later style,' but the last shows no greater change than the first. Don't you consider these facts very striking and significant?"

I reflected a few moments, trying to make out the deep significance to which Thorndyke was directing my attention — and not succeeding very triumphantly.

"You mean," I said, "that the occasional reversions to the earlier form convey some material suggestion?"

"Yes; but more than that. What we learn from an inspection of this series is this: that there was a change in the character of the signature; a very slight change, but quite recognizable. Now that change was not gradual or insidious nor was it progressive. It occurred at a certain definite time. At first there were one or two reversions to the earlier form, but after number six the new style continued to the end; and you notice that it continued without any increase in the change and without any variation. There are no intermediate forms. Some of the signatures are in the 'old style' and some in the 'new,' but there are none that are half and half. So that, to repeat: We have here two types of signature, very much alike, but distinguishable. They alternate, but do not merge into one another to produce intermediate forms. The change occurs abruptly, but shows no tendency to increase as time goes on; it is not a progressive change. What do you make of that, Jervis?"

"It is very remarkable," I said, poring over the cards to verify Thorndyke's statements. "I don't quite know what to make of it. If the circumstances admitted of the idea of forgery, one would suspect the genuineness of some of the signatures. But they don't — at any rate, in the case of the later will, to say nothing of Mr. Britton's opinion on the signatures."

"Still," said Thorndyke, "there must be some explanation of the change in the character of the signatures, and that explanation cannot be the failing eyesight of the writer; for that is a gradually progressive and continuous condition, whereas the change in the writing is abrupt and intermittent."

I considered Thorndyke's remark for a few moments; and then a light — though not a very brilliant one — seemed to break on me.

"I think I see what you are driving at," said I. "You mean that the change in the writing must be associated with some new condition affecting the writer, and that that condition existed intermittently?"

Thorndyke nodded approvingly, and I continued:

"The only intermittent condition that we know of is the effect of opium. So that we might consider the clearer signatures to have been made when Jeffrey was in his normal state, and the less distinct ones after a bout of opium-smoking."

"That is perfectly sound reasoning," said Thorndyke. "What further conclusion does it lead to?"

"It suggests that the opium habit had been only recently acquired, since the change was noticed only about the time he went to live at New Inn; and, since the change in the writing is at first intermittent and then continuous, we may infer that the opium-smoking was at first occasional and later became a confirmed habit."

"Quite a reasonable conclusion and very clearly stated," said Thorndyke. "I don't say that I entirely agree with you, or that you have exhausted the information that these signatures offer. But you have started in the right direction."

"I may be on the right road," I said gloomily; "but I am stuck fast in one place and I see no chance of getting any farther."

"But you have a quantity of data," said Thorndyke. "You have all the facts that I had to start with, from which I constructed the hypothesis that I am now busily engaged in verifying. I have a few more data now, for 'as money makes money' so knowledge begets knowledge, and I put my original capital out to interest. Shall we tabulate the facts that are in our joint possession and see what they suggest?"

I grasped eagerly at the offer, though I had conned over my notes again and again.

Thorndyke produced a slip of paper from a drawer, and, uncapping his fountain-pen, proceeded to write down the leading facts, reading each aloud as soon as it was written.

"1. The second will was unnecessary since it contained no new matter, expressed no new intentions and met no new conditions, and the first will was quite clear and efficient.

"2. The evident intention of the testator was to leave the bulk of his property to Stephen Blackmore.

"3. The second will did not, under existing circumstances, give effect to this intention, whereas the first will did.

"4. The signature of the second will differs slightly from that of the first, and also from what had hitherto been the testator's ordinary signature.

"And now we come to a very curious group of dates, which I will advise you to consider with great attention.

"5. Mrs. Wilson made her will at the beginning of September last year, without acquainting Jeffrey Blackmore, who seems to have been unaware of the existence of this will.

"6. His own second will was dated the twelfth of November of last year.

"7. Mrs. Wilson died of cancer on the twelfth of March this present year.

"8. Jeffrey Blackmore was last seen alive on the fourteenth of March.

"9. His body was discovered on the fifteenth of March.

"10. The change in the character of his signature began about September last year and became permanent after the middle of October.

"You will find that collection of facts repay careful study, Jervis, especially when considered in relation to the further data:

"11. That we found in Blackmore's chambers a framed inscription of large size, hung upside down, together with what appeared to be the remains of a watch-glass and a box of stearine candles and some other objects."

He passed the paper to me and I pored over it intently, focusing my attention on the various items with all the power of my will. But, struggle as I would, no general conclusion could be made to emerge from the mass of apparently disconnected facts.

"Well?" Thorndyke said presently, after watching with grave interest my unavailing efforts; "what do you make of it?"

"Nothing!" I exclaimed desperately, slapping the paper down on the table. "Of course, I can see that there are some queer coincidences. But how do they bear on the case? I understand that you want to upset this will; which we know to have been signed without compulsion or even suggestion in the presence of two respectable men, who have sworn to the identity of the document. That is your object, I believe?"

"Certainly it is."

"Then I am hanged if I see how you are going to do it. Not, I should say, by offering a group of vague coincidences that would muddle any brain but your own."

Thorndyke chuckled softly but pursued the subject no farther.

"Put that paper in your file with your other notes," he said, "and think it over at your leisure. And now I want a little help from you. Have you a good memory for faces?"

"Fairly good, I think. Why?"

"Because I have a photograph of a man whom I think you may have met. Just look at it and tell me if you remember the face."

He drew a cabinet size photograph from an envelope that had come by the morning's post and handed it to me.

"I have certainly seen this face somewhere," said I, taking the portrait over to the window to examine it more thoroughly, "but I can't, at the moment, remember where."

"Try," said Thorndyke. "If you have seen the face before, you should be able to recall the person."

I looked intently at the photograph, and the more I looked, the more familiar did the face appear. Suddenly the identity of the man flashed into my mind and I exclaimed in astonishment:

"It can't be that poor creature at Kennington, Mr. Graves?"

"I think it can," replied Thorndyke, "and I think it is. But could you swear to the identity in a court of law?"

"It is my firm conviction that the photograph is that of Mr. Graves. I would swear to that."

"No man ought to swear to more," said Thorndyke. "Identification is always a matter of opinion or belief. The man who will swear unconditionally to identity from memory only is a man whose evidence should be discredited. I think your sworn testimony would be sufficient."

It is needless to say that the production of this photograph filled me with amazement and curiosity as to how Thorndyke had obtained it. But, as he replaced it impassively in its envelope without volunteering any explanation, I felt that I could not question him directly. Nevertheless, I ventured to approach the subject in an indirect manner.

"Did you get any information from those Darmstadt people?" I asked.

"Schnitzler? Yes. I learned, through the medium of an official acquaintance, that Dr. H. Weiss was a stranger to them; that they knew nothing about him excepting that he had ordered from them, and been supplied with, a hundred grams of pure hydrochlorate of morphine."

"All at once?"

"No. In separate parcels of twenty-five grams each."

"Is that all you know about Weiss?"

"It is all that I actually know; but it is not all that I suspect — on very substantial grounds. By the way, what did you think of the coachman?"

"I don't know that I thought very much about him. Why?"

"You never suspected that he and Weiss were one and the same person?"

"No. How could they be? They weren't in the least alike. And one was a Scotchman and the other a German. But perhaps you know that they were the same?"

"I only know what you have told me. But considering that you never saw them together, that the coachman was never available for messages or assistance when Weiss was with you; that Weiss always made his appearance some time after you arrived, and disappeared some time before you left; it has seemed to me that they might have been the same person."

"I should say it was impossible. They were so very different in appearance. But supposing that they were the same; would the fact be of any importance?"

"It would mean that we could save ourselves the trouble of looking for the coachman. And it would suggest some inferences, which will occur to you if you think the matter over. But being only a speculative opinion, at present, it would not be safe to infer very much from it."

"You have rather taken me by surprise," I remarked. "It seems that you have been working at this Kennington case, and working pretty actively I imagine, whereas I supposed that your entire attention was taken up by the Blackmore affair."

"It doesn't do," he replied, "to allow one's entire attention to be taken up by anyone case. I have half a dozen others — minor cases, mostly — to which I am attending at this moment. Did you think I was proposing to keep you under lock and key indefinitely?"

"Well, no. But I thought the Kennington case would have to wait its turn. And I had no idea that you were in possession of enough facts to enable you to get any farther with it."

"But you knew all the very striking facts of the case, and you saw the further evidence that we extracted from the empty house."

"Do you mean those things that we picked out from the rubbish under the grate?"

"Yes. You saw those curious little pieces of reed and the pair of spectacles. They are lying in the top drawer of that cabinet at this moment, and I should recommend you to have another look at them. To me they are most instructive. The pieces of reed offered an extremely valuable suggestion, and the spectacles enabled me to test that suggestion and turn it into actual information."

"Unfortunately," said I, "the pieces of reed convey nothing to me. I don't know what they are or of what they have formed a part."

"I think," he replied, "that if you examine them with due consideration, you will find their use pretty obvious. Have a good look at them and the spectacles too. Think over all that you know of that mysterious group of people who lived in that house, and see if you cannot form some coherent theory of their actions. Think, also, if we have not some information in our possession by which we might be able to identify some of them, and infer the identity of the others. You will have a quiet day, as I shall not be home until the evening; set yourself this task. I assure you that you have the material for identifying — or rather for testing the identity of — at least one of those persons. Go over your material systematically, and let me know in the evening what further investigations you would propose."

"Very well," said I. "It shall be done according to your word. I will addle my brain afresh with the affair of Mr. Weiss and his patient, and let the Blackmore case rip."

"There is no need to do that. You have a whole day before you. An hour's really close consideration of the Kennington case ought to show you what your next move should be, and then you could devote yourself to the consideration of Jeffrey Blackmore's will."

With this final piece of advice, Thorndyke collected the papers for his day's work, and, having deposited them in his brief bag, took his departure, leaving me to my meditations.

Chapter XIII

The Statement of Samuel Wilkins

As soon as I was alone, I commenced my investigations with a rather desperate hope of eliciting some startling and unsuspected facts. I opened the drawer and taking from it the two pieces of reed and the shattered remains of the spectacles, laid them on the table. The repairs that Thorndyke had contemplated in the case of the spectacles, had not been made. Apparently they had not been necessary. The battered wreck that lay before me, just as we had found it, had evidently furnished the necessary information; for, since Thorndyke was in possession of a portrait of Mr. Graves, it was clear that he had succeeded in identifying him so far as to get into communication with someone who had known him intimately.

The circumstance should have been encouraging. But somehow it was not. What was possible to Thorndyke was, theoretically, possible to me — or to anyone else. But the possibility did not realize itself in practice. There was the personal equation. Thorndyke's brain was not an ordinary brain. Facts of which his mind instantly perceived the relation remained to other people unconnected and without meaning. His powers of observation and rapid inference were almost incredible, as I had noticed again and again, and always with undiminished wonder. He seemed to take in everything at a single glance and in an instant to appreciate the meaning of everything that he had seen.

Here was a case in point. I had myself seen all that he had seen, and, indeed, much more; for I had looked on the very people and witnessed their actions, whereas he had never set eyes on any of them. I had examined the little handful of rubbish that he had gathered up so carefully, and would have flung it back under the grate without a qualm. Not a glimmer of light had I perceived in the cloud of mystery, nor even a hint of the direction in which to seek enlightenment. And yet Thorndyke had, in some incomprehensible manner, contrived to piece together facts that I had probably not even observed, and that so completely that he had already, in these few days, narrowed down the field of inquiry to quite a small area.

From these reflections I returned to the objects on the table. The spectacles, as things of which I had some expert knowledge, were not so profound a mystery to me. A pair of spectacles might easily afford good evidence for identification; that I perceived clearly enough. Not a ready-made pair, picked up casually at a shop, but a pair constructed by a skilled optician to remedy a particular defect of vision and to fit a particular face. And such were the spectacles before me. The build of the frames was peculiar; the existence of a cylindrical lens — which I could easily make out from the remaining fragments — showed that one glass had been cut to a prescribed shape and almost certainly ground to a particular formula, and also that the distance between centers must have been carefully secured. Hence these spectacles had an individual character. But it was manifestly impossible to inquire of all the spectacle-makers in Europe — for the glasses were not necessarily made in England. As confirmation the spectacles might be valuable; as a starting-point they were of no use at all.

From the spectacles I turned to the pieces of reed. These were what had given Thorndyke his start. Would they give me a leading hint too? I looked at them and wondered what it was that they had told Thorndyke. The little fragment of the red paper label had a dark-brown or thin black border ornamented with a fret-pattern, and on it I detected a couple of tiny points of gold like the dust from leaf-gilding. But I learned nothing from that. Then the shorter piece of reed was artificially hollowed to fit on the longer piece. Apparently it formed a protective sheath or cap. But what did it protect? Presumably a point or edge of some kind. Could this be a pocket-knife of any sort, such as a small stencil-knife? No; the material was too fragile for a knife-handle. It could not be an etching-needle for the same reason; and it was not a surgical appliance — at least it was not like any surgical instrument that was known to me.

I turned it over and over and cudgeled my brains; and then I had a brilliant idea. Was it a reed pen of which the point had been broken off? I knew that reed pens were still in use by draftsmen of decorative leanings with an affection for the "fat line." Could any of our friends be draftsmen? This seemed the most probable solution of the difficulty, and the more I thought about it the more likely it seemed. Draftsmen usually sign their work intelligibly, and even when they use a device instead of a signature their identity is easily traceable. Could it be that Mr. Graves, for instance, was an illustrator, and that Thorndyke had established his identity by looking through the works of all the well-known thick-line draftsmen?

This problem occupied me for the rest of the day. My explanation did not seem quite to fit Thorndyke's description of his methods; but I could think of no other. I turned it over during my solitary lunch; I meditated on it with the aid of several pipes in the afternoon; and having refreshed my brain with a cup of tea, I went forth to walk in the Temple gardens — which I was permitted to do without breaking my parole — to think it out afresh.

The result was disappointing. I was basing my reasoning on the assumption that the pieces of reed were parts of a particular appliance, appertaining to a particular craft; whereas they might be the remains of something quite different, appertaining to a totally different craft or to no craft at all. And in no case did they point to any known individual or indicate any but the vaguest kind of search. After pacing the pleasant walks for upwards of two hours, I at length turned back towards our chambers, where I arrived as the lamp-lighter was just finishing his round.

My fruitless speculations had left me somewhat irritable. The lighted windows that I had noticed as I approached had given me the impression that Thorndyke had returned. I had intended to press him for a little further information. When, therefore, I let myself into our chambers and found, instead of my colleague, a total stranger — and only a back view at that — I was disappointed and annoyed.

The stranger was seated by the table, reading a large document that looked like a lease. He made no movement when I entered, but when I crossed the room and wished him "Good evening," he half rose and bowed silently. It was then that I first saw his face, and a mighty start he gave me. For one moment I actually thought he was Mr. Weiss, so close was the resemblance, but immediately I perceived that he was a much smaller man.

I sat down nearly opposite and stole an occasional furtive glance at him. The resemblance to Weiss was really remarkable. The same flaxen hair, the same ragged beard and a similar red nose, with the patches of *acne rosacea* spreading to the adjacent cheeks. He wore spectacles, too, through which he took a quick glance at me now and again, returning immediately to his document.

After some moments of rather embarrassing silence, I ventured to remark that it was a mild evening; to which he assented with a sort of Scotch "Hm – hm" and nodded slowly. Then came another interval of silence, during which I speculated on the possibility of his being a relative of Mr. Weiss and wondered what the deuce he was doing in our chambers.

"Have you an appointment with Dr. Thorndyke?" I asked, at length.

He bowed solemnly, and by way of reply – in the affirmative, as I assumed – emitted another "hm – hm."

I looked at him sharply, a little nettled by his lack of manners; whereupon he opened out the lease so that it screened his face, and as I glanced at the back of the document, I was astonished to observe that it was shaking rapidly.

The fellow was actually laughing! What he found in my simple question to cause him so much amusement I was totally unable to imagine. But there it was. The tremulous movements of the document left me in no possible doubt that he was for some reason convulsed with laughter.

It was extremely mysterious. Also, it was rather embarrassing. I took out my pocket file and began to look over my notes. Then the document was lowered and I was able to get another look at the stranger's face. He was really extraordinarily like Weiss. The shaggy eyebrows, throwing the eye-sockets into shadow, gave him, in conjunction with the spectacles, the same owlish, solemn expression that I had noticed in my Kennington acquaintance; and which, by the way, was singularly out of character with the frivolous behavior that I had just witnessed.

From time to time as I looked at him, he caught my eye and instantly averted his own, turning rather red. Apparently he was a shy, nervous man, which might account for his giggling; for I have noticed that shy or nervous people have a habit of smiling inopportunely and even giggling when embarrassed by meeting an oversteady eye. And it seemed my own eye had this disconcerting quality, for even as I looked at him, the document suddenly went up again and began to shake violently.

I stood it for a minute or two, but, finding the situation intolerably embarrassing, I rose, and brusquely excusing myself, went up to the laboratory to look for Polton and inquire at what time Thorndyke was expected home. To my surprise, however, on entering, I discovered

Thorndyke himself just finishing the mounting of a microscopical specimen.

"Did you know that there is someone below waiting to see you?" I asked.

"Is it anyone you know?" he inquired.

"No," I answered. "It is a red-nosed, sniggering fool in spectacles. He has got a lease or a deed or some other sort of document which he has been using to play a sort of idiotic game of Peep-Bo! I couldn't stand him, so I came up here."

Thorndyke laughed heartily at my description of his client.

"What are you laughing at?" I asked sourly; at which he laughed yet more heartily and added to the aggravation by wiping his eyes.

"Our friend seems to have put you out," he remarked.

"He put me out literally. If I had stayed much longer I should have punched his head."

"In that case," said Thorndyke, "I am glad you didn't stay. But come down and let me introduce you."

"No, thank you. I've had enough of him for the present."

"But I have a very special reason for wishing to introduce you. I think you will get some information from him that will interest you very much; and you needn't quarrel with a man for being of a cheerful disposition."

"Cheerful be hanged!" I exclaimed. "I don't call a man cheerful because he behaves like a gibbering idiot."

To this Thorndyke made no reply but a broad and appreciative smile, and we descended to the lower floor. As we entered the room, the stranger rose, and, glancing in an embarrassed way from one of us to the other, suddenly broke out into an undeniable snigger. I looked at him sternly, and Thorndyke, quite unmoved by his indecorous behavior, said in a grave voice:

"Let me introduce you, Jervis; though I think you have met this gentleman before."

"I think not," I said stiffly.

"Oh yes, you have, sir," interposed the stranger; and, as he spoke, I started; for the voice was uncommonly like the familiar voice of Polton.

I looked at the speaker with sudden suspicion. And now I could see that the flaxen hair was a wig; that the beard had a decidedly artificial look, and that the eyes that beamed through the spectacles were remarkably like the eyes of our factotum. But the blotchy face, the bulbous nose and the shaggy, overhanging eyebrows were alien features that I could not reconcile with the personality of our refined and aristocratic-looking little assistant.

"Is this a practical joke?" I asked.

"No," replied Thorndyke; "it is a demonstration. When we were talking this morning it appeared to me that you did not realize the extent to which it is possible to conceal identity under suitable conditions of light. So I arranged, with Polton's rather reluctant assistance, to give you ocular evidence. The conditions are not favorable — which makes the demonstration more convincing. This is a very well-lighted room and Polton is a very poor actor; in spite of which it has been possible for you to sit opposite him for several minutes and look at him, I have no doubt, very attentively, without discovering his identity. If the room had been lighted only with a candle, and Polton had been equal to the task of supporting his make-up with an appropriate voice and manner, the deception would have been perfect."

"I can see that he has a wig on, quite plainly," said I.

"Yes; but you would not in a dimly lighted room. On the other hand, if Polton were to walk down Fleet Street at mid-day in this condition, the make-up would be conspicuously evident to any moderately observant passer-by. The secret of making up consists in a careful adjustment to the conditions of light and distance in which the make-up is to be seen. That in use on the stage would look ridiculous in an ordinary room; that which would serve in an artificially lighted room would look ridiculous out of doors by daylight."

"Is any effective make-up possible out of doors in ordinary daylight?" I asked.

"Oh, yes," replied Thorndyke. "But it must be on a totally different scale from that of the stage. A wig, and especially a beard or moustache, must be joined up at the edges with hair actually stuck on the skin with transparent cement and carefully trimmed with scissors. The same applies to eyebrows; and alterations in the color of the skin must be carried out much more subtly. Polton's nose has been built up with a small covering of toupée-paste, the pimples on the cheeks produced with little particles of the same material; and the general tinting has been done with grease-paint with a very light scumble of powder color to take off some of the shine. This would be possible in outdoor make-up, but it would have to be done with the greatest care and delicacy; in fact, with what the art-critics call 'reticence.' A very little make-up is sufficient and too much is fatal. You would be surprised to see how little paste is required to alter the shape of the nose and the entire character of the face."

At this moment there came a loud knock at the door; a single, solid dab of the knocker which Polton seemed to recognize, for he ejaculated:

"Good lord, sir! That'll be Wilkins, the cabman! I'd forgotten all about him. Whatever's to be done?"

He stared at us in ludicrous horror for a moment or two, and then, snatching off his wig, beard and spectacles, poked them into a cupboard. But his appearance was now too much even for Thorndyke — who hastily got behind him — for he had now resumed his ordinary personality — but with a very material difference.

"Oh, it's nothing to laugh at, sir," he exclaimed indignantly as I crammed my handkerchief into my mouth. "Somebody's got to let him in, or he'll go away."

"Yes; and that won't do," said Thorndyke. "But don't worry, Polton. You can step into the office. I'll open the door."

Polton's presence of mind, however, seemed to have entirely forsaken him, for he only hovered irresolutely in the wake of his principal. As the door opened, a thick and husky voice inquired:

"Gent of the name of Polton live here?"

"Yes, quite right," said Thorndyke. "Come in. Your name is Wilkins, I think?"

"That's me, sir," said the voice; and in response to Thorndyke's invitation, a typical "growler" cabman of the old school, complete even to imbricated cape and dangling badge, stalked into the room, and glancing round with a mixture of embarrassment and defiance, suddenly fixed on Polton's nose a look of devouring curiosity.

"Here you are, then," Polton remarked nervously.

"Yus," replied the cabman in a slightly hostile tone. "Here I am. What am I wanted to do? And where's this here Mr. Polton?"

"I am Mr. Polton," replied our abashed assistant.

"Well, it's the other Mr. Polton what I want," said the cabman, with his eyes still riveted on the olfactory prominence.

"There isn't any other Mr. Polton," our subordinate replied irritably. "I am the — er — person who spoke to you in the shelter."

"Are you though?" said the manifestly incredulous cabby. "I shouldn't have thought it; but you ought to know. What do you want me to do?"

"We want you," said Thorndyke, "to answer one or two questions. And the first one is, Are you a teetotaler?"

The question being illustrated by the production of a decanter, the cabman's dignity relaxed somewhat.

"I ain't bigoted," said he.

"Then sit down and mix yourself a glass of grog. Soda or plain water?"

"May as well have all the extries," replied the cabman, sitting down and grasping the decanter with the air of a man who means business. "Per'aps you wouldn't mind squirtin' out the soda, sir, bein' more used to it."

While these preliminaries were being arranged, Polton silently slipped out of the room, and when our visitor had fortified himself with a gulp of the uncommonly stiff mixture, the examination began.

"Your name, I think, is Wilkins?" said Thorndyke.

"That's me, sir. Samuel Wilkins is my name."

"And your occupation?"

"Is a very tryin' one and not paid for as it deserves. I drives a cab, sir; a four-wheeled cab is what I drives; and a very poor job it is."

"Do you happen to remember a very foggy day about a month ago?"

"Do I not, sir! A regler sneezer that was! Wednesday, the fourteenth of March. I remember the date because my benefit society came down on me for arrears that morning."

"Will you tell us what happened to you between six and seven in the evening of that day?"

"I will, sir," replied the cabman, emptying his tumbler by way of bracing himself up for the effort. "A little before six I was waiting on the arrival side of the Great Northern Station, King's Cross, when I see a gentleman and a lady coming out. The gentleman he looks up and down and then he sees me and walks up to the cab and opens the door and helps the lady in. Then he says to me: 'Do you know New Inn?' he says. That's what he says to me what was born and brought up in White Horse Alley, Drury Lane.

"'Get inside,' says I.

"'Well,' says he, 'you drive in through the gate in Wych Street,' he says, as if he expected me to go in by Houghton Street and down the steps, 'and then,' he says, 'you drive nearly to the end and you'll see a house with a large brass plate at the corner of the doorway. That's where we want to be set down,' he says, and with that he nips in and pulls up the windows and off we goes.

"It took us a full half-hour to get to New Inn through the fog, for I had to get down and lead the horse part of the way. As I drove in under the archway, I saw it was half-past six by the clock in the porter's lodge. I drove down nearly to the end of the inn and drew up opposite a house where there was a big brass plate by the doorway. It was number thirty-one. Then the gent crawls out and hands me five bob — two 'arf-crowns — and then he helps the lady out, and away they waddles to the doorway and I see them start up the stairs very slow — regler Pilgrim's Progress. And that was the last I see of 'em."

Thorndyke wrote down the cabman's statement verbatim together with his own questions, and then asked:

"Can you give us any description of the gentleman?"

"The gent," said Wilkins, "was a very respectable-looking gent, though he did look as if he'd had a drop of something short, and small blame to him on a day like that. But he was all there, and he knew what was the proper fare for a foggy evening, which is more than some of 'em do. He was a elderly gent, about sixty, and he wore spectacles, but he didn't seem to be able to see much through 'em. He was a funny 'un to look at; as round in the back as a turtle and he walked with his head stuck forward like a goose."

"What made you think he had been drinking?"

"Well, he wasn't as steady as he might have been on his pins. But he wasn't drunk, you know. Only a bit wobbly on the plates."

"And the lady; what was she like?"

"I couldn't see much of her because her head was wrapped up in a sort of woolen veil. But I should say she wasn't a chicken. Might have been about the same age as the gent, but I couldn't swear to that. She seemed a trifle rickety on the pins too; in fact they were a rum-looking couple. I watched 'em tottering across the pavement and up the stairs, hanging on to each other, him peering through his blinkers and she trying to see through her veil, and I thought it was a jolly good job they'd got a nice sound cab and a steady driver to bring 'em safe home."

"How was the lady dressed?"

"Can't rightly say, not being a hexpert. Her head was done up in this here veil like a pudden in a cloth and she had a small hat on. She had a dark brown mantle with a fringe of beads round it and a black dress; and I noticed when she got into the cab at the station that one of her stockings looked like the bellows of a concertina. That's all I can tell you."

Thorndyke wrote down the last answer, and, having read the entire statement aloud, handed the pen to our visitor.

"If that is all correct," he said, "I will ask you to sign your name at the bottom."

"Do you want me to swear a affidavy that it's all true?" asked Wilkins.

"No, thank you," replied Thorndyke. "We may have to call you to give evidence in court, and then you'll be sworn; and you'll also be paid for your attendance. For the present I want you to keep your own counsel and say nothing to anybody about having been here. We have to make some other inquiries and we don't want the affair talked about."

"I see, sir," said Wilkins, as he laboriously traced his signature at the foot of the statement; "you don't want the other parties for to ogle your lay. All right, sir; you can depend on me. I'm fly, I am."

"Thank you, Wilkins," said Thorndyke. "And now what are we to give you for your trouble in coming here?"

"I'll leave the fare to you, sir. You know what the information's worth; but I should think 'arf a thick-un wouldn't hurt you."

Thorndyke laid on the table a couple of sovereigns, at the sight of which the cabman's eyes glistened.

"We have your address, Wilkins," said he. "If we want you as a witness we shall let you know, and if not, there will be another two pounds for you at the end of a fortnight, provided you have not let this little interview leak out."

Wilkins gathered up the spoils gleefully. "You can trust me, sir," said he, "for to keep my mouth shut. I knows which side my bread's buttered. Good night, gentlemen all."

With this comprehensive salute he moved towards the door and let himself out.

"Well, Jervis; what do you think of it?" Thorndyke asked, as the cabman's footsteps faded away in a creaky diminuendo.

"I don't know what to think. This woman is a new factor in the case and I don't know how to place her."

"Not entirely new," said Thorndyke. "You have not forgotten those beads that we found in Jeffrey's bedroom, have you?"

"No, I had not forgotten them, but I did not see that they told us much excepting that some woman had apparently been in his bedroom at some time."

"That, I think, is all that they did tell us. But now they tell us that a particular woman was in his bedroom at a particular time, which is a good deal more significant."

"Yes. It almost looks as if she must have been there when he made away with himself."

"It does, very much."

"By the way, you were right about the colors of those beads, and also about the way they were used."

"As to their use, that was a mere guess; but it has turned out to be correct. It was well that we found the beads, for, small as is the amount of information they give, it is still enough to carry us a stage further."

"How so?"

"I mean that the cabman's evidence tells us only that this woman entered the house. The beads tell us that she was in the bedroom; which, as you say, seems to connect her to some extent with Jeffrey's death. Not necessarily, of course. It is only a suggestion; but a rather strong suggestion under the peculiar circumstances."

"Even so," said I, "this new fact seems to me so far from clearing up the mystery, only to add to it a fresh element of still deeper mystery. The porter's evidence at the inquest could leave no doubt that Jeffrey contemplated suicide, and his preparations pointedly suggest this particular night as the time selected by him for doing away with himself. Is not that so?"

"Certainly. The porter's evidence was very clear on that point."

"Then I don't see where this woman comes in. It is obvious that her presence at the inn, and especially in the bedroom, on this occasion and in these strange, secret circumstances, has a rather sinister look; but yet I do not see in what way she could have been connected with the tragedy. Perhaps, after all, she has nothing to do with it. You remember that Jeffrey went to the lodge about eight o'clock, to pay his rent, and chatted for some time with the porter. That looks as if the lady had already left."

"Yes," said Thorndyke. "But, on the other hand, Jeffrey's remarks to the porter with reference to the cab do not quite agree with the account that we have just heard from Wilkins. Which suggests — as does Wilkins's account generally — some secrecy as to the lady's visit to his chambers."

"Do you know who the woman was?" I asked.

"No, I don't know," he replied. "I have a rather strong suspicion that I can identify her, but I am waiting for some further facts."

"Is your suspicion founded on some new matter that you have discovered, or is it deducible from facts that are known to me?"

"I think," he replied, "that you know practically all that I know, although I have, in one instance, turned a very strong suspicion into a certainty by further inquiries. But I think you ought to be able to form some idea as to who this lady probably was."

"But no woman has been mentioned in the case at all."

"No; but I think you should be able to give this lady a name, notwithstanding."

"Should I? Then I begin to suspect that I am not cut out for medico-legal practice, for I don't see the faintest glimmer of a suggestion."

Thorndyke smiled benevolently. "Don't be discouraged, Jervis," said he. "I expect that when you first began to go round the wards, you doubted whether you were cut out for medical practice. I did. For special work one needs special knowledge and an acquired faculty for making use of it. What does a second year's student make of a small thoracic aneurysm? He knows the anatomy of the chest; he begins to know the normal heart sounds and areas of dullness; but he cannot yet fit his various items of knowledge together. Then comes the experienced physician and perhaps makes a complete diagnosis without any examination at all, merely from hearing the patient speak or cough. He has the same facts as the student, but he has acquired the faculty of instantly connecting an abnormality of function with its correlated anatomical change. It is a matter of experience. And, with your previous training, you will soon acquire the faculty. Try to observe everything. Let nothing escape you. And try constantly to find some connection between facts and events that seem to be unconnected. That is my advice to you; and with that we will put away the Blackmore case for the present and consider our day's work at an end."

Chapter XIV

Thorndyke Lays the Mine

*T*he information supplied by Mr. Samuel Wilkins, so far from dispelling the cloud of mystery that hung over the Blackmore case, only enveloped it in deeper obscurity, so far as I was concerned. The new problem that Thorndyke offered for solution was a tougher one than any of the others. He proposed that I should identify and give a name to this mysterious woman. But how could I? No woman, excepting Mrs. Wilson, had been mentioned in connection with the case. This new *dramatis persona* had appeared suddenly from nowhere and straightway vanished without leaving a trace, excepting the two or three beads that we had picked up in Jeffrey's room.

Nor was it in the least clear what part, if any, she had played in the tragedy. The facts still pointed as plainly to suicide as before her appearance. Jeffrey's repeated hints as to his intentions, and the very significant preparations that he had made, were enough to negative any idea of foul play. And yet the woman's presence in the chambers at that time, the secret manner of her arrival and her precautions against recognition, strongly suggested some kind of complicity in the dreadful event that followed.

But what complicity is possible in the case of suicide? The woman might have furnished him with the syringe and the poison, but it would not have been necessary for her to go to his chambers for that purpose. Vague ideas of persuasion and hypnotic suggestion floated through my brain; but the explanations did not fit the case and the hypnotic suggestion of crime is not very convincing to the medical mind. Then I thought of blackmail in connection with some disgraceful secret; but though this was a more hopeful suggestion, it was not very probable, considering Jeffrey's age and character.

And all these speculations failed to throw the faintest light on the main question: "Who was this woman?"

A couple of days passed, during which Thorndyke made no further reference to the case. He was, most of the time, away from home, though how he was engaged I had no idea. What was rather more unusual was that Polton seemed to have deserted the laboratory and taken to outdoor pursuits. I assumed that he had seized the opportunity of leaving me in charge, and I dimly surmised that he was acting as Thorndyke's private inquiry agent, as he seemed to have done in the case of Samuel Wilkins.

On the evening of the second day Thorndyke came home in obviously good spirits, and his first proceedings aroused my expectant curiosity. He went to a cupboard and brought forth a box of Trichinopoly cheroots. Now the Trichinopoly cheroot was Thorndyke's one dissipation, to be enjoyed only on rare and specially festive occasions; which, in practice, meant those occasions on which he had scored some important point or solved some unusually tough problem. Wherefore I watched him with lively interest.

"It's a pity that the 'Trichy' is such a poisonous beast," he remarked, taking up one of the cheroots and sniffing at it delicately. "There is no other cigar like it, to a really abandoned smoker." He laid the cigar back in the box and continued: "I think I shall treat myself to one after dinner to celebrate the occasion."

"What occasion?" I asked.

"The completion of the Blackmore case. I am just going to write to Marchmont advising him to enter a caveat."

"Do you mean to say that you have discovered a flaw in the will, after all?"

"A flaw!" he exclaimed. "My dear Jervis, that second will is a forgery."

I stared at him in amazement; for his assertion sounded like nothing more or less than arrant nonsense.

"But the thing is impossible, Thorndyke," I said. "Not only did the witnesses recognize their own signatures and the painter's greasy fingermarks, but they had both read the will and remembered its contents."

"Yes; that is the interesting feature in the case. It is a very pretty problem. I shall give you a last chance to solve it. Tomorrow evening we shall have to give a full explanation, so you have another twenty-four hours in which to think it over. And, meanwhile, I am going to take you to my club to dine. I think we shall be pretty safe there from Mrs. Schallibaum."

He sat down and wrote a letter, which was apparently quite a short one, and having addressed and stamped it, prepared to go out.

"Come," said he, "let us away to 'the gay and festive scenes and halls of dazzling light.' We will lay the mine in the Fleet Street pillar box. I should like to be in Marchmont's office when it explodes."

"I expect, for that matter," said I, "that the explosion will be felt pretty distinctly in these chambers."

"I expect so, too," replied Thorndyke; "and that reminds me that I shall be out all day tomorrow, so, if Marchmont calls, you must do all that you can to persuade him to come round after dinner and bring Stephen Blackmore, if possible. I am anxious to have Stephen here, as he will be able to give us some further information and confirm certain matters of fact."

I promised to exercise my utmost powers of persuasion on Mr. Marchmont which I should certainly have done on my own account, being now on the very tiptoe of curiosity to hear Thorndyke's explanation of the unthinkable conclusion at which he had arrived — and the subject dropped completely; nor could I, during the rest of the evening, induce my colleague to reopen it even in the most indirect or allusive manner.

Our explanations in respect of Mr. Marchmont were fully realized; for, on the following morning, within an hour of Thorndyke's departure from our chambers, the knocker was plied with more than usual emphasis, and, on my opening the door, I discovered the solicitor in company with a somewhat older gentleman. Mr. Marchmont appeared somewhat out of humor, while his companion was obviously in a state of extreme irritation.

"How d'you do, Dr. Jervis?" said Marchmont as he entered at my invitation. "Your friend, I suppose, is not in just now?"

"No; and he will not be returning until the evening."

"Hm; I'm sorry. We wished to see him rather particularly. This is my partner, Mr. Winwood."

The latter gentleman bowed stiffly and Marchmont continued:

"We have had a letter from Dr. Thorndyke, and it is, I may say, a rather curious letter; in fact, a very singular letter indeed."

"It is the letter of a madman!" growled Mr. Winwood.

"No, no, Winwood; nothing of the kind. Control yourself, I beg you. But really, the letter is rather incomprehensible. It relates to the will of the late Jeffrey Blackmore — you know the main facts of the case; and we cannot reconcile it with those facts."

"This is the letter," exclaimed Mr. Winwood, dragging the document from his wallet and slapping it down on the table. "If you are acquainted with the case, sir, just read that, and let us hear what *you* think."

I took up the letter and read aloud:

"Jeffrey Blackmore, Decd.

"Dear Mr. Marchmont, —

"I have gone into this case with great care and have now no doubt that the second will is a forgery. Criminal proceedings will, I think, be inevitable, but meanwhile it would be wise to enter a caveat.

"If you could look in at my chambers tomorrow evening we could talk the case over; and I should be glad if you could bring Mr. Stephen Blackmore; whose personal knowledge of the events and the parties concerned would be of great assistance in clearing up obscure details.

"I am,

"Yours sincerely,
"John Evelyn Thorndyke
"C.F. Marchmont, Esq."

"Well!" exclaimed Mr. Winwood, glaring ferociously at me, "what do you think of the learned counsel's opinion?"

"I knew that Thorndyke was writing to you to this effect," I replied, "but I must frankly confess that I can make nothing of it. Have you acted on his advice?"

"Certainly not!" shouted the irascible lawyer. "Do you suppose that we wish to make ourselves the laughingstock of the courts? The thing is impossible — ridiculously impossible!"

"It can't be that, you know," I said, a little stiffly, for I was somewhat nettled by Mr. Winwood's manner, "or Thorndyke would not have written this letter. The conclusion looks as impossible to me as it does to you; but I have complete confidence in Thorndyke. If he says that the will is a forgery, I have no doubt that it is a forgery."

"But how the deuce can it be?" roared Winwood. "You know the circumstances under which the will was executed."

"Yes; but so does Thorndyke. And he is not a man who overlooks important facts. It is useless to argue with me. I am in a complete fog about the case myself. You had better come in this evening and talk it over with him as he suggests."

"It is very inconvenient," grumbled Mr. Winwood. "We shall have to dine in town."

"Yes," said Marchmont, "but it is the only thing to be done. As Dr. Jervis says, we must take it that Thorndyke has something solid to base his opinion on. He doesn't make elementary mistakes. And, of course, if what he says is correct, Mr. Stephen's position is totally changed."

"Bah!" exclaimed Winwood, "he has found a mare's nest, I tell you. Still, I agree that the explanation should be worth hearing."

"You mustn't mind Winwood," said Marchmont, in an apologetic undertone; "he's a peppery old fellow with a rough tongue, but he doesn't mean any harm." Which statement Winwood assented to — or dissented from; for it was impossible to say which — by a prolonged growl.

"We shall expect you then," I said, "about eight tonight, and you will try to bring Mr. Stephen with you?"

"Yes," replied Marchmont; "I think we can promise that he shall come with us. I have sent him a telegram asking him to attend."

With this the two lawyers took their departure, leaving me to meditate upon my colleague's astonishing statement; which I did, considerably to the prejudice of other employment. That Thorndyke would be able to justify the opinion that he had given, I had no doubt whatever; but yet there was no denying that his proposition was what Mr. Dick Swiveller would call "a staggerer."

When Thorndyke returned, I informed him of the visit of our two friends, and acquainted him with the sentiments that they had expressed; whereat he smiled with quiet amusement.

"I thought," he remarked, "that letter would bring Marchmont to our door before long. As to Winwood, I have never met him, but I gather that he is one of those people whom you 'mustn't mind.' In a general way, I object to people who tacitly claim exemption from the ordinary rules of conduct that are held to be binding on their fellows. But, as he promises to give us what the variety artists call 'an extra turn,' we will make the best of him and give him a run for his money."

Here Thorndyke smiled mischievously — I understood the meaning of that smile later in the evening — and asked: "What do you think of the affair yourself?"

"I have given it up," I answered. "To my paralyzed brain, the Blackmore case is like an endless algebraical problem propounded by an insane mathematician."

Thorndyke laughed at my comparison, which I flatter myself was a rather apt one.

"Come and dine," said he, "and let us crack a bottle, that our hearts may not turn to water under the frown of the disdainful Winwood. I think the old 'Bell' in Holborn will meet our present requirements better than the club. There is something jovial and roistering about an ancient tavern; but we must keep a sharp lookout for Mrs. Schallibaum."

Thereupon we set forth; and, after a week's close imprisonment, I once more looked upon the friendly London streets, the cheerfully lighted shop windows and the multitudes of companionable strangers who moved unceasingly along the pavements.

Chapter XV

Thorndyke Explodes the Mine

*W*e had not been back in our chambers more than a few minutes when the little brass knocker on the inner door rattled out its summons. Thorndyke himself opened the door, and, finding our three expected visitors on the threshold, he admitted them and closed the "oak."

"We have accepted your invitation, you see," said Marchmont, whose manner was now a little flurried and uneasy. "This is my partner, Mr. Winwood; you haven't met before, I think. Well, we thought we should like to hear some further particulars from you, as we could not quite understand your letter."

"My conclusion, I suppose," said Thorndyke, "was a little unexpected?"

"It was more than that, sir," exclaimed Winwood. "It was absolutely irreconcilable either with the facts of the case or with common physical possibilities."

"At the first glance," Thorndyke agreed, "it would probably have that appearance."

"It has that appearance still to me." said Winwood, growing suddenly red and wrathful, "and I may say that I speak as a solicitor who was practicing in the law when you were an infant in arms. You tell us, sir, that this will is a forgery; this will, which was executed in broad daylight in the presence of two unimpeachable witnesses who have sworn, not only to their signatures and the contents of the document, but to their very finger-marks on the paper. Are those finger-marks forgeries, too? Have you examined and tested them?"

"I have not," replied Thorndyke. "The fact is they are of no interest to me, as I am not disputing the witnesses' signatures."

At this, Mr. Winwood fairly danced with irritation.

"Marchmont!" he exclaimed fiercely, "you know this good gentleman, I believe. Tell me, is he addicted to practical jokes?"

"Now, my dear Winwood," groaned Marchmont, "I pray you – I beg you to control yourself. No doubt –"

"But confound it!" roared Winwood, "you have, yourself, heard him say that the will is a forgery, but that he doesn't dispute the signatures; which," concluded Winwood, banging his fist down on the table, "is damned nonsense."

"May I suggest," interposed Stephen Blackmore, "that we came here to receive Dr. Thorndyke's explanation of his letter. Perhaps it would be better to postpone any comments until we have heard it."

"Undoubtedly, undoubtedly," said Marchmont. "Let me entreat you, Winwood, to listen patiently and refrain from interruption until we have heard our learned friend's exposition of the case."

"Oh, very well," Winwood replied sulkily; "I'll say no more."

He sank into a chair with the manner of a man who shuts himself up and turns the key; and so remained – excepting when the internal pressure approached bursting-point – throughout the subsequent proceedings, silent, stony and impassive, like a seated statue of Obstinacy.

"I take it," said Marchmont, "that you have some new facts that are not in our possession?"

"Yes," replied Thorndyke; "we have some new facts, and we have made some new use of the old ones. But how shall I lay the case before you? Shall I state my theory of the sequence of events and furnish the verification afterwards? Or shall I retrace the actual course of my investigations and give you the facts in the order in which I obtained them myself, with the inferences from them?"

"I almost think," said Mr. Marchmont, "that it would be better if you would put us in possession of the new facts. Then, if the conclusions that follow from them are not sufficiently obvious, we could hear the argument. What do you say, Winwood?"

Mr. Winwood roused himself for an instant, barked out the one word "Facts," and shut himself up again with a snap.

"You would like to have the new facts by themselves?" said Thorndyke.

"If you please. The facts only, in the first place, at any rate."

"Very well," said Thorndyke; and here I caught his eye with a mischievous twinkle in it that I understood perfectly; for I had most of the facts myself and realized how much these two lawyers were likely to extract from them. Winwood was going to "have a run for his money," as Thorndyke had promised.

My colleague, having placed on the table by his side a small cardboard box and the sheets of notes from his file, glanced quickly at Mr. Winwood and began:

"The first important new facts came into my possession on the day on which you introduced the case to me. In the evening, after you left, I availed myself of Mr. Stephen's kind invitation to look over his uncle's chambers in New Inn. I wished to do so in order to ascertain, if possible, what had been the habits of the deceased during his residence there. When I arrived with Dr. Jervis, Mr. Stephen was in the chambers, and I learned from him that his uncle was an Oriental scholar of some position and that he had a very thorough acquaintance with the cunei-form writing. Now, while I was talking with Mr. Stephen I made a very curious discovery. On the wall over the fireplace hung a large framed photograph of an ancient Persian inscription in the cuneiform charac-ter; and that photograph was upside down."

"Upside down!" exclaimed Stephen. "But that is really very odd."

"Very odd indeed," agreed Thorndyke, "and very suggestive. The way in which it came to be inverted is pretty obvious and also rather suggestive. The photograph had evidently been in the frame some years but had apparently never been hung up before."

"It had not," said Stephen, "though I don't know how you arrived at the fact. It used to stand on the mantelpiece in his old rooms in Jermyn Street."

"Well," continued Thorndyke, "the frame-maker had pasted his label on the back of the frame, and as this label hung the right way up, it appeared as if the person who fixed the photograph on the wall had adopted it as a guide."

"It is very extraordinary," said Stephen. "I should have thought the person who hung it would have asked Uncle Jeffrey which was the right way up; and I can't imagine how on earth it could have hung all those months without his noticing it. He must have been practically blind."

Here Marchmont, who had been thinking hard, with knitted brows, suddenly brightened up.

"I see your point," said he. "You mean that if Jeffrey was as blind as that, it would have been possible for some person to substitute a false will, which he might sign without noticing the substitution."

"That wouldn't make the will a forgery," growled Winwood. "If Jeffrey signed it, it was Jeffrey's will. You could contest it if you could prove the fraud. But he said: 'This is my will,' and the two witnesses read it and have identified it."

"Did they read it aloud?" asked Stephen.

"No, they did not," replied Thorndyke.

"Can you prove substitution?" asked Marchmont.

"I haven't asserted it," answered Thorndyke, "My position is that the will is a forgery."

"But it is not," said Winwood.

"We won't argue it now," said Thorndyke. "I ask you to note the fact that the inscription was upside down. I also observed on the walls of the chambers some valuable Japanese color-prints on which were recent damp-spots. I noted that the sitting room had a gas-stove and that the kitchen contained practically no stores or remains of food and hardly any traces of even the simplest cooking. In the bedroom I found a large box that had contained a considerable stock of hard stearine candles, six to the pound, and that was now nearly empty. I examined the clothing of the deceased. On the soles of the boots I observed dried mud, which was unlike that on my own and Jervis's boots, from the gravelly square of the inn. I noted a crease on each leg of the deceased man's trousers as if they had been turned up halfway to the knee; and in the waistcoat pocket I found the stump of a 'Contango' pencil. On the floor of the bedroom, I found a portion of an oval glass somewhat like that of a watch or locket, but ground at the edge to a double bevel. Dr. Jervis and I also found one or two beads and a bugle, all of dark brown glass."

Here Thorndyke paused, and Marchmont, who had been gazing at him with growing amazement, said nervously:

"Er — yes. Very interesting. These observations of yours — er — are —"

"Are all the observations that I made at New Inn."

The two lawyers looked at one another and Stephen Blackmore stared fixedly at a spot on the hearthrug. Then Mr. Winwood's face contorted itself into a sour, lopsided smile.

"You might have observed a good many other things, sir," said he, "if you had looked. If you had examined the doors, you would have noted that they had hinges and were covered with paint; and, if you had looked up the chimney you might have noted that it was black inside."

"Now, now, Winwood," protested Marchmont in an agony of uneasiness as to what his partner might say next, "I must really beg you — er — to refrain from — what Mr. Winwood means, Dr. Thorndyke, is that — er — we do not quite perceive the relevancy of these — ah — observations of yours."

"Probably not," said Thorndyke, "but you will perceive their relevancy later. For the present, I will ask you to note the facts and bear them in mind, so that you may be able to follow the argument when we come to that.

"The next set of data I acquired on the same evening, when Dr. Jervis gave me a detailed account of a very strange adventure that befell him.

I need not burden you with all the details, but I will give you the substance of his story."

He then proceeded to recount the incidents connected with my visits to Mr. Graves, dwelling on the personal peculiarities of the parties concerned and especially of the patient, and not even forgetting the very singular spectacles worn by Mr. Weiss. He also explained briefly the construction of the chart, presenting the latter for the inspection of his hearers. To this recital our three visitors listened in utter bewilderment, as, indeed did I also; for I could not conceive in what way my adventures could possibly be related to the affairs of the late Mr. Blackmore. This was manifestly the view taken by Mr. Marchmont, for, during a pause in which the chart was handed to him, he remarked somewhat stiffly:

"I am assuming, Dr. Thorndyke, that the curious story you are telling us has some relevance to the matter in which we are interested."

"You are quite correct in your assumption," replied Thorndyke. "The story is very relevant indeed, as you will presently be convinced."

"Thank you," said Marchmont, sinking back once more into his chair with a sigh of resignation.

"A few days ago," pursued Thorndyke, "Dr. Jervis and I located, with the aid of this chart, the house to which he had been called. We found that the late tenant had left somewhat hurriedly and that the house was to let; and, as no other kind of investigation was possible, we obtained the keys and made an exploration of the premises."

Here he gave a brief account of our visit and the conditions that we observed, and was proceeding to furnish a list of the articles that we had found under the grate, when Mr. Winwood started from his chair.

"Really, sir!" he exclaimed, "this is too much! Have I come here, at great personal inconvenience, to hear you read the inventory of a dust-heap?"

Thorndyke smiled benevolently and caught my eye, once more, with a gleam of amusement.

"Sit down, Mr. Winwood," he said quietly. "You came here to learn the facts of the case, and I am giving them to you. Please don't interrupt needlessly and waste time."

Winwood stared at him ferociously for several seconds; then, somewhat disconcerted by the unruffled calm of his manner, he uttered a snort of defiance, sat down heavily and shut himself up again.

"We will now," Thorndyke continued, with unmoved serenity, "consider these relics in more detail, and we will begin with this pair of spectacles. They belonged to a person who was near-sighted and astigmatic in the left eye and almost certainly blind in the right. Such a description agrees entirely with Dr. Jervis's account of the sick man."

He paused for the moment, and then, as no one made any comment, proceeded:

"We next come to these little pieces of reed, which you, Mr. Stephen, will probably recognize as the remains of a Japanese brush, such as is used for writing in Chinese ink or for making small drawings."

Again he paused, as though expecting some remark from his listeners; but no one spoke, and he continued:

"Then there is this bottle with the theatrical wig-maker's label on it, which once contained cement such as is used for fixing on false beards, moustaches or eyebrows."

He paused once more and looked round expectantly at his audience, none of whom, however, volunteered any remark.

"Do none of these objects that I have described and shown you, seem to have any significance for us?" he asked, in a tone of some surprise.

"They convey nothing to me," said Mr. Marchmont, glancing at his partner, who shook his head like a restive horse.

"Nor to you, Mr. Stephen?"

"No," replied Stephen. "Under the existing circumstances they convey no reasonable suggestion to me."

Thorndyke hesitated as if he were half inclined to say something more; then, with a slight shrug, he turned over his notes and resumed:

"The next group of new facts is concerned with the signatures of the recent checks. We have photographed them and placed them together for the purpose of comparison and analysis."

"I am not prepared to question the signatures." said Winwood. "We have had a highly expert opinion, which would override ours in a court of law even if we differed from it; which I think we do not."

"Yes," said Marchmont; "that is so. I think we must accept the signatures, especially as that of the will has been proved, beyond any question to be authentic."

"Very well," agreed Thorndyke; "we will pass over the signatures. Then we have some further evidence in regard to the spectacles, which serves to verify our conclusions respecting them."

"Perhaps," said Marchmont, "we might pass over that, too, as we do not seem to have reached any conclusions."

"As you please," said Thorndyke. "It is important, but we can reserve it for verification. The next item will interest you more, I think. It is the signed and witnessed statement of Samuel Wilkins, the driver of the cab in which the deceased came home to the inn on the evening of his death."

My colleague was right. An actual document, signed by a tangible witness, who could be put in the box and sworn, brought both lawyers to a state of attention; and when Thorndyke read out the cabman's evidence, their attention soon quickened into undisguised astonishment.

"But this is a most mysterious affair," exclaimed Marchmont. "Who could this woman have been, and what could she have been doing in Jeffrey's chambers at this time? Can you throw any light on it, Mr. Stephen?"

"No, indeed I can't," replied Stephen. "It is a complete mystery to me. My uncle Jeffrey was a confirmed old bachelor, and, although he did not dislike women, he was far from partial to their society, wrapped up as he was in his favorite studies. To the best of my belief, he had not a single female friend. He was not on intimate terms even with his sister, Mrs. Wilson."

"Very remarkable," mused Marchmont; "most remarkable. But, perhaps, you can tell us, Dr. Thorndyke, who this woman was?"

"I think," replied Thorndyke, "that the next item of evidence will enable you to form an opinion for yourselves. I only obtained it yesterday, and, as it made my case quite complete, I wrote off to you immediately. It is the statement of Joseph Ridley, another cabman, and unfortunately, a rather dull, unobservant fellow, unlike Wilkins. He has not much to tell us, but what little he has is highly instructive. Here is the statement, signed by the deponent and witnessed by me:

"'My name is Joseph Ridley. I am the driver of a four-wheeled cab. On the fourteenth of March, the day of the great fog, I was waiting at Vauxhall Station, where I had just set down a fare. About five o'clock a lady came and told me to drive over to Upper Kennington Lane to take up a passenger. She was a middle-sized woman. I could not tell what her age was, or what she was like, because her head was wrapped up in a sort of knitted, woolen veil to keep out the fog. I did not notice how she was dressed. She got into the cab and I led the horse over to Upper Kennington Lane and a little way up the lane, until the lady tapped at the front, window for me to stop.

"'She got out of the cab and told me to wait. Then she went away and disappeared in the fog. Presently a lady and gentleman came from the direction in which she had gone. The lady looked like the same lady, but I won't answer to that. Her head was wrapped up in the same kind of veil or shawl, and I noticed that she had on a dark colored mantle with bead fringe on it.

"'The gentleman was clean shaved and wore spectacles, and he stooped a good deal. I can't say whether his sight was good or bad. He helped the lady into the cab and told me to drive to the Great Northern Station, King's Cross. Then he got in himself and I drove off. I got to the station about a quarter to six and the lady and gentleman got out. The gentleman paid my fare and they both went into the station. I did not notice anything unusual about either of them. Directly after they had gone, I got a fresh fare and drove away.'

"That," Thorndyke concluded, "is Joseph Ridley's statement; and I think it will enable you to give a meaning to the other facts that I have offered for your consideration."

"I am not so sure about that," said Marchmont. "It is all exceedingly mysterious. Your suggestion is, of course, that the woman who came to New Inn in the cab was Mrs. Schallibaum!"

"Not at all," replied Thorndyke. "My suggestion is that the woman was Jeffrey Blackmore."

There was deathly silence for a few moments. We were all absolutely thunderstruck, and sat gaping at Thorndyke in speechless-astonishment. Then — Mr. Winwood fairly bounced out of his chair.

"But — my — good — sir!" he screeched. "Jeffrey Blackmore was with her at the time!"

"Naturally," replied Thorndyke, "my suggestion implies that the person who was with her was not Jeffrey Blackmore."

"But he was!" bawled Winwood. "The porter saw him!"

"The porter saw a person whom he believed to be Jeffrey Blackmore. I suggest that the porter's belief was erroneous."

"Well," snapped Winwood, "perhaps you can prove that it was. I don't see how you are going to; but perhaps you can."

He subsided once more into his chair and glared defiantly at Thorndyke.

"You seemed," said Stephen, "to suggest some connection between the sick man, Graves, and my uncle. I noted it at the time, but put it aside as impossible. Was I right. Did you mean to suggest any connection?"

"I suggest something more than a connection. I suggest identity. My position is that the sick man, Graves, was your uncle."

"From Dr. Jervis's description," said Stephen, "this man must have been very like my uncle. Both were blind in the right eye and had very poor vision with the left; and my uncle certainly used brushes of the kind that you have shown us, when writing in the Japanese character, for I have watched him and admired his skill; but —"

"But," said Marchmont, "there is the insuperable objection that, at the very time when this man was lying sick in Kennington Lane, Mr. Jeffrey was living at New Inn."

"What evidence is there of that?" asked Thorndyke.

"Evidence!" Marchmont exclaimed impatiently. "Why, my dear sir —"

He paused suddenly, and, leaning forward, regarded Thorndyke with a new and rather startled expression.

"You mean to suggest —" he began.

"I suggest that Jeffrey Blackmore never lived at New Inn at all."

For the moment, Marchmont seemed absolutely paralyzed by astonishment.

"This is an amazing proposition!" he exclaimed, at length. "Yet the thing is certainly not impossible, for, now that you recall the fact, I realize that no one who had known him previously — excepting his brother, John — ever saw him at the inn. The question of identity was never raised."

"Excepting," said Mr. Winwood, "in regard to the body; which was certainly that of Jeffrey Blackmore."

"Yes, yes. Of course," said Marchmont. "I had forgotten that for the moment. The body was identified beyond doubt. You don't dispute the identity of the body, do you?"

"Certainly not," replied Thorndyke.

Here Mr. Winwood grasped his hair with both hands and stuck his elbows on his knees, while Marchmont drew forth a large handkerchief and mopped his forehead. Stephen Blackmore looked from one to the other expectantly, and finally said:

"If I might make a suggestion, it would be that, as Dr. Thorndyke has shown us the pieces now of the puzzle, he should be so kind as to put them together for our information."

"Yes," agreed Marchmont, "that will be the best plan. Let us have the argument, Doctor, and any additional evidence that you possess."

"The argument," said Thorndyke, "will be a rather long one, as the data are so numerous, and there are some points in verification on which I shall have to dwell in some detail. We will have some coffee to clear our brains, and then I will bespeak your patience for what may seem like a rather prolix demonstration."

Chapter XVI

An Exposition and a Tragedy

"You may have wondered," Thorndyke commenced, when he had poured out the coffee and handed round the cups, "what induced me to undertake the minute investigation of so apparently simple and straightforward a case. Perhaps I had better explain that first and let you see what was the real starting-point of the inquiry.

"When you, Mr. Marchmont and Mr. Stephen, introduced the case to me, I made a very brief précis of the facts as you presented them, and of these there were one or two which immediately attracted my attention. In the first place, there was the will. It was a very strange will. It was perfectly unnecessary. It contained no new matter; it expressed no changed intentions; it met no new circumstances, as known to the testator. In short it was not really a new will at all, but merely a repetition of the first one, drafted in different and less suitable language. It differed only in introducing a certain ambiguity from which the original was free. It created the possibility that, in certain circumstances, not known to or anticipated by the testator, John Blackmore might become the principal beneficiary, contrary to the obvious wishes of the testator.

"The next point that impressed me was the manner of Mrs. Wilson's death. She died of cancer. Now people do not die suddenly and unexpectedly of cancer. This terrible disease stands almost alone in that it marks out its victim months in advance. A person who has an incurable cancer is a person whose death may be predicted with certainty and its date fixed within comparatively narrow limits.

"And now observe the remarkable series of coincidences that are brought into light when we consider this peculiarity of the disease. Mrs. Wilson died on the twelfth of March of this present year. Mr. Jeffrey's second will was signed on the twelfth of November of last year; at a time, that is to say, when the existence of cancer must have been known to Mrs. Wilson's doctor, and might have been known to any of her relatives who chose to inquire after her.

"Then you will observe that the remarkable change in Mr. Jeffrey's habits coincides in the most singular way with the same events. The cancer must have been detectable as early as September of last year; about the time, in fact, at which Mrs. Wilson made her will. Mr. Jeffrey went to the inn at the beginning of October. From that time his habits were totally changed, and I can demonstrate to you that a change — not a gradual, but an abrupt change — took place in the character of his signature.

"In short, the whole of this peculiar set of curcumstances — the change in Jeffrey's habits, the change in his signature, and the execution of his strange will — came into existence about the time when Mrs. Wilson was first known to be suffering from cancer.

"This struck me as a very suggestive fact.

"Then there is the extraordinarily opportune date of Mr. Jeffrey's death. Mrs. Wilson died on the twelfth of March. Mr. Jeffrey was found dead on the fifteenth of March, having apparently died on the fourteenth, on which day he was seen alive. If he had died only three days sooner, he would have predeceased Mrs. Wilson, and her property would never have devolved on him at all; while, if he had lived only a day or two longer, he would have learned of her death and would certainly have made a new will or codicil in his nephew's favor.

"Circumstances, therefore, conspired in the most singular manner in favor of John Blackmore.

"But there is yet another coincidence. Jeffrey's body was found, by the merest chance, the day after his death. But it might have remained undiscovered for weeks, or even months; and if it had, it would have been impossible to fix the date of his death. Then Mrs. Wilson's next of kin would certainly have contested John Blackmore's claim — and probably with success — on the ground that Jeffrey died before Mrs. Wilson. But all this uncertainty is provided for by the circumstance that Mr. Jeffrey paid his rent personally — and prematurely — to the porter on the fourteenth of March, thus establishing beyond question the fact that he was alive on that date; and yet further, in case the porter's memory should be untrustworthy or his statement doubted, Jeffrey furnished a signed and dated document — the check — which could be produced in a court to furnish incontestable proof of survival.

"To sum up this part of the evidence. Here was a will which enabled John Blackmore to inherit the fortune of a man who, almost certainly, had no intention of bequeathing it to him. The wording of that will seemed to be adjusted to the peculiarities of Mrs. Wilson's disease; and the death of the testator occurred under a peculiar set of circumstances which seemed to be exactly adjusted to the wording of the will. Or, to put it in another way: the wording of the will and the time, the manner and the circumstances of the testator's death, all seemed to be precisely adjusted to the fact that the approximate date of Mrs. Wilson's death was known some months before it occurred.

"Now you must admit that this compound group of coincidences, all conspiring to a single end — the enrichment of John Blackmore — has a very singular appearance. Coincidences are common enough in real life; but we cannot accept too many at a time. My feeling was that there were too many in this case and that I could not accept them without searching inquiry."

Thorndyke paused, and Mr. Marchmont, who had listened with close attention, nodded, as he glanced at his silent partner.

"You have stated the case with remarkable clearness," he said; "and I am free to confess that some of the points that you have raised had escaped my notice."

"My first idea," Thorndyke resumed, "was that John Blackmore, taking advantage of the mental enfeeblement produced by the opium habit, had dictated this will to Jeffrey, It was then that I sought permission to inspect Jeffrey's chambers; to learn what I could about him and to see for myself whether they presented the dirty and disorderly appearance characteristic of the regular opium-smoker's den. But when, during a walk into the City, I thought over the case, it seemed to me that this explanation hardly met the facts. Then I endeavored to think of some other explanation; and looking over my notes I observed two points that seemed worth considering. One was that neither of the witnesses to the will was really acquainted with Jeffrey Blackmore; both being strangers who had accepted his identity on his own statement. The other was that no one who had previously known him, with the single exception of his brother John, had ever seen Jeffrey at the inn.

"What was the import of these two facts? Probably they had none. But still they suggested the desirability of considering the question: Was the person who signed the will really Jeffrey Blackmore? The contrary supposition — that someone had personated Jeffrey and forged his signature to a false will — seemed wildly improbable, especially in view of the identification of the body; but it involved no actual impossibility; and it offered a complete explanation of the, otherwise inexplicable, coincidences that I have mentioned.

"I did not, however, for a moment, think that this was the true explanation, but I resolved to bear it in mind, to test it when the opportunity arose, and consider it by the light of any fresh facts that I might acquire.

"The new facts came sooner than I had expected. That same evening I went with Dr. Jervis to New Inn and found Mr. Stephen in the chambers. By him I was informed that Jeffrey was a learned Orientalist, with a quite expert knowledge of the cuneiform writing; and even as he was telling me this, I looked over his shoulder and saw a cuneiform inscription hanging on the wall upside down.

"Now, of this there could be only one reasonable explanation. Disregarding the fact that no one would screw the suspension plates on a frame without ascertaining which was the right way up, and assuming it to be hung up inverted, it was impossible that the misplacement could have been overlooked by Jeffrey. He was not blind, though his sight was defective. The frame was thirty inches long and the individual characters nearly an inch in length — about the size of the D 18 letters of Snellen's test-types, which can be read by a person of ordinary sight at a distance of fifty-five feet. There was, I repeat, only one reasonable explanation; which was that the person who had inhabited those chambers was not Jeffrey Blackmore.

"This conclusion received considerable support from a fact which I observed later, but mention in this place. On examining the soles of the shoes taken from the dead man's feet, I found only the ordinary mud of the streets. There was no trace of the peculiar gravelly mud that adhered to my own boots and Jervis's, and which came from the square of the inn. Yet the porter distinctly stated that the deceased, after paying the rent, walked back towards his chambers across the square; the mud of which should, therefore, have been conspicuous on his shoes.

"Thus, in a moment, a wildly speculative hypothesis had assumed a high degree of probability.

"When Mr. Stephen was gone, Jervis and I looked over the chambers thoroughly; and then another curious fact came to light. On the wall were a number of fine Japanese color-prints, all of which showed recent damp-spots. Now, apart from the consideration that Jeffrey, who had been at the trouble and expense of collecting these valuable prints, would hardly have allowed them to rot on his walls, there arose the question: How came they to be damp? There was a gas stove in the room, and a gas stove has at least the virtue of preserving a dry atmosphere. It was winter weather, when the stove would naturally be pretty constantly alight. How came the walls to be so damp? The answer seemed to be that the stove had not been constantly alight, but had been lighted only occasionally. This suggestion was borne out by a further examination of the rooms. In the kitchen there were practically no stores and hardly any arrangements even for simple bachelor cooking; the bedroom offered the same suggestion; the soap in the wash-stand was shriveled and cracked; there was no cast-off linen, and the shirts in the drawers, though clean, had the peculiar yellowish, faded appearance that linen acquires when long out of use. In short, the rooms had the appearance of not having been lived in at all, but only visited at intervals.

"Against this view, however, was the statement of the night porter that he had often seen a light in Jeffrey's sitting room at one o'clock in the morning, with the apparent implication that it was then turned out. Now a light may be left in an empty room, but its extinction implies the presence of some person to extinguish it; unless some automatic device be adopted for putting it out at a given time. Such a device – the alarm movement of a clock, for instance, with a suitable attachment – is a simple enough matter, but my search of the rooms failed to discover anything of the kind. However, when looking over the drawers in the bedroom, I came upon a large box that had held a considerable quantity of hard stearine candles. There were only a few left, but a flat candlestick with numerous wick-ends in its socket accounted for the remainder.

"These candles seemed to dispose of the difficulty. They were not necessary for ordinary lighting, since gas was laid on in all three rooms. For what purpose, then, were they used, and in such considerable quantities? I subsequently obtained some of the same brand – Price's stearine candles, six to the pound – and experimented with them. Each candle was seven and a quarter inches in length, not counting the cone at the top, and I found that they burned in still air at the rate of a fraction over one inch in an hour. We may say that one of these candles would burn in still air a little over six hours. It would thus be possible for the person who inhabited these rooms to go away at seven o'clock in the evening and leave a light which would burn until past one in the morning and then extinguish itself. This, of course, was only surmise, but it destroyed the significance of the night porter's statement.

"But, if the person who inhabited these chambers was not Jeffrey, who was he?

"The answer to that question seemed plain enough. There was only one person who had a strong motive for perpetrating a fraud of this kind, and there was only one person to whom it was possible. If this person was not Jeffrey, he must have been very like Jeffrey; sufficiently like for the body of the one to be mistaken for the body of the other. For the production of Jeffrey's body was an essential part of the plan and must have been contemplated from the first. But the only person who fulfills the conditions is John Blackmore.

"We have learned from Mr. Stephen that John and Jeffrey, though very different in appearance in later years, were much alike as young men. But when two brothers who are much alike as young men, become unlike in later life, we shall find that the unlikeness is produced by superficial differences and that the essential likeness remains. Thus, in the present case, Jeffrey was clean shaved, had bad eyesight, wore spectacles and stooped as he walked; John wore a beard and moustache, had good eyesight, did not wear spectacles and had a brisk gait and upright carriage. But supposing John to shave off his beard and moustache, to put on spectacles and to stoop in his walk, these conspicuous but superficial differences would vanish and the original likeness reappear.

"There is another consideration. John had been an actor and was an actor of some experience. Now, any person can, with some care and practice, make up a disguise; the great difficulty is to support that disguise by a suitable manner and voice. But to an experienced actor this difficulty does not exist. To him, personation is easy; and, moreover, an actor is precisely the person to whom the idea of disguise and impersonation would occur.

"There is a small item bearing on this point, so small as to be hardly worth calling evidence, but just worth noting. In the pocket of the waistcoat taken from the body of Jeffrey I found the stump of a 'Contango' pencil; a pencil that is sold for the use of stock dealers and brokers. Now John was an outside broker and might very probably have used such a pencil, whereas Jeffrey had no connection with the stock markets and there is no reason why he should have possessed a pencil of this kind. But the fact is merely suggestive; it has no evidential value.

"A more important inference is to be drawn from the collected signatures. I have remarked that the change in the signature occurred abruptly, with one or two alterations of manner, last September, and that there are two distinct forms with no intermediate varieties. This is, in itself, remarkable and suspicious. But a remark made by Mr. Britton furnishes a really valuable piece of evidence on the point we are now considering. He admitted that the character of the signature had undergone a change, but observed that the change did not affect the individual or personal character of the writing. This is very important; for handwriting is, as it were, an extension of the personality of the writer. And just as a man to some extent snares his personality with his near blood-relations in the form of family resemblances, so his handwriting often shows a subtle likeness to that of his near relatives. You must have noticed, as I have, how commonly the handwriting of one brother resembles that of another, and in just this peculiar and subtle way. The inference, then, from Mr. Britton's statement is, that if the signature of the will was forged, it was probably forged by a relative of the deceased. But the only relative in question is his brother John.

"All the facts, therefore, pointed to John Blackmore as the person who occupied these chambers, and I accordingly adopted that view as a working hypothesis."

"But this was all pure speculation," objected Mr. Winwood.

"Not speculation," said Thorndyke. "Hypothesis. It was ordinary inductive reasoning such as we employ in scientific research. I started with the purely tentative hypothesis that the person who signed the will was not Jeffrey Blackmore. I assumed this; and I may say that I did not believe it at the time, but merely adopted it as a proposition that was worth testing. I accordingly tested it, 'Yes?' or 'No?' with each new fact; but as each new fact said 'Yes,' and no fact said definitely 'No,' its probability increased rapidly by a sort of geometrical progression. The probabilities multiplied into one another. It is a perfectly sound method, for one knows that if a hypothesis be true, it will lead one, sooner or later, to a crucial fact by which its truth can be demonstrated.

"To resume our argument. We have now set up the proposition that John Blackmore was the tenant of New Inn and that he was personating Jeffrey. Let us reason from this and see what it leads to.

"If the tenant of New Inn was John, then Jeffrey must be elsewhere, since his concealment at the inn was clearly impossible. But he could not have been far away, for he had to be producible at short notice whenever the death of Mrs. Wilson should make the production of his body necessary. But if he was producible, his person must have been in the possession or control of John. He could not have been at large, for that would have involved the danger of his being seen and recognized. He could not have been in any institution or place where he would be in contact with strangers. Then he must be in some sort of confinement. But it is difficult to keep an adult in confinement in an ordinary house. Such a proceeding would involve great risk of discovery and the use of violence which would leave traces on the body, to be observed and commented on at the inquest. What alternative method could be suggested?

"The most obvious method is that of keeping the prisoner in such a state of debility as would confine him to his bed. But such debility could be produced by only starvation, unsuitable food, or chronic poisoning. Of these alternatives, poisoning is much more exact, more calculable in its effect and more under control. The probabilities, then, were in favor of chronic poisoning.

"Having reached this stage, I recalled a singular case which Jervis had mentioned to me and which seemed to illustrate this method. On our return home I asked him for further particulars, and he then gave me a very detailed description of the patient and the circumstances. The upshot was rather startling. I had looked on his case as merely illustrative, and wished to study it for the sake of the suggestions that it might offer. But when I had heard his account, I began to suspect that there was something more than mere parallelism of method. It began to look as if his patient, Mr. Graves, might actually be Jeffrey Blackmore.

"The coincidences were remarkable. The general appearance of the patient tallied completely with Mr. Stephen's description of his uncle Jeffrey. The patient had a tremulous iris in his right eye and had clearly suffered from dislocation of the crystalline lens. But from Mr. Stephen's account of his uncle's sudden loss of sight in the right eye after a fall, I judged that Jeffrey had also suffered from dislocation of the lens and therefore had a tremulous iris in the right eye. The patient, Graves, evidently had defective vision in his left eye, as proved by the marks made behind his ears by the hooked side-bars of his spectacles; for it is only on spectacles that are intended for constant use that we find hooked side-bars. But Jeffrey had defective vision in his left eye and wore spectacles constantly. Lastly, the patient Graves was suffering from chronic morphine poisoning, and morphine was found in the body of Jeffrey.

"Once more, it appeared to me that there were too many coincidences.

"The question as to whether Graves and Jeffrey were identical admitted of fairly easy disproof; for if Graves was still alive, he could not be Jeffrey. It was an important question and I resolved to test it without delay. That night, Jervis and I plotted out the chart, and on the following morning we located the house. But it was empty and to let. The birds had flown, and we failed to discover whither they had gone.

"However, we entered the house and explored. I have told you about the massive bolts and fastenings that we found on the bedroom doors and window, showing that the room had been used as a prison. I have told you of the objects that we picked out of the dust-heap under the grate. Of the obvious suggestion offered by the Japanese brush and the bottle of 'spirit gum' or cement, I need not speak now; but I must trouble you with some details concerning the broken spectacles. For here we had come upon the crucial fact to which, as I have said, all sound inductive reasoning brings one sooner or later.

"The spectacles were of a rather peculiar pattern. The frames were of the type invented by Mr. Stopford of Moorfields and known by his name. The right eye-piece was fitted with plain glass, as is usual in the case of a blind, or useless, eye. It was very much shattered, but its character was obvious. The glass of the left eye was much thicker and fortunately less damaged, so that I was able accurately to test its refraction.

"When I reached home, I laid the pieces of the spectacles together, measured the frames very carefully, tested the left eye-glass, and wrote down a full description such as would have been given by the surgeon to the spectacle-maker. Here it is, and I will ask you to note it carefully.

"'Spectacles for constant use. Steel frame, Stopford's pattern, curl sides, broad bridge with gold lining. Distance between centers, 6.2 centimeters; extreme length of side-bars, 13.3 centimeters.

"'Right eye,   plain glass.
"'Left eye,   <u>-5.75 D. spherical</u>
                -3.25 D. cylindrical, axis 35°.'

"The spectacles, you see, were of a very distinctive character and seemed to offer a good chance of identification. Stopford's frames are, I believe, made by only one firm of opticians in London, Parry & Cuxton of Regent Street. I therefore wrote to Mr. Cuxton, who knows me, asking him if he had supplied spectacles to the late Jeffrey Blackmore, Esq. — here is a copy of my letter — and if so, whether he would mind letting me have a full description of them, together with the name of the oculist who prescribed them.

"He replied in this letter, which is pinned to the copy of mine, that, about four years ago, he supplied a pair of glasses to Mr. Jeffrey Blackmore, and described them thus: 'The spectacles were for constant use and had steel frames of Stopford's pattern with curl sides, the length of the side-bars including the curled ends being 13.3 cm. The bridge was broad with a gold lining-plate, shaped as shown by the enclosed tracing from the diagram on the prescription. Distance between centers 6.2 cm.

"'Right eye,   plain glass.
"'Left eye,   <u>-5.75 D. spherical</u>
                -3.25 D. cylindrical, axis 35°.'

"'The spectacles were prescribed by Mr. Hindley of Wimpole Street.'

"You see that Mr. Cuxton's description is identical with mine. However, for further confirmation, I wrote to Mr. Hindley, asking certain questions, to which he replied thus:

"'You are quite right. Mr. Jeffrey Blackmore had a tremulous iris in his right eye (which was practically blind), due to dislocation of the lens. The pupils were rather large; certainly not contracted.'

"Here, then, we have three important facts. One is that the spectacles found by us at Kennington Lane were undoubtedly Jeffrey's; for it is as unlikely that there exists another pair of spectacles exactly identical with those as that there exists another face exactly like Jeffrey's face. The second fact is that the description of Jeffrey tallies completely with that of the sick man, Graves, as given by Dr. Jervis; and the third is that when Jeffrey was seen by Mr. Hindley, there was no sign of his being addicted to the taking of morphine. The first and second facts, you will agree, constitute complete identification."

"Yes," said Marchmont; "I think we must admit the identification as being quite conclusive, though the evidence is of a kind that is more striking to the medical than to the legal mind."

"You will not have that complaint to make against the next item of evidence," said Thorndyke. "It is after the lawyer's own heart, as you shall hear. A few days ago I wrote to Mr. Stephen asking him if he possessed a recent photograph of his uncle Jeffrey. He had one, and he sent it to me by return. This portrait I showed to Dr. Jervis and asked him if he had ever seen the person it represented. After examining it attentively, without any hint whatever from me, he identified it as the portrait of the sick man, Graves."

"Indeed!" exclaimed Marchmont. "This is most important. Are you prepared to swear to the identity, Dr. Jervis?"

"I have not the slightest doubt," I replied, "that the portrait is that of Mr. Graves."

"Excellent!" said Marchmont, rubbing his hands gleefully; "this will be much more convincing to a jury. Pray go on, Dr. Thorndyke."

"That," said Thorndyke, "completes the first part of my investigation. We had now reached a definite, demonstrable fact; and that fact, as you see, disposed at once of the main question — the genuineness of the will. For if the man at Kennington Lane was Jeffrey Blackmore, then the man at New Inn was not. But it was the latter who had signed the will. Therefore the will was not signed by Jeffrey Blackmore; that is to say, it was a forgery. The case was complete for the purposes of the civil proceedings; the rest of my investigations had reference to the criminal prosecution that was inevitable. Shall I proceed, or is your interest confined to the will?"

"Hang the will!" exclaimed Stephen. "I want to hear how you propose to lay hands on the villain who murdered poor old uncle Jeffrey — for I suppose he did murder him?"

"I think there is no doubt of it," replied Thorndyke.

"Then," said Marchmont, "we will hear the rest of the argument, if you please."

"Very well," said Thorndyke. "As the evidence stands, we have proved that Jeffrey Blackmore was a prisoner in the house in Kennington Lane and that someone was personating him at New Inn. That someone, we have seen, was, in all probability, John Blackmore. We now have to consider the man Weiss. Who was he? and can we connect him in any way with New Inn?

"We may note in passing that Weiss and the coachman were apparently one and the same person. They were never seen together. When Weiss was present, the coachman was not available even for so urgent a service as the obtaining of an antidote to the poison. Weiss always appeared some time after Jervis's arrival and disappeared some time before his departure, in each case sufficiently long to allow of a change of disguise. But we need not labor the point, as it is not of primary importance.

"To return to Weiss. He was clearly heavily disguised, as we see by his unwillingness to show himself even by the light of a candle. But there is an item of positive evidence on this point which is important from having other bearings. It is furnished by the spectacles worn by Weiss, of which you have heard Jervis's description. These spectacles had very peculiar optical properties. When you looked *through* them they had the properties of plain glass; when you looked *at* them they had the appearance of lenses. But only one kind of glass possesses these properties; namely, that which, like an ordinary watch-glass, has curved, parallel surfaces. But for what purpose could a person wear 'watch-glass' spectacles? Clearly, not to assist his vision. The only alternative is disguise.

"The properties of these spectacles introduce a very curious and interesting feature into the case. To the majority of persons, the wearing of spectacles for the purpose of disguise or personation, seems a perfectly simple and easy proceeding. But, to a person of normal eyesight, it is nothing of the kind. For, if he wears spectacles suited for long sight he cannot see distinctly through them at all; while, if he wears concave, or near sight, glasses, the effort to see through them produces such strain and fatigue that his eyes become disabled altogether. On the stage the difficulty is met by using spectacles of plain window-glass, but in real life this would hardly do; the 'property' spectacles would be detected at once and give rise to suspicion.

"The personator is therefore in this dilemma: if he wears actual spectacles, he cannot see through them; if he wears sham spectacles of plain glass, his disguise will probably be detected. There is only one way out of the difficulty, and that not a very satisfactory one; but Mr. Weiss seems to have adopted it in lieu of a better. It is that of using watch-glass spectacles such as I have described.

"Now, what do we learn from these very peculiar glasses? In the first place they confirm our opinion that Weiss was wearing a disguise. But, for use in a room so very dimly lighted, the ordinary stage spectacles would have answered quite well. The second inference is, then, that these spectacles were prepared to be worn under more trying conditions of light — out of doors, for instance. The third inference is that Weiss was a man with normal eyesight; for otherwise he could have worn real spectacles suited to the state of his vision.

"These are inferences by the way, to which we may return. But these glasses furnish a much more important suggestion. On the floor of the bedroom at New Inn I found some fragments of glass which had been trodden on. By joining one or two of them together, we have been able to make out the general character of the object of which they formed parts. My assistant — who was formerly a watch-maker — judged that object to be the thin crystal glass of a lady's watch, and this, I think, was Jervis's opinion. But the small part which remains of the original edge furnishes proof in two respects that this was not a watch-glass. In the first place, on taking a careful tracing of this piece of the edge, I found that its curve was part of an ellipse; but watch-glasses, nowadays, are invariably circular. In the second place, watch-glasses are ground on the edge to a single bevel to snap into the bezel or frame; but the edge of this object was ground to a double bevel, like the edge of a spectacle-glass, which fits into a groove in the frame and is held by the side-bar screw. The inevitable inference was that this was a spectacle-glass. But, if so, it was part of a pair of spectacles identical in properties with those worn by Mr. Weiss.

"The importance of this conclusion emerges when we consider the exceptional character of Mr. Weiss's spectacles. They were not merely peculiar or remarkable; they were probably unique. It is exceedingly likely that there is not in the entire world another similar pair of spectacles. Whence the finding of these fragments of glass in the bedroom establishes a considerable probability that Mr. Weiss was, at some time, in the chambers at New Inn.

"And now let us gather up the threads of this part of the argument. We are inquiring into the identity of the man Weiss. Who was he?

"In the first place, we find him committing a secret crime from which John Blackmore alone will benefit. This suggests the *prima-facie* probability that he was John Blackmore.

"Then we find that he was a man of normal eyesight who was wearing spectacles for the purpose of disguise. But the tenant of New Inn, whom we have seen to be, almost certainly, John Blackmore — and whom we will, for the present, assume to have been John Blackmore — was a man with normal eyesight who wore spectacles for disguise.

"John Blackmore did not reside at New Inn, but at some place within easy reach of it. But Weiss resided at a place within easy reach of New Inn.

"John Blackmore must have had possession and control of the person of Jeffrey. But Weiss had possession and control of the person of Jeffrey.

"Weiss wore spectacles of a certain peculiar and probably unique character. But portions of such spectacles were found in the chambers at New Inn.

"The overwhelming probability, therefore, is that Weiss and the tenant of New Inn were one and the same person; and that that person was John Blackmore."

"That," said Mr. Winwood, "is a very plausible argument. But, you observe, sir, that it contains an undistributed middle term."

Thorndyke smiled genially. I think he forgave Winwood everything for that remark.

"You are quite right, sir," he said. "It does. And, for that reason, the demonstration is not absolute. But we must not forget, what logicians seem occasionally to overlook: that the 'undistributed middle,' while it interferes with absolute proof, may be quite consistent with a degree of probability that approaches very near to certainty. Both the Bertillon system and the English fingerprint system involve a process of reasoning in which the middle term is undistributed. But the great probabilities are accepted in practice as equivalent to certainties."

Mr. Winwood grunted a grudging assent, and Thorndyke resumed:

"We have now furnished fairly conclusive evidence on three heads: we have proved that the sick man, Graves, was Jeffrey Blackmore; that the tenant of New Inn was John Blackmore; and that the man Weiss was also John Blackmore. We now have to prove that John and Jeffrey were together in the chambers at New Inn on the night of Jeffrey's death.

"We know that two persons, and two persons only, came from Kennington Lane to New Inn. But one of those persons was the tenant of New Inn — that is, John Blackmore. Who was the other? Jeffrey is known by us to have been at Kennington Lane. His body was found on the following morning in the room at New Inn. No third person is known to have come from Kennington Lane; no third person is known to have arrived at New Inn. The inference, by exclusion, is that the second person — the woman — was Jeffrey.

"Again; Jeffrey had to be brought from Kennington to the inn by John. But John was personating Jeffrey and was made up to resemble him very closely. If Jeffrey were undisguised the two men would be almost exactly alike; which would be very noticeable in any case and suspicious after the death of one of them. Therefore Jeffrey would have to be disguised in some way; and what disguise could be simpler and more effective than the one that I suggest was used?

"Again; it was unavoidable that someone — the cabman — should know that Jeffrey was not alone when he came to the inn that night. If the fact had leaked out and it had become known that a man had accompanied him to his chambers, some suspicion might have arisen, and that suspicion would have pointed to John, who was directly interested in his brother's death. But if it had transpired that Jeffrey was accompanied by a woman, there would have been less suspicion, and that suspicion would not have pointed to John Blackmore.

"Thus all the general probabilities are in favor of the hypothesis that this woman was Jeffrey Blackmore. There is, however, an item of positive evidence that strongly supports this view. When I examined the clothing of the deceased, I found on the trousers a horizontal crease on each leg as if the trousers had been turned up halfway to the knees. This appearance is quite understandable if we suppose that the trousers were worn under a skirt and were turned up so that they should not be accidentally seen. Otherwise it is quite incomprehensible."

"Is it not rather strange," said Marchmont, "that Jeffrey should have allowed himself to be dressed up in this remarkable manner?"

"I think not," replied Thorndyke. "There is no reason to suppose that he knew how he was dressed. You have heard Jervis's description of his condition; that of a mere automaton. You know that without his spectacles he was practically blind, and that he could not have worn them since we found them at the house in Kennington Lane. Probably his head was wrapped up in the veil, and the skirt and mantle put on afterwards; but, in any case, his condition rendered him practically devoid of will power. That is all the evidence I have to prove that the unknown woman was Jeffrey. It is not conclusive but it is convincing enough for our purpose, seeing that the case against John Blackmore does not depend upon it."

"Your case against him is on the charge of murder, I presume?" said Stephen.

"Undoubtedly. And you will notice that the statements made by the supposed Jeffrey to the porter, hinting at suicide, are now important evidence. By the light of what we know, the announcement of intended suicide becomes the announcement of intended murder. It conclusively disproves what it was intended to prove; that Jeffrey died by his own hand."

"Yes, I see that," said Stephen, and then after a pause he asked: "Did you identify Mrs. Schallibaum? You have told us nothing about her."

"I have considered her as being outside the case as far as I am concerned," replied Thorndyke. "She was an accessory; my business was with the principal. But, of course, she will be swept up in the net. The evidence that convicts John Blackmore will convict her. I have not troubled about her identity. If John Blackmore is married, she is probably his wife. Do you happen to know if he is married?"

"Yes; but Mrs. John Blackmore is not much like Mrs. Schallibaum, excepting that she has a cast in the left eye. She is a dark woman with very heavy eyebrows."

"That is to say that she differs from Mrs. Schallibaum in those peculiarities that can be artificially changed and resembles her in the one feature that is unchangeable. Do you know if her Christian name happens to be Pauline?"

"Yes, it is. She was a Miss Pauline Hagenbeck, a member of an American theatrical company. What made you ask?"

"The name which Jervis heard poor Jeffrey struggling to pronounce seemed to me to resemble Pauline more than any other name."

"There is one little point that strikes me," said Marchmont. "Is it not rather remarkable that the porter should have noticed no difference between the body of Jeffrey and the living man whom he knew by sight, and who must, after all, have been distinctly different in appearance?"

"I am glad you raised that question," Thorndyke replied, "for that very difficulty presented itself to me at the beginning of the case. But on thinking it over, I decided that it was an imaginary difficulty, assuming, as we do, that there was a good deal of resemblance between the two men. Put yourself in the porter's place and follow his mental processes. He is informed that a dead man is lying on the bed in Mr. Blackmore's rooms. Naturally, he assumes that the dead man is Mr. Blackmore — who, by the way, had hinted at suicide only the night before. With this idea he enters the chambers and sees a man a good deal like Mr. Blackmore and wearing Mr. Blackmore's clothes, lying on Mr. Blackmore's bed. The idea that the body could be that of some other person has never entered his mind. If he notes any difference of appearance he will put that down to the effects of death; for everyone knows that a man dead looks somewhat different from the same man alive. I take it as evidence of great acuteness on the part of John Blackmore that he should have calculated so cleverly, not only the mental process of the porter, but the erroneous reasoning which everyone would base on the porter's conclusions. For, since the body was actually Jeffrey's, and was identified by the porter as that of his tenant, it has been assumed by everyone that no question was possible as to the identity of Jeffrey Blackmore and the tenant of New Inn."

There was a brief silence, and then Marchmont asked:

"May we take it that we have now heard all the evidence?"

"Yes," replied Thorndyke. "That is my case."

"Have you given information to the police?" Stephen asked eagerly.

"Yes. As soon as I had obtained the statement of the cabman, Ridley, and felt that I had enough evidence to secure a conviction, I called at Scotland Yard and had an interview with the Assistant Commissioner. The case is in the hands of Superintendent Miller of the Criminal Investigation Department, a most acute and energetic officer. I have been expecting to hear that the warrant has been executed, for Mr. Miller is usually very punctilious in keeping me informed of the progress of the cases to which I introduce him. We shall hear tomorrow, no doubt."

"And, for the present," said Marchmont, "the case seems to have passed out of our hands."

"I shall enter a caveat, all the same," said Mr. Winwood.

"That doesn't seem very necessary," Marchmont objected. "The evidence that we have heard is amply sufficient to ensure a conviction and there will be plenty more when the police go into the case. And a conviction on the charges of forgery and murder would, of course, invalidate the second will."

"I shall enter a caveat, all the same," repeated Mr. Winwood.

As the two partners showed a disposition to become heated over this question, Thorndyke suggested that they might discuss it at leisure by the light of subsequent events. Acting on this hint — for it was now close upon midnight — our visitors prepared to depart; and were, in fact, just making their way towards the door when the bell rang. Thorndyke flung open the door, and, as he recognized his visitor, greeted him with evident satisfaction.

"Ha! Mr. Miller; we were just speaking of you. These gentlemen are Mr. Stephen Blackmore and his solicitors, Mr. Marchmont and Mr. Winwood. You know Dr. Jervis, I think."

The officer bowed to our friends and remarked:

"I am just in time, it seems. A few minutes more and I should have missed these gentlemen. I don't know what you'll think of my news."

"You haven't let that villain escape, I hope," Stephen exclaimed.

"Well," said the Superintendent, "he is out of my hands and yours too; and so is the woman. Perhaps I had better tell you what has happened."

"If you would be so kind," said Thorndyke, motioning the officer to a chair.

The superintendent seated himself with the manner of a man who has had a long and strenuous day, and forthwith began his story.

"As soon as we had your information, we procured a warrant for the arrest of both parties, and then I went straight to their flat with Inspector Badger and a sergeant. There we learned from the attendant that they were away from home and were not expected back until today about noon. We kept a watch on the premises, and this morning, about the time appointed, a man and a woman, answering to the description, arrived at the flat. We followed them in and saw them enter the lift, and we were going to get into the lift too, when the man pulled the rope, and away they went. There was nothing for us to do but run up the stairs, which we did as fast as we could race; but they got to their landing first, and we were only just in time to see them nip in and shut the door. However, it seemed that we had them safe enough, for there was no dropping out of the windows at that height; so we sent the sergeant to get a locksmith to pick the lock or force the door, while we kept on ringing the bell.

"About three minutes after the sergeant left, I happened to look out of the landing window and saw a hansom pull up opposite the flats. I put my head out of the window, and, hang me if I didn't see our two friends getting into the cab. It seems that there was a small lift inside the flat communicating with the kitchen, and they had slipped down it one at a time.

"Well, of course, we raced down the stairs like acrobats, but by the time we got to the bottom the cab was off with a fine start. We ran out into Victoria Street, and there we could see it halfway down the street and going like a chariot race. We managed to pick up another hansom and told the cabby to keep the other one in sight, and away we went like the very deuce; along Victoria Street and Broad Sanctuary, across Parliament Square, over Westminster Bridge and along York Road; we kept the other beggar in sight, but we couldn't gain an inch on him. Then we turned into Waterloo Station, and, as we were driving up the slope we met another hansom coming down; and when the cabby kissed his hand and smiled at us, we guessed that he was the sportsman we had been following.

"But there was no time to ask questions. It is an awkward station with a lot of different exits, and it looked a good deal as if our quarry had got away. However, I took a chance. I remembered that the Southampton express was due to start about this time, and I took a short cut across the lines and made for the platform that it starts from. Just as Badger and I got to the end, about thirty yards from the rear of the train, we saw a man and a woman running in front of us. Then the guard blew his whistle and the train began to move. The man and the woman managed to scramble into one of the rear compartments and Badger and I raced up the platform like mad. A porter tried to head us off, but Badger capsized him and we both sprinted harder than ever, and just hopped on the foot-board of the guard's van as the train began to get up speed. The guard couldn't risk putting us off, so he had to let us into his van, which suited us exactly, as we could watch the train on both sides from the look-out. And we did watch, I can tell you; for our friend in front had seen us. His head was out of the window as we climbed on to the foot-board.

"However, nothing happened until we stopped at Southampton West. There, I need not say, we lost no time in hopping out, for we naturally expected our friends to make a rush for the exit. But they didn't. Badger watched the platform, and I kept a look-out to see that they didn't slip away across the line from the off-side. But still there was no sign of them. Then I walked up the train to the compartment which I had seen them enter. And there they were, apparently fast asleep in the corner by the off-side window, the man leaning back with his mouth open and the woman resting against him with her head on his shoulder. She gave me quite a turn when I went in to look at them, for she had her eyes half-closed and seemed to be looking round at me with a most horrible expression; but I found afterwards that the peculiar appearance of looking round was due to the cast in her eye."

"They were dead, I suppose?" said Thorndyke.

"Yes, sir. Stone dead; and I found these on the floor of the carriage."

He held up two tiny yellow glass tubes, each labeled "Hypodermic tabloids. Aconitine Nitrate gr. 1/640."

"Ha!" exclaimed Thorndyke, "this fellow was well up in alkaloidal poisons, it seems; and they appear to have gone about prepared for emergencies. These tubes each contained twenty tabloids, a thirty-second of a grain altogether, so we may assume that about twelve times the medicinal dose was swallowed. Death must have occurred in a few minutes, and a merciful death too."

"A more merciful death than they deserved," exclaimed Stephen, "when one thinks of the misery and suffering that they inflicted on poor old uncle Jeffrey. I would sooner have had them hanged."

"It's better as it is, sir," said Miller. "There is no need, now, to raise any questions in detail at the inquest. The publicity of a trial for murder would have been very unpleasant for you. I wish Dr. Jervis had given the tip to me instead of to that confounded, overcautious — but there, I mustn't run down my brother officers: and it's easy to be wise after the event.

"Good night, gentlemen. I suppose this accident disposes of your business as far as the will is concerned?"

"I suppose it does," agreed Mr. Winwood. "But I shall enter a caveat, all the same."

THE END